Matcha Murder

A Tearoom Mystery
Kirsten Weiss

misterio press

Contents

Copyright	V
About the Book	VI
Special Offer!	VII
Chapter 1	1
Chapter 2	10
Chapter 3	20
Chapter 4	26
Chapter 5	34
Chapter 6	43
Chapter 7	50
Chapter 8	56
Chapter 9	67
Chapter 10	76
Chapter 11	82
Chapter 12	90
Chapter 13	96
Chapter 14	105
Chapter 15	112
Chapter 16	120
Chapter 17	128
Chapter 18	137

Chapter 19	145
Chapter 20	152
Chapter 21	161
Chapter 22	165
Chapter 23	172
Chapter 24	179
Chapter 25	185
Chapter 26	192
Chapter 27	198
Chapter 28	205
Chapter 29	211
Chapter 30	216
Chapter 31	222
Cherry Lemonade Scones	227
Birthday Cake Scones	229
Matcha and Almond Scones	231
More Kirsten Weiss	233
Beanblossom's Swag Shop!	236
Other misterio press books	237
About the Author	239

Copyright

COPYRIGHT © 2025 BY Kirsten Weiss

All rights reserved.

No part of this publication may be reproduced, distributed, or transmitted in any form or by any means, including photocopying, recording, or other electronic or mechanical methods, without the prior written permission of the publisher, except as permitted by U.S. copyright law. For permission requests, contact kweiss2001@kirstenweiss.com.

The story, all names, characters, and incidents portrayed in this production are fictitious. No identification with actual persons (living or deceased), places, buildings, and products is intended or should be inferred. AI has not been used in the conceptualization, generation, or drafting of this work.

NO AI TRAINING: Without in any way limiting the author's [and publisher's] exclusive rights under copyright, any use of this publication to "train" generative artificial intelligence (AI) technologies to generate text is expressly prohibited. The author reserves all rights to license uses of this work for generative AI training and development of machine learning language models.

Book Cover by Dar Albert

Visit the author website to sign up for updates on upcoming books and fun, free stuff: KirstenWeiss.com

About the Book

MURDER'S BREWING...

Tearoom owner Abigail will have to read between the leaves before she's the next ingredient in a deadly draught.

A storm's raging over the California coast. Abigail's boyfriend has gone AWOL. And her most annoying acquaintance is the prime suspect in a murder.

Abigail and her quirky Tarot-reading partner, Hyperion, will have to sift through a whirlwind of lies to crack this twisty crime. But the power's flickering, and emotions are boiling. Can they decipher the murderer's bitter blend before it's too late, or will this be their final cup?

Join this wacky detecting duo and unravel *Matcha Murder*. Grab your copy now and immerse yourself in this hilarious cozy mystery!

Cherry Lemonade, Birthday Cake, and Matcha and Almond Scone recipes in the back of the book!

Special Offer!

THANK YOU FOR BUYING *Matcha Murder*! I have a free gift if you'd like to read more light paranormal mystery! You can download *Fortune Favors the Grave*, a novella in my Tea and Tarot series, FREE right here —> Get the Book.

Will Abigail become a hostage to fortune?

Independent Abigail Beanblossom finally has the tearoom of her dreams, even if it is chock full of eccentric Tarot readers. But when her Tarot reading business partner, Hyperion Night, becomes embroiled in a rival's murder, Abigail discovers that true partnership is about more than profit and loss.

Escape into this hilarious mystery today!

Fortune Favors the Grave

KIRSTEN WEISS

Chapter 1

When tourists think California *beach town*, they usually think something along the lines of sunshine, sunglasses, and sunburn.

The point is *sun*.

But every few years, the jet stream over the Pacific gets shifty. Then a watery hellscape of landslides and demented driving breaks loose.

Rain drummed on the flat roof of Beanblossom's Tea and Tarot for the fifth day in a row. Outside our windows, the sloping street had turned into a raging river.

That river was rising. My grip tightened on the hostess stand's wooden sides, as if its flimsy wooden sides could anchor the tearoom.

A Tesla rolled down the street. The car skidded, fishtailing frighteningly close to a Buick. The Tesla corrected, then sped up, sheeting our windows with water. A trio of white-haired women at a window table flinched.

Conversation hit a lull as customers, Tarot readers, and waitstaff studied the water cascading down the windows. Then there was a collective breath, and the clatter of teacups and chatter of Saturday morning diners resumed.

"You're going to have to do something about that," Verbena said from behind me. "Your tearoom's going to flood."

I rolled my eyes. *Sure. I'll just wave my magic wand and make the rain stop, the sun shine, and the water drain. No problem.*

I released my grip on the hostess stand. "More sandbags are on the way," I said shortly.

Verbena Pillbrow, tea witch and all-around pill, jammed her hands on her skinny hips. She was five-foot-eight-inches of annoyance, which made her four inches more annoying than me.

As a self-proclaimed tea witch—someone who incorporated tea into her magical rituals—she considered herself a higher authority when it came to tea. Water dampened the fringe of her tie-dyed brown yoga duster over her usual stretchy festival wear—a droopy tank top and thick tights.

"They'd better get here soon, Abigail." Verbena angled her pointed chin. "And I'd like a refill of my Chariot *tisane.*" She thrust an empty white mug in my face. "I've told you before, if it doesn't use leaves from the camellia sinensis, it's not a tea. If you're going to sell tisanes, at least learn about the topic."

My fingers twitched. It was an old argument. Technically, herbal teas were called *tisanes*. But the common phraseology in America was "herbal tea," so I stuck with that so as not to confuse my customers. And I'd explained this to Verbena.

Repeatedly.

Cleansing breaths. I glanced toward the counter. My manager, Maricel, brewed tea with one hand and wiped down the white quartz with the other. Her long, black braid cascaded down the back of her t-shirt, the slogan on it hidden by her apron.

Verbena *could* have asked Maricel for a refill, since that's where the tea witch had been sitting. But for some reason known only to Verbena and her pagan gods, she preferred pestering me.

A Tarot reader dealt cards at one of the tables. A second reader, Sierra, sat at the bar, her toe tapping the restored wood base. Casually, she scanned the crowd for any interest in a reading.

I returned my attention to the front windows. Umbrellas wobbling, two elderly women in raincoats and matching plastic caps clambered over the sandbags protecting the front door.

They had to throw their weight into it to pull it open. A gust of wind ripped through the tearoom and snatched the door from their hands, slamming it shut. They stumbled.

Hurrying around the hostess stand, I pushed the door open. A gust of wind caught it, carrying me onto the brick sidewalk with a splash.

One of the women smiled. "Thank you, young lady." She moved cautiously across the threshold. Her friend waited, balancing on the sandbags, one hand braced on the white stucco wall.

A black monster truck roared up the street. Water arced from its enormous tires in a muddy tidal wave.

"Look out!" I leapt over the sandbags and extended my hand to her.

But instead of taking my hand and moving forward, she stared, transfixed by the oncoming truck. "Oh, dear."

A surfer's pipe of water curled toward us. I turned my back, shielding her. Water iced my blouse and khakis. My shoulders rocketed to my ears, and I winced. The truck roared past.

Stupid, inconsiderate... I shook my fist at the pickup, because it beat shouting curses. As much as I wanted to swear—and I *really* wanted to—that wouldn't mesh with the tearoom's elegant, genteel vibe.

Oblivious, the black truck zoomed down Main. It turned the corner onto Front Street—so named because it fronted the ocean—and vanished.

The second woman tottered inside. I followed, tugging the blue door shut behind us.

Aghast, she studied the water puddling at my feet on the laminate floor. "It was a noble gesture, my dear," she said. "But we *are* wearing raincoats."

It had been an idiotic gesture, and my cheeks heated. Those two were more thoroughly cloaked against the elements than the guy on the fish sticks package. I, in my blouse and slacks, was not.

I swiped up the mess with a towel then went to drip behind the hostess station. Water trickled down the back of my neck. I touched the net containing my brunette curls, done up in a bun. No surprise—it was drenched.

Peeling off their raincoats, they deposited their umbrellas in the stand beside the door. "Reservations for two," the silver-haired woman said. "Name of Samuels."

I scanned the reservation book. Theirs were the last reservations for the morning seating. "Yes, here you—"

"My tisane?" Verbena tossed her long brown hair over one shoulder.

I stretched my mouth into a smile. "Why don't you have a seat at the bar, Verbena?" As *far away from me as possible*. "I'll be right with you."

Without waiting for her response, I whisked two paper menus from their plastic holder. I led the newcomers to their white-clothed table. "Here you go. Your server will be with you in a moment."

A broad-shouldered man in a sopping navy hoodie, his golden hair plastered to his head, emerged from the rear hallway. My annoyance at Verbena fled and was replaced by a golden warmth.

I forgot my sodden clothes and the rising waters. Brik. I hurried to greet him. "Hey."

Brik and I had been dating for nearly a year, and we'd reached the easy phase of our relationship. I trusted him. He trusted me. There was no struggle, no strife. Everything just clicked. I loved that we'd gotten here.

He pulled me into a damp kiss. "Hey." His neat beard tickled my cheeks, and I inhaled his faint, musky odor.

There was another brief fall in the volume of the tearoom, and I knew guests were watching us. My face heated, along with the rest of my body.

"Did Hyperion get you with the sink hose again?" he asked.

I scowled. "No." In fairness, we'd been goofing around in a post-holiday season high, so I was as guilty as Hyperion. But I'd gotten *very* wet.

"Then why are you so wet?" he asked.

"Some jerk in a truck splashed me." Fortunately, I kept a spare change of clothing in anticipation of kitchen disasters.

Brik grimaced.

"What are you doing here?" I asked.

"I was just stacking more sandbags out back. Your parking lot's not looking good."

"Will the sandbags hold?" I asked anxiously. Brik was a contractor. If he thought there was a problem, there was a problem.

His blue eyes twinkled. "Don't worry, I've got you. This isn't a real flood—it's only a few inches. And I've got more sandbags for the front door."

I gripped his calloused hand, rough against mine, and warmth flowed between us. I hadn't asked him to take time out of his day to help. But he knew how important Beanblossom's was to me, and so he had. "My hero."

"My *tisane*," Verbena shouted over her shoulder at me.

Behind the bar, Maricel poured more herbal tea into Verbena's cup. My manager shot me an apologetic look, and I shrugged a response. I couldn't control Verbena. There was no reason to hope my manager could either.

"Is Verbena still hanging around here?" Brik asked in a low voice. "I thought she hated the tearoom."

"That's *why* she comes. To tell me everything that's wrong with it." She'd let the world know it too, in her many reviews. The weird thing was, the reviews were all five stars—five stars followed by a load of complaints.

"Where's Hyperion?" He scanned the tearoom.

I peeled the fabric of my wet blouse from my back. "Hiding in his office, the coward." I glanced past him down the hallway. The faint glow of twinkle lights surrounded Hyperion's office door.

"Hiding from what?"

I jerked my head toward Verbena, who seemed to be lecturing the Tarot reader at the bar. Sierra nodded politely, her gaze darting around the tearoom for an escape. "Three guesses from whom," I said, "and the first two don't count."

"Then your partner can help me with the sandbags."

Oh, I want to see that. Hyperion would get drenched, and after the kitchen sprayer incident, it would serve him right. I followed Brik past the kitchen and to Hyperion's door. Brik knocked.

"Is it safe?" Hyperion called.

Brik opened the office door and walked inside. I trailed after him.

Electric candles flickered around the room, the gold-painted crown molding glinting in their light. Against one wall, a narrow table had been decorated like an altar with driftwood, crystals, and his tabby, Bastet. The cat yawned.

My business partner had turned what had been a glorified closet into a Tarot-reading room that a world-classic psychic could be proud of. Hyperion was quite clear with clients he wasn't psychic though. He only read the cards.

"Water's still rising," Brik said. "I need your help sandbagging the front door."

"I meant safe from you-know-who." Hyperion slouched in his throne-like, red-velvet chair at the round, scarlet-clothed table. "That cackling fury, that hapless, insipid, decomposition—"

The orange, striped cat lifted one leg and groomed himself.

Hyperion narrowed his coffee-colored eyes at the cat. "Rude." He rose and peeled off his slim-fitting charcoal suit jacket. "Is Verbena still in the tearoom?" he asked me.

"At the tea bar," I said.

"Right." He rolled up the sleeves of his white, button-up shirt. Hyperion always dressed like a male model, probably because with his high cheekbones and perfect, near-black hair, he looked like one. "Let's keep the sandbags out of Beanblossom's then. Don't want to disrupt the elegant and genteel atmosphere." He smirked.

My eyes narrowed. Hyperion didn't want to be hassled by Verbena. But I was fine with them hauling the sandbags around the outside of the building rather than through it. That would just get Hyperion wetter.

Feeling more upbeat, I changed into a dry blue peasant top and jeans, returned to the tearoom, and walked behind the bar. "Maricel, would you take over in the kitchen for a while?"

Shooting me a grateful look, my manager dropped her dish towel in a bin beneath the bar. She practically tripped over herself in her hurry to get away from the counter.

Verbena sipped her Chariot tea, one of our Tarot-themed brews. "Trouble in paradise?" she asked, arch.

"Since I don't know what you're talking about, no." I grabbed my apron from behind the counter.

She braced her elbows on the white counter. Her pointed nose quivered. "You and Brik have been seeing each other nearly a year. The bloom of romance must have worn off by now. But what did you expect from such a boringly patriarchal relationship?"

"It isn't boring," I said, tying the apron around me. "And the romance is fine. Sure, things have settled down a bit—"

"A bit?"

"I mean, of course some of the excitement has worn off. But we love each other."

So what if the excitement of fresh love had faded? Excitement wasn't love. It was *excitement*. I didn't need that—at least not *all* the time. We had something more—love built on shared values.

She tapped the back of one finger. "Unless he puts a ring on it, you're in the danger zone. Men get bored easily. If you don't step it up, he'll be onto the next hot young thing." She swiveled on her barstool and pointed at the windows.

Brik, sandbags on each shoulder, was talking to a dripping redhead. The woman laughed at something he said and splashed down the street.

"He was probably giving her directions," I said.

"She seemed awfully charmed by his *directions*."

I scowled. Not because I was jealous—because Verbena was trying to make trouble. Brik couldn't help it if he was six-foot-two and built like a Viking marauder.

Hyperion staggered into view carrying a sandbag with both hands. He dropped it on the sidewalk, and water splashed the front window.

The women at the nearby table winced. Hyperion gave them an apologetic wave, and the men trooped past the window and out of sight.

"I trust Brik." He'd proven himself to me in more ways than I could count. Not that he needed to prove anything. But actions really do speak louder than words.

"Of course, not *all* men are dogs, but today's societal structure perpetuates male dominance and female subjugation." Verbena sniffed. "That said, maybe it wouldn't hurt to put some extra effort in?" She eyed me.

I looked down at my outfit. Okay, maybe my *Happy New Year* apron (courtesy of an apron-of-the-month club Hyperion had gifted me) was a bit much. But it was January, and the blue fabric did match my peasant top.

My jaw firmed. The customer might *almost* always be right, but enough was enough. "Listen, Verbena—"

The blue front door opened. Rain and wind whipped through the tearoom. A man roughly the size and shape of a gorilla strode inside without bothering to close the door.

Annoyed, I hurried around the counter. "Door!"

A woman at a nearby table leapt to her feet and shut it for me. The tablecloths floated into place.

My face heated. I'd been shouting at the detective, not the customers.

The woman skidded on the wet floor and grasped the hostess stand for balance.

"Thanks," I said, embarrassed, and bent to wipe up the muddy mess with a fresh towel. "I didn't mean for you to—"

"I know," she said, "but I was closest. And it was cold."

"Verbena Pillbrow?" Ignoring me, Detective Baranko strode toward the counter. "I was told I'd find you here." Rivulets of water trickled down his flattened brown hair and ruddy face.

Crumpling the towel in my hand, I straightened and lifted a single brow. Detective Baranko wanted Verbena?

Baranko was my bête noir, the thorn in my side, the fly in my wine. Since Verbena fit those categories as well, I wasn't overly concerned on her behalf. I wanted to see how this would play out.

It was sort of like choosing which movie monster to root for—the building-sized lizard or the giant robot? Either way, I'd be entertained.

"Told by whom?" Verbena swiveled on her barstool and lifted her chin. "And who are you?"

What had she done? Unpaid parking tickets? Ignoring a jury summons? San Borromeo was a small town. The detective might have gotten stuck with that sort of drudge work. I made for the tea bar.

"Detective Baranko, San Borromeo PD." He reached inside his dripping trench coat and pulled out a badge. "I'd like you to come to the station with me."

"Why?" she asked.

I slowed, my eyebrows pinching together. *The station?* That... actually sounded serious.

"I've got some questions," he rumbled. "It'd be better if we talked privately."

"No." Verbena sipped her tea. "It wouldn't. You can ask what you want to ask right here."

I had to hand it to the tea witch. She was a lot more direct with the detective than I usually was. Baranko wasn't incompetent or crooked. I just didn't like him on principle.

"It's about Falkner Fiore," the detective said.

Verbena crossed her arms over her flat chest. "If you have questions about Falkner, why not just ask Falkner?"

I stumbled to a halt, a cold weight filling my gut. *Oh, no. Oh, no, no, no.* There was only one good reason why a cop would—

"Because he's dead," Baranko said. "Murdered."

Chapter 2

"Where's Verbena?" Hyperion looked warily around the tearoom. Even though he'd been out in the pouring rain, Hyperion's white shirt was pristine. It was super irritating.

Laughter and chatter rose and fell. Tarot readers ambled between white-clothed tables.

I drummed my fingers on the hostess stand and stared at the tearoom's blue front door. "Detective Baranko just took her in for questioning. For murder."

"Seriously? I managed to miss Baranko, *and* he removed Verbena from the tearoom? Talk about two birds with one stone." My partner rubbed his hands together. "Now did I hear something about your grandfather's horseradish being involved in today's roast beef sandwich?"

Verbena would never be on my birthday list, but being taken in for questioning was not good. "Aren't you curious about the murder?"

"No," Hyperion said flatly. "If we get curious, we'll never get rid of Verbena. And if we rescue her from a false charge—which will no doubt resolve itself—she'll be our friend for life whether we like it or not."

"How can you be sure it's a false charge?"

Hyperion gave me a look. "Really? Verbena? She might annoy someone to death, but can you really see her committing murder? It's a shame in a way. If Verbena was in prison, she wouldn't be in Beanblossom's."

"No." I sighed. Not that I'd wish prison on Verbena. But a few weeks break from her would be nice.

"Besides, you said she was taken in for questioning, not arrested."

I shifted my weight. "Yeah, but when the police take you in for questioning—"

"Uh, uh. Do not go there." He clapped his hands to his ears. "No more. Don't want to hear it. Not involved. Not listening." Singing loudly, he hurried into the hallway. His office door slammed.

I shook myself. Hyperion was right. There was no reason to make this my problem.

Zero.

None.

Brik returned inside to kiss me goodbye, and I didn't mention Verbena. I might be a snoop, but I wasn't a gossip. So, I got back to the business of running a tea and Tarot room.

Maybe because it was raining, Beanblossom's seemed cozier. It might have been my leftover New Year's optimism. Or it might have been because Verbena wasn't perched at the bar like a vulture, critiquing my every move.

But that afternoon, the tearoom had a flow to it I hadn't felt in months. Which perhaps not coincidentally happened to be the amount of time she'd been hanging around.

It felt... wonderful. I chatted with diners, poured tea, and made sandwiches. And I was happy.

The tearoom's existence seemed miraculous. We'd almost failed on more than one occasion. But Hyperion and I had done it. We'd built something special. Beanblossom's Tea and Tarot was more than a restaurant. It was a community. And I fell in love with it all over again. Life was good.

I should have known better. Just when you think everything is going great, that's when life drop-kicks you into a tax audit with your ex as the auditor.

I sat the last reservations for our mid-day seating, a young couple. The male half of the pair looked uneasily around the tearoom.

"Don't worry." His girlfriend unfurled her white napkin with a snap. "Your masculinity will remain intact."

He shot me an embarrassed glance. "It's just that I'm pretty hungry."

"The Royal Tea is a lot of food." I handed them paper menus. "But you can always just go for a sandwich."

From the hostess station, Maricel motioned toward me with the receiver of the retro phone.

"Your server will be right with you." I wove through the white-clothed tables to the front of the tearoom.

"It's for you," Maricel said in a low voice. "Verbena."

Uh, oh. Verbena never called. She just appeared, unannounced, like a flying monkey with a curse on the wing. Uneasy, I pressed the receiver to my ear. "Hello?"

"You need to get me out of here," Verbena hissed.

I jerked down on the apron strings tied at my stomach. *So much for not getting involved.* But what could I do? You don't leave an innocent person at a cop shop, even if she *was* annoying.

"Are you still at the police station?" I asked her, just to be sure.

"Where *else* would I be? You need to get me out. *Right now.*"

My neck muscles tightened. "I don't need to do any—" My hand spasmed on the phone. "Wait. This isn't your one phone call, is it?"

She disconnected.

I bit back a curse. Why the hell didn't she call her lawyer? Why call *me*? Probably because she knew I was sap enough to help her.

No. I didn't owe Verbena anything. We weren't friends. We weren't even frenemies.

"What's wrong?" Maricel asked.

Still... I'd been in the crosshairs of a murder investigation once. It had been awful. I wouldn't wish it on my worst enemy, and Verbena was far from that.

I gnawed my bottom lip. "I think... I need to spring Verbena from jail."

As police stations go, San Borromeo's is kind of charming—on the outside, at least. It had been built in the Spanish style, with white stucco walls and a red tile roof. I hesitated beneath one of the arches marching along its promenade.

Across the street, water streamed down the wavy, shingled roof of a candy shop. Its decorative half-timbering funneled the liquid down smooth white stucco walls and into the street. San Borromeo had a dozen or so of these fairytale-style buildings—knock-offs of the famous Comstock homes in nearby Carmel.

I shut my pink umbrella, opened the arched wooden door, and walked into the police station. Unlike its quaint exterior, the interior was seventies grunge, complete with a drunk sagging in one of the plastic chairs.

Inhaling through my mouth, I looked around. Worried, I started for the front desk.

I wasn't exactly flush with bail money. All I would do was get the situation from Verbena and help her figure out next steps. Maybe call around for a lawyer. But that was it.

The toe of my right boot hooked a rucked-up floor mat. I stumbled on the wet linoleum. "Wha—" My boots skidded from beneath me, and I landed on my assets in an inglorious heap.

Clutching my umbrella, I gasped, staring at the white tile ceiling. "Ow." I groaned and gave myself a mental check-up. I'd landed mostly on my butt, and that hurt. But I didn't think I'd done permanent damage.

A fall of brown hair cascaded toward my face. I jerked away.

Verbena frowned down at me. "What are you doing on the floor?"

"Assessing my options. What are you doing out of jail?" I rolled to my side on the muddy floor and clambered to standing.

"Jail? I was never in jail."

My jaw clenched. *What the...?* Why had Verbena dragged me up here in the rain?

I brushed at the mud on the back of my raincoat. All that accomplished was smearing it around and dirtying my hands. "You said you needed me to get you out of here."

"I do need to get out of here. I need a ride."

"You could have walked to the tearoom," I said, outraged. The police station was only a couple blocks away.

"In this weather?" Verbena asked. "Didn't *you* drive here?"

"Of course I did," I snapped, "but—"

"Then what's the problem? And I need a ride to my apartment, not to the tearoom." She strode out the arched door, the hems of her brown knit coat flapping.

"You can't just..." I said to her departing back.

The drunk belched and slumped lower in his chair.

Never mind. I scuttled from the police station.

Verbena was nowhere in sight on the sloping street. She'd no doubt deduced, correctly, that I'd parked in the station's rear lot.

I jogged through the rain to my Mazda hatchback. Verbena was already inside, in the passenger's seat.

"You should keep your doors locked," she said as I got in. "Crime's rising. It's no surprise in a society where male aggression is normalized. Go south on El Camino."

"I'm not your taxi driver," I said. "And I have to get back to the tearoom."

"Why? You're mid-way through your second seating. Maricel has everything under control. Doesn't she?" Verbena asked, arch.

Dammit. She had a point. And if I suggested Maricel *didn't* have everything under control, that would be an insult to my manager. An insult Verbena would make sure she heard about.

"Fine," I snarled and started the small car. I headed east toward El Camino and cleared my throat. "How'd it go with Baranko?" Not that I cared. I was just making conversation.

"*Him?* The murder will never get solved with that lug nut in charge." She tossed her long, brown hair.

"Why do you say that?"

"Because he was wasting his time talking to me. What do *I* know about murder? And I can't believe you didn't bring a carafe of hot chamomile tisane after my ordeal."

Like *that* was going to happen. "Maybe Baranko thought you had some useful, ah, intel about the victim."

"I was only one of Falkner's clients. I never got *close* to him. I never trusted the man."

"What did Falkner do for a living?" No, I wasn't investigating, because Hyperion was right. If we got involved, we'd never get rid of her. But I couldn't help being curious.

"Nice." Her mouth twisted. "For a *living*? There's no need to emphasize he's dead."

"That wasn't—" My grip tightened on the wheel. "What was his career?"

"Spiritual business coaching."

"What's that?"

She swiveled in her seat and gaped at me. "Are you kidding me? Isn't it obvious? You do know what a coach is, don't you?"

"Well, yes, but—"

"And you know what a spiritual business is, don't you?"

"I imagine it's like Tarot reading?"

She braced one hand on my gray dashboard. "Oh. My. God. This explains everything."

My hand twisted on the wheel. *Don't ask. Don't ask. If you ask, you'll never hear the end of it.*

I asked. "Explains what?"

"To be successful," she said, "you need to bring spirit to your work—to *all* your work. I suppose people in our community are more attuned to that, but if you aren't, no wonder Beanblossom's is struggling."

I sucked in my cheeks. *Struggling*? The tearoom was full most days. "We're in the black."

"And how long did *that* take you?"

My brow lowered. "It usually takes at least a year for a restaurant to break even."

"Hm." Her thin lips compressed. "Turn right here."

I turned. "Beanblossom's is doing fine."

"Oh. Right. Sure. Of course, you know best."

"We are!" Did she have any idea how challenging making it in the restaurant business was? Most failed within their twelve months.

"Make a right... There. Stop there."

I pulled up in front of a shabby, two-story apartment building. A man sheltered from the rain beneath a set of exterior stairs. He could have been the twin of the drunk in the police station.

A dull weight filled my chest. Verbena lived *here*?

Some people think that because California is so expensive, the housing must all be deluxe. It isn't. A lot of apartments are just overpriced slums. The working class was getting pushed out of the state. I hated the situation, but I didn't see an obvious solution.

"Verbena—"

"What?" The look she turned on me was challenging. And then, for a fraction of a second, her bravado faltered, and I saw fear behind her brown eyes—fear and something else. Anguish.

Verbena looked down and sniffed. She made a business of unbuckling her seatbelt.

"It's okay," I said quietly. "I'd be rattled too. Once, I was accused—"

"I didn't do anything," she said, shrill, and opened the car door.

I also understood putting up a front, faking it until you made it. Because when the machine of the law was steamrolling toward you, knowing you were innocent wasn't the morale booster it should be. "I know you didn't—"

"I'll see you tomorrow."

"Okay, but—Wait. Tomorrow?" She usually came to Beanblossom's on alternate days. Knowing I didn't have to deal with her daily was the only thing keeping me sane.

She stepped from my Mazda.

I leaned across the passenger seat. "Tomorr—?"

Verbena slammed the door and dashed through the rain, up the steps. I waited until she'd closed the door to her second-floor apartment behind her.

Thoughtful, I navigated the return trip to Beanblossom's. Verbena had never complained about money problems. We'd both attended a Tarot retreat at an expensive resort. Hyperion and I had got in free as vendors and speakers.

Verbena hadn't been speaking, though. I tried to square her down-market apartment with that sort of expenditure and couldn't. No wonder she'd called me instead of a lawyer. The thought was depressing.

I dropped my umbrella in the stand beside Beanblossom's rear door and walked into the kitchen. Nothing was on fire or flooding, so I tied on my *Happy New Year* apron and ambled into the dining area.

As Verbena had predicted, Maricel had everything under control. Waitresses cleared tables for the next seating. A few customers lingered over tea and scones. All normal.

"Your friend Razzzor called." Maricel handed me a slip of paper. "He wanted to know if you were still working here. And some other guy called but wouldn't leave a message."

I made a face. Razzzor was my ex-boss. He'd tried to get me to return to work for him on more than one occasion. Razzzor was terrific, and working with him had been fun. But I wouldn't give up being my own boss for anything.

"Thanks." I slipped the note into my apron pocket.

Three familiar figures stood outside the window beside the front door. They frowned down at the sidewalk, and warmth radiated from my chest.

I jogged to the door, opened it, and stuck my head outside. "Gramps? Tomas? Archer? What's going on? Why aren't you at the Farmers' Market?"

My grandfather and his best friend—my honorary uncle, Tomas—studied the sandbags damming the brick sidewalk at my front door. Rain streamed off Tomas's *Giants* windbreaker and down my grandfather's checked, cabby-style hat.

Beneath his umbrella, their friend Archer patted his silver hair. He minced over the sandbags and strolled past me into the tearoom. "At least I have the sense not to stand out in the rain."

Neither of the other men were carrying umbrellas. Tomas had once told me they were unmanly.

"The farmers' market is canceled." Tomas wiped rain from his leathery face. "The city thought that many people on the pier in all this rain would be a hazard. They're wrong. Hardly anyone will come out in this weather. But I'd rather stay dry, so I'm enjoying the break."

I nodded. The San Borromeo pier was massive—big enough to host the weekly farmers' market where Gramps and Tomas sold horseradish and salsa, respectively. Torrential rain plus hundreds of people might well equal a hazard.

"You're enjoying not watching me outsell you with my horseradish," Gramps said.

"Ha!" Tomas sneered. "As if you could. My salsa is the best south of Silicon Valley."

"Who stacked these sandbags?" Gramps lifted up his flat cap and rubbed his balding head. Water stained the shoulders of his tweedy sports jacket, buttons straining across his broad stomach.

"Brik. And Hyperion," I added belatedly.

"That explains it," Tomas said. He was tall and lanky and had begun to walk with a slight hunch, which was worrying. He was also my landlord. "These are the best-stacked sandbags I've ever seen."

"Professional job," my grandfather agreed.

"Archer was right," I said. "Come inside before you drown." Holding the door for them, I retreated into the tearoom.

The two older men bellied up to the bar beside Archer, who had divested himself of his elegant raincoat and was adjusting his mercury cravat. I took the other men's dripping outwear.

Hyperion plunked down beside Gramps. He set his favorite deck of Tarot cards on the counter. "Hey, ho."

"How was the police station?" Archer asked me.

I blinked. "How did you—?"

"Maricel told me *everything*," Archer said. "She's a doll. An arrest in the tearoom? This town is going to pot."

"It is not," I said. If anything, the latter was true. San Borromeo had gone from a middle-class beach town to a playground for the affluent. It was depressing.

"Police station?" Gramps asked. "What were you doing at the police station?"

"Giving Verbena Pillbrow a ride. It turned out, she wasn't arrested," I explained to Hyperion. "Just questioned."

"Over what?" Tomas asked.

"The murder of a spiritual business coach named Falkner something—"

Hyperion paled. "Falkner? Not Falkner Fiore?"

"Yeah," I said. "You know him?"

"Oh, damn." Hyperion clutched the counter's edge.

"What?" My stomach did an uneasy flip. "What's wrong?"

My partner cleared his throat. "I, uh, *might* be a suspect."

Chapter 3

ANOTHER ONE OF THOSE odd, inconvenient silences fell. A waitress, heading toward the kitchen, brushed silently past us. Two white-haired ladies rose and made their way to the blue front door.

"Why would you be a suspect?" I asked Hyperion.

"I mean, I'm probably not. I just was kind of vocal about calling him out on his business practices."

"How vocal?" I asked. *And what practices?*

"Falkner might have threatened to sue me," Hyperion mumbled. "He wasn't serious though. Libel is hard to prove."

"You put it in writing?" Tomas yelped. An ex-lawyer, Tomas had given us all sorts of helpful advice when we'd started up the tea and Tarot room.

"Er, no," Hyperion said.

Tomas's shoulders relaxed beneath his orange and black jacket. "Then that's slander. You're right—it's hard to prove. You're probably in the clear."

I glanced at Archer. Head cocked, the gossip columnist leaned forward, his navy sports jacket wrinkling against the counter.

"You got any of those roast beef sandwiches left, Abigail?" Gramps asked.

"We'd better," I said.

"Don't change the subject," Archer said. "I want *all* the hot goss."

Hyperion glared. "I don't want to *be* the *hot goss.*"

Tomas shot me a questioning look.

"Gossip," I explained and eyed Archer uneasily. The older man had an online "society" column. After a lifetime in the newspaper business, he'd made the switch to independent, online media. He was terrifyingly good at it. "And who has time for gossip in this storm?"

"I *know*," Archer said. "Did you hear that that old cemetery up the hill is starting to wash out? Just imagine—coffins rampaging down Main Street. And that cemetery has the most *exclusive* bodies," he finished gleefully.

Or maybe we *should* talk about the murder. "How do you know Falkner?" I asked Hyperion.

"Everyone in the spiritual community knew him," Hyperion said. "He started out as a Tarot reader, then realized he could make more money business coaching other Tarot readers."

It was an age-old story, and the consultants always came out on top. "Did he ever coach you?" I asked.

Archer drew a pen and leather notebook from the inside pocket of his navy blazer. He clicked open the pen.

Hyperion gave me a look. "Why do you think I let *you* handle the financial side of the tearoom?"

I adjusted my apron. "I'm not sure how to answer that."

"I was one of his early clients," Hyperion admitted. "Falkner over-promised and under-delivered. But what got me were his manipulative sales tactics. How can you call yourself a spiritual business advisor when you mislead clients from the jump?"

Archer scribbled frantically.

"And you got fooled." Tomas clapped my partner's shoulder. "It happens to the best of us every now and again."

"The unkindest cut of all," Hyperion agreed. "His useless marketing banalogies were one thing. Feeling like a sucker was worse."

"Banalogy?" Archer cocked his head.

"I made it up. Banal plus analogy. Like it?"

"When I can figure out how to use it in a sentence," Archer said, "I will."

Behind the counter, I poured cups of cinnamon and orange tea for the men. "I wonder if Verbena had the same experience? She was one of Falkner's clients. She told me she never trusted him."

"I hope she didn't tell the cops that," Tomas said. "Did she have a lawyer with her?"

"It didn't look like it." I met Hyperion's brown-eyed gaze. "I don't know if she can afford a lawyer." Not if she lived in those apartments.

Archer straightened on his seat. "Oooh. Are you two going to—?"

"No," my partner said. "No, no, no. Definitely not. *Verily* not. Not in the least. No. We are *not* helping Verbena get out of whatever trouble she's gotten herself into."

I lowered my head and got busy wiping down the bar. "I didn't say we should." *But we kind of should.* Verbena was irritating, but that didn't mean she should go to jail for a crime she didn't commit. And I couldn't shake the memory of that brief flash of fear in her eyes.

Hyperion reached across the counter for the honey pot. "Good, because we're staying out of it. Both the victim and the suspect were fluctuating, yammering, maggoty furies."

I eyed him. Hyperion's Lovecraft Word a Day calendar might be gone, but it had not been forgotten. "Yes," I said, "Verbena is irritating and... maladroit, and—"

"Maladroit?" Hyperion's dark brows rocketed toward the ceiling. "She's intentional with her insults."

"All right," I said, "maybe she is. Maybe I *have* fantasized about throwing her out on her ear. Or watching her wash down the street into the Pacific, but—"

"You're not exactly selling me on getting involved." Hyperion arched a dark brow.

"But that just makes her more likely to be found guilty, when we both know Verbena's no killer. We need to help her. She's scared."

"Why?" Hyperion's eyes widened, pleading. "Let the police do their thing."

"We haven't solved a crime since Thanksgiving," I wheedled. Hyperion *had* to be getting antsy. I knew he was getting frustrated hearing about his boyfriend Tony's tales of crime and deception and not having any of his own to share.

Plus, Hyperion and I had once been in the crosshairs of a police investigation. The both of us had looked guilty as hell. We'd only gotten through it because we'd had each other.

"Boredom is no reason to get involved in a crime," Hyperion said loftily.

"Are you kidding me? How many times have you dragged me into trouble for exactly that reason?"

Hyperion rubbed his jaw. "It can't have been that many."

"Oh, that's rich. What about the time you talked me into going to the park at midnight to catch the newest yarn bomber?"

"That was totally legit."

I set my hands on my hips. "Or the time you set up a UFO observatory in my backyard?"

"What?" Tomas asked.

"Or the time—?"

"Fine," Hyperion said hastily, glancing at Tomas. "We'll do it, but I'm totally holding this over you if anything goes wrong."

The odds of things going wrong were close to a hundred percent, but I smiled. We were getting involved.

―――― ℓℓℓ ――――

We might be getting involved, but I still had a day job. Hyperion and I didn't get a chance to do any actual snooping until after we'd closed up and cleaned up and the rest of the staff had gone home.

Resting one arm on the back of his throne-like office chair, I read the laptop screen over his shoulder. Bastet lolled on the red-clothed table. The cat knocked a deck of Tarot cards sideways and started at the sound, orange ears flicking.

Transform yourself. Transform your business. Transform your life.

Are you a psychic, tarot reader, or lightworker looking to take your business to the next level?

I'm Falkner Fiore, and I specialize in helping spiritual entrepreneurs like you skyrocket your business to new heights. My blend of spirit-based coaching and practical strategies will make manifesting clients natural and easy.

If you want to:

- *Unblock your flow and get seen.*

- Attract A-list clients.

- Craft a spiritually based business plan that will drive clients and profits.

- Network with other like-minded entrepreneurs.

- Learn the art of "manifestation marketing."

Sign up now and receive a free Spiritual Business Analysis call (a $99 value) to uncover the hidden potential in your business.

"It's the call where he sucks you in," Hyperion said darkly. He gathered up the fallen cards.

"Oh, look." I pointed. "Scroll down to the testimonials. Any locals we know?"

There were three at the bottom of the elegant page, complete with photos:

Working with Falkner has been nothing short of transformative. He helped me tackle the core issues inside me and my metaphysical bookstore. I've seen a significant increase in client engagement online and a newfound sense of purpose in my work. I highly recommend Falkner to anyone looking for a coach who resonates. — Katey Molina, The Metaphysical Bookshop

I was skeptical at first, but after just a few sessions with Falkner, I'm a believer! His unique blend of business sense and spiritual insight has helped me overcome obstacles I didn't know I had. My apothecary shop has not only grown financially, but I also feel more connected to my higher purpose. — Anna Ogawa, Anna's Arcane Apothecary

I was at a crossroads in my business when I found Falkner. His intuitive approach helped me tap into my inner wisdom and make decisions that felt right on a soul level. As a result, my work as a psychic advisor has flourished, and I've attracted clients who are truly aligned with my values and mission. I'm forever grateful for Falkner's guidance and support! — Tad Trzaskalski, Psychic

I angled my head. "They seemed to like him."

"Because he asks for reviews after the first two weeks of coaching, when you're still on a high." Absently, Hyperion shuffled the deck of Tarot cards. Bastet started at the sound. "Falkner was a sales Svengali. And after you pay his overpriced fees, it's hard to admit it was for nothing."

"Do you recognize any of their names?"

"Yeah, you know how small the spiritual community is on the NorCal coast. We know each other. They're all close, in the Santa Cruz area."

Santa Cruz was basically San Borromeo adjacent. But it was bigger, funkier, and had a lot more going on in the woo-woo world. It also had multiple tearooms, which was one of the reasons why Beanblossom's was in San Borromeo.

Thunder rumbled, and I glanced at the white-painted ceiling. "Then I guess Santa Cruz is where we start."

Chapter 4

I LOVE BOOKSTORES.

I love the smell of the books. I love the quiet. I love the magic.

And there *is* magic in bookstores. Not the *abracadabra* kind, but the promise, the mystery of the words and worlds hidden between the covers.

And even though Katey Molina's metaphysical bookstore was only half books and the rest Tarot cards and crystals and potions, a part of me loved it too.

The other part of me was uneasy. Ironically, for someone who is part-owner in a tea and Tarot room, I had mixed feelings about the metaphysical.

And Katey looked a lot like the mother who'd abandoned me at the San Francisco airport for a spiritual guru. The resemblance plus the dreamcatchers dangling in the window set my teeth on edge.

Rain drummed on the windows overlooking the street, giving the shop a cozy feel. Automatically, I drifted away from the glass counter where Katey stood. I figured Hyperion knew her. He could take the lead. I moved toward a large clearance section.

Katey wore a tie-dyed caftan—a garment I've noticed looks best on tall, willowy women, which she was not. She was slender but at least two inches shorter than me. Her mid-length, silvering hair hung loose about her shoulders.

She looked up from writing in a hardback journal. Her face was make-up-free, and only the faintest of lines spoked from the corners of her gray eyes. "Good morning. How can I help you?"

"Katey, it's *me*," Hyperion said.

She blinked. "Oh. I... I'm sorry, I recognize you, but I'm terrible with names. You read Tarot, don't you?"

"Exactly." He pressed his hand to the front of his charcoal sweater. "I'm Hyperion, Hyperion Night. This is my business partner, Abigail Beanblossom."

I shifted my weight on the thin, gray carpet. Sunday mornings were busy in the tearoom, and I felt guilty sneaking away. I hoped the reacquaintance portion of this interview didn't take too long.

"Right. Hyperion. How could I forget?" She clasped his hand between two of hers, her silvery rings flashing beneath the pendant lights. Their red shades turned her hands orange. "Are you looking for some new cards?"

"Oooh. Have you got—?" He shook his head. "No. I'm on a budget. This is business. Have you heard about Falkner?"

Her face spasmed. The expression was gone in a blink.

"What about him?" she asked.

There's no good way to give someone that kind of bad news. And though I knew it was gutless of me, I was glad Hyperion was the one delivering it. He was better at that sort of thing.

"Then you haven't heard." He glanced at me and lowered his voice. "I'm sorry, but Falkner's dead."

Katey stepped backward, hand to her throat. Her face turned the color of old parchment. "Dead? But... that's impossible."

"Why?" I asked.

"Because... Sorry. That was a stupid reaction. But..." Katey turned back to Hyperion. Her tongue flicked across her bottom lip. "Are you sure? He's dead?"

"I wouldn't joke about that," Hyperion said flatly.

"No," she said faintly. "I don't suppose you would. How... How did it happen? Was it... a heart attack?"

"I don't know." Hyperion frowned and whisked his hand over his damp, near-black hair. "Did he have heart problems?"

"No, but... I don't think so." She tugged on a gold hoop earring. "It's just that he's a man of a certain age... I need to tell the others."

"What others?" I asked, and she hesitated. "Sorry," I said. "I'm being nosy."

Hyperion glared at me. "We ask because Falkner's death has been such a shock."

"No, no," she said, nodding to me. "It's natural to wonder. I meant the others in our group coaching." Katey glanced at a wall, its shelves lined with candles and smudging bundles. "Group was more cost-effective for me than individual coaching."

"I understand about wanting to save money," I said. It was nothing to be embarrassed about. It was just smart. "When you're a small business owner—"

"You're one too?" she asked me.

"Hyperion and I run Beanblossom's Tea and Tarot."

She smiled. "Then you understand. It's more than just a business."

I understood all right. Beanblossom's was my passion, my livelihood.

Katey nodded, her silvery hair swinging. "I don't know what else I'd do. I can't imagine..." She blinked rapidly. "Poor Falkner."

"How long have you had the bookstore?" I asked.

"Fifteen years," she said.

"What inspired you to open it?" All of the small, local bookstores in San Borromeo had closed. In the online era, selling paper books was a tough business model.

"My mother used to work in a bookstore," she said. "I'd spend afternoons there, after school, when I wasn't working at my dad's place." A shadow fell across her face.

"Your dad's...?" I prompted.

"He died young."

My heart pinched. My parents were still alive, if incommunicado. But I'd lost my grandmother when I was little, and she and my grandfather had been the ones to raise me. I understood the pain of parental loss at a young age. "I'm sorry."

Katey fingered her bead necklace. "I should probably tell the others what happened," she said uncertainly.

"Which others?" I prompted.

"Anna, Jose, and Tad. And Verbena," she added forbiddingly.

I smothered a smile. Clearly, I wasn't the only one Verbena drove batty.

"Sorry," Katey said quickly. "I didn't mean it that way. Verbena is... Ah..."

"Verbena is Verbena," Hyperion said, and she shot him a relieved smile. "Who's Jose? Not Jose Hidalgo?"

"Yes, he's new to the group," Katey said.

I looked around the empty store. Crystals gleamed dully on a central table. "Do you run this place all by yourself?"

"Yes," she said. "It's hard to find good help."

"It must be a challenge," I said, "doing everything yourself."

"Sometimes, but not today. Sundays are always a bit slow."

I'd have thought weekends would be best for selling books. But the storm was keeping a lot of people home.

"Was there something else you wanted?" Katey asked.

Hyperion snapped his fingers. "Do you have that new book by Robert Place?"

"Sorry. We just sold our last copy."

"What about Corinne Kenner?"

"She'd be in the Tarot section, over there." Katey pointed.

"Thanks." Hyperion ambled into a nook of bookshelves, and I followed.

Hyperion ran his fingers down a line of colorful paperback spines. "I'm torn," he said in a low voice. "Baranko hasn't been here yet, but who's to say he'll *ever* get here?"

"He found Verbena," I murmured and glanced over the shelf at Katey. We couldn't interrogate her if the police hadn't done it first. That might be considered interfering in an investigation. We may have *already* crossed the line.

"He didn't just find her; he brought her in for questioning. That's serious. Baranko must have reason to think Verbena's a real suspect."

"And Katey isn't one?" I stuck my head from the alcove. Katey scribbled in her journal and closed it.

"Exactly," he said. "Which means he may not show up here at all."

"Or he might." I pulled my purse closer.

Katey drifted into the nook, her caftan billowing. "Find the book you wanted?"

"No," Hyperion said. "All you've got is her old stuff. Which is terrific, BTW, but I've got all of these." He motioned toward a row of colorful spines.

"Would you like me to order it for you?" she asked.

"No." Hyperion sighed. "Still on a budget, and my impulse for impulse purchases is dying."

I bought a nettle tincture for my blood pressure. Over the last few months, it had unaccountably been rising. We left the bookstore and darted through the rain to Hyperion's yellow Jeep.

Hyperion started the car. "That was a bust." He jammed his foot on the accelerator, and the Jeep sped forward.

Hastily, I buckled my seatbelt. "Not entirely. We got a new name—Jose Hidalgo. And we learned Katey's bookstore isn't doing well." The massive clearance section and lack of customers, employees, and new books were all signs of that.

"Are *any* bookstores doing well?" He swerved around a slow-moving Tesla.

"They're a dying breed," I agreed sadly and displayed the label on the small blue bottle. "From Anna's Arcane Apothecary."

Out of the corner of my eye, a black shape skimmed close.

"I'd have thought you could make your own tinc— Whoa!"

A horn blared. Hyperion jerked the wheel to the left, his shoulders hunched.

The Jeep skidded, hydroplaning across the three-lane road. I grabbed the door handle, my fingers digging in, my heart jumping. A black monster truck honked and sped past, spraying my window with water.

Hyperion wrestled the car back into our proper lane. He exhaled slowly.

Releasing the door handle, I drew a deep breath and exhaled. My heartrate resumed normal operations, fear replaced by irritation. What *was* it with big trucks? Or had that been the same big truck?

He cleared his throat. "As I was saying, I think... What was I saying? Oh, yeah. Should we go to Anna's apothecary shop?"

I was pretty sure I wasn't imagining the reluctance in his tone. And I couldn't blame him for wanting to stay in. The streets were a mess. "I should get back to the tearoom." I pocketed the bottle in my oversized hoodie.

While Hyperion piloted us through the wet streets, I called my grandfather. He assured me his house had not gone surfing down his hillside.

"Do you need me to pick up any groceries for you on the way home?" I asked. "I'm out and about already. No sense in you getting wet."

"I'm fully stocked. Don't worry about me."

"I could bring lasagna over—"

"I do *not* want you driving me lasagna tonight. Not in this weather. Stay home."

I grimaced. The one thing I'd sworn I'd never do was baby my grandfather. "Well, good then," I said. "More lasagna for me."

He laughed. "Stay dry, Abigail." He disconnected.

Hyperion and I returned to Beanblossom's rear parking lot. It was inch-deep in water, and I tiptoed through it, my worry growing. Was the storm drain backing up?

I stepped over the sandbags, and Hyperion opened the heavy door for me. Peeling off my wet jacket, I hung it in the kitchen closet then hurried into the dining area.

Hyperion's boyfriend, ex-cop and current PI, Tony Chase, leaned one elbow on the white quartz counter. Verbena, in a green and brown paisley tunic, batted her eyes up at him.

I couldn't blame her for trying. In his fitted jacket, jeans, and cowboy hat, Tony was a long, tall drink of Texan water. He was also very taken.

I walked behind the counter. "Hyperion's in his office," I told the PI.

Tony touched the rim of his cowboy hat, darkened with rain. "Thanks. If you'll excuse me," he said to Verbena and strode into the hallway.

She frowned, twisting the string of green beads around her neck. They matched her tights and leggings. Verbena turned to me. "It's almost the lunch rush. Where have you been?"

"Researching tinctures." It wasn't a lie. But I wasn't going to tell her the whole truth.

"They're simply herbal extracts made by soaking herbs in alcohol or vinegar. The liquid pulls the active ingredients from the herbs and concentrates them. They're cheap and easy to make. What's to research?"

Verbena was right on all counts, and why was I surprised? The tea witch was an irritant, but she wasn't ignorant—not when it came to herbalism.

"I'm researching suppliers," I said.

"I'd have thought you'd already have access to bulk herbs. But if you're looking for tinctures to sell, there's a woman in my coaching group who wholesales."

"Anna Ogawa?"

Verbena blew into her teacup. "You know her?" she asked, not meeting my gaze.

"No, but I've heard of her apothecary shop."

"Then maybe Falkner's coaching was working after all." She tossed a length of her brown hair over one shoulder.

"What was she getting coached on, exactly?" I asked.

"I *told* you. Spirit-based marketing."

"Uh, huh."

"Don't roll your eyes. Ethical marketing matters. I don't want to have to trick people into paying for my services."

My face warmed. What was she implying? I'd never tricked anyone into visiting Beanblossom's. I wouldn't know how. "Neither do I."

"Then what's the problem?"

"No problem. Spiritual marketing just seems like a... gimmick."

"It's *absolutely* a gimmick," she said, "and it works. How do you think Falkner got me to sign up for it? He may be—may have been gimmicky, but he knew his stuff."

I grabbed a towel from beneath the counter and wiped a splotch of brown liquid from it. "You told me you never trusted him."

"That's different."

"How?"

"I never trusted him *personally*," she said. "Professionally, I took what I could get from him and that was it."

My hand spasmed on the towel. Well, that was just... Actually, it wasn't too terrible a philosophy. "Tell me more about his coaching."

"I was doing group coaching with him. You can learn a lot from listening to other people's challenges. And one-on-one would have been more expensive."

So I'd heard. "When's the next meeting?"

"There's usually a meeting Sunday night," she said. "But obviously, it won't happen tonight."

"Where?"

"Why? Like I said, with Falkner dead, there's no meeting."

Because I'm trying to help you. "I think... maybe... we should make an appearance anyway. The others might not know he's dead." Or they might, if Katey had called them. Either way, it was time to meet some of the other people who'd known the dead man.

"I don't want to go. It will be a waste of time without Falkner."

"You don't have to go, but I'd like to," I said patiently.

The adrenaline rush from our near traffic accident had faded. It was only rain, and I could drive in that. And I wanted to know if Baranko had gotten in touch with any of Falkner's other clients yet.

If he hadn't... I bit my bottom lip. Maybe the detective really was focused exclusively on Verbena.

And that was a problem.

Chapter 5

"Go where?" Hyperion ambled from the hallway and into the tearoom. Casually, he slid his hands into the pockets of his black, skinny slacks. I noticed he maintained a safe sprinting distance from Verbena at the tea bar.

"I'm not going to a coaching meeting in the middle of a bomb cyclone when the coach is dead," Verbena huffed. "And I'd better be able to get a refund for the rest of the meetings."

"Bomb cyclone?" I asked blankly. "What's that?"

"I thought we were in an atmospheric river," Hyperion said. A waitress bustled past him.

"No." Verbena blew on her tea. "Explosive cyclogenesis occurs when an extratropical cyclonic low-pressure area experiences a rapid deepening, causing winds up to 95 miles per hour. Bomb cyclone. *Duh*."

"Ah, okay," I said. "But what's—?"

Hyperion placed a hand on my arm. "I think that's enough questions, Abigail."

Verbena slid from the stool. "It's supposed to hit San Borromeo tonight. If you're smart, you'll get home before it does. Can one of you give me a ride?"

"Tearoom duties," I said quickly. "I'm stuck here until closing." And clean-up never looked so good.

She looked at Hyperion.

He glared at me, his mouth pinching. But it wasn't my fault I'd been quicker. "Fine," he finally said. "My Jeep's in the back."

I smiled. He'd get the address of the coaching meeting out of Verbena. And the rain was blowing harder, so he'd also get very, very wet.

So. This was a bomb cyclone.

Hyperion piloted his Jeep through a puddle, and water fanned from the wheels onto the side windows. Involuntarily, I pressed deeper into the seat. We wound up a narrow, hillside road, and my grip on the door handle tightened.

Wind howled around the car. Rain blotted out the light from the rare streetlamp, sinking the winter night into even deeper gloom.

"I can't believe you made me drive Verbena home on my own," he grumped for the third time. A gust of wind buffeted the Jeep.

"I had to work in the tearoom 'til closing," I said. "Thanks for coming back to pick me up though."

For once, I was glad Hyperion was at the wheel. The storm slowed his usual enthusiastic driving, and the Jeep rode higher than my Mazda. We'd already encountered two intersections that had become minor rivers.

Lightning flashed, illuminating a black and white chiaroscuro of tossing trees and brush.

CRACK!

A dark shape crashed in front of the Jeep, and I sucked in a sharp breath. Hyperion hit the brakes hard, lifting out of his seat.

Momentum flung my upper body forward, straining against the seatbelt. The Jeep skidded to a halt. I gaped at the fallen eucalyptus tree, inches from his front bumper.

Eucalyptus trees are no joke. The wood is hard and heavy. There's no question as to the outcome when it's car vs. tree. The Eucalyptus always wins.

This one had nearly crushed us. If Hyperion had been a second slower to react...

"What I like about you," Hyperion said evenly, "is you're not a screamer."

Only because I'd been too startled to scream. The idea of starting now was tempting.

I swallowed and started breathing again. "That was close. Did lightning hit it?"

"That would have been louder," Hyperion said. "The wind must have blown over the tree."

Feeling foolish, I nodded. Trees had been falling all week, their roots loosened by erosion and the rain-soaked earth. "How long will it take us to go back and around the other way?"

"Everyone else will be long gone by the time we get to Falkner's house," he fretted.

"Can we get around the tree?"

In answer, he stepped from the car and walked to the edge of the road. Hyperion peered over the hillside, then turned and gave me a thumbs up.

He returned inside the Jeep and shook himself like a wet dog, splattering me with droplets. "We can make it. Get the reciprocating saw out of the back, will ya?"

"Ah..." I angled my head. "Why do you have a reciprocating saw in the back of your Jeep?"

"In case I want to cut up a body, obvs."

I stared.

He heaved a breath. "Your grandfather wanted to borrow it," he said. "There are a lot of branches down around his house."

Were there? I bit my bottom lip. I hadn't visited Gramps since the storm had started a week ago, but he'd told me his house was fine.

I pressed my lips together. And if he said his place was okay, it was okay. A few branches down did not a disaster make.

We got the orange saw out of its case, and Hyperion cut through the tree branches at its top in record time. I piled them as neatly as I could, but the wind kept dashing branches down the hill. They smelled like a day spa.

"Good enough," Hyperion bellowed over the roaring wind. "Let's bounce."

Headlights swept around the curve of the hillside. I winced and shielded my eyes with one dripping hand.

The headlights stopped two car-lengths behind the Jeep. They glowed electric blue and slanted demonically. A sapphire ribbon of light stretched between its headlights like a wicked smile.

I shifted uneasily. Silicon Valley now went all the way to Santa Barbara, and there was a lot of money in it. Money meant fancy sports cars. But there was something disturbing about this one, with its sly blue smile.

And why was it just sitting there? Why hadn't the driver checked to see what was going on?

Likely the rich kid driving it just didn't want to get wet. But a chill trailed down the back of my neck.

Ignoring the newcomer, Hyperion strode to the back of the Jeep and deposited the saw inside. He slammed the rear door.

The headlights edged forward. The car stopped a length away.

"Get in," Hyperion said shortly.

I scrambled into the Jeep.

Hyperion backed up a few feet then crawled toward the gap he'd made between the branches and the steep drop. "Don't look."

I looked.

I looked into an inky maw, a chasm of infinite darkness. Gripping my purse against my stomach, I tried not to think of the Jeep tumbling into that void. The fall might not kill us. A tree *might* stop our descent. *Eventually.*

The interior of the Jeep brightened, and I looked over my shoulder. The sports car rolled toward us, too fast. Hyperion yelped and stepped on the gas.

We roared forward. I lurched against my seat, my heart slammed into my throat, and we passed the fallen tree. Hyperion braked and pulled to the side of the dark road.

"What are you—?"

"Letting this idiot pass," he gritted out.

The sports car pulled up beside ours and stopped. I tensed. This was not normal driving behavior. The passenger window rolled down. *Not normal.*

A man whose skin had only seen the light of computer screens leaned toward the opening. He adjusted his spectacles, his brown eyes serious. "You two okay?" he shouted.

I sagged against the seat. Hyperion rolled down the window.

"Razzzor?" my partner asked. "What the hell are you doing? I thought you were trying to run us off the road."

Razzzor was more than my past employer. He was also a tech multi-gazillionaire who'd retired early, made a video game for fun, and then had gotten sucked back into the work world when the game had accidentally become a hit.

My ex-boss blushed. "Sorry. I thought I was tapping the brake, but I hit the gas instead."

"What are you doing here?" I asked.

"I heard there was a murder," he shouted cheerfully.

My eyes narrowed. "Did you put a tracker on Hyperion's car again?"

"No," he said in an injured voice. "I'm all about healthy boundaries. I followed you from the tearoom."

I stared. Rain pattered on the black road. For not the first time, I wanted to wring Razzzor's neck.

"You could have called," Hyperion said. "And what kind of car is that?"

"I didn't want to distract your driving in the middle of an explosive cyclogenesis," my ex-boss said. "And it's a Mazda Furai."

"That's a *Mazda*?" I asked. It could have come from a different planet than my Mazda, and I felt offended on my hatchback's behalf. If Mazda could create something like that, couldn't it have made my hatchback a *little* sexier?

"Yep," Razzzor said. "How can I help?"

"I haven't been able to find anything online about the murder," I said across Hyperion. "How did you?"

"Eh, you know," Razzzor said shiftily. "I pick things up."

"Anything you can pick up about Falkner Fiore and who might have a motive to kill him would be useful," I shouted. Razzzor had an uncanny ability for cyberstalking. The world was lucky he only used his powers for good.

"Where are you going?" my ex-boss asked.

"To Falkner's house," Hyperion said. "There's supposed to be a coaching meeting there tonight. We're hoping not all of his clients got word that it's off. Want to come?"

"Uh... No," Razzzor said. "Not really an IRL person."

A silence fell. "Anything else?" Hyperion asked.

"No. Uh... no." The sports car didn't move. Rain lashed down, rattling on the Jeep's rooftop and pattering on the street.

"You sure?" I asked.

"I was just, uh, wondering, if anything unusual has happened recently," Razzzor said.

"Aside from the murder?" I asked.

"Yeah, aside from that," Razzzor said, oblivious to my sarcasm. "Did anyone say anything, uh, unusual to you?"

"No," I said, baffled. "I mean, Verbena is a murder suspect—"

"No, no, not that," he said absently. "I'll get on that deep research for you." Razzzor rolled up the window and turned the sports car around on the narrow road. His car vanished around the fallen tree.

I cocked my head. "Do you think Razzzor was acting a little... weird?"

"Weirder than usual?" Hyperion snorted. "The guy launched a private space agency for cats."

"That was a joke," I said. Though in fairness, it seemed to have taken on a life of its own. A lot of people thought it was real.

"He has a team of memeologists."

I brushed back a lock of hair. "Controlling the meme cycle is the next frontier in digital influence."

"Smell-o-vision?"

"Okay," I admitted. "That was a bad idea."

We continued up the hillside. My shoes had filled with water and my feet begun to itch by the time we reached Falkner's house.

Did I say house? I meant villa.

The place was massive—a Spanish-style estate with white adobe walls and red-tiled roofs. The lights were on inside and out, and three cars sat parked in the driveway. Three people hunched beneath the front door's arched entry.

They straightened eagerly as we pulled up. Hyperion and I stepped from the Jeep and jogged through the rain, joining them beneath the shelter.

Their faces fell. They looked at each other in confusion.

"Falkner's not coming," Hyperion said. "I'm sorry, but we have bad news. He's dead."

Anna Ogawa let out a soft cry and pressed a hand to her mouth. I was glad again for those photos beside the testimonials on Falkner's website. I recognized her and one of the other people sheltering from the rain.

Anna was significantly shorter than me—five-foot-nothing, I guessed. Slender, she looked to be in her early forties. She hugged her pale blue raincoat cinched about her waist.

Tad Trzaskalski was there too. The thirty-something stood over six-feet tall. The bulk beneath his trench coat seemed to be more pudge than muscle. His curling brown hair had been flattened to his head by the rain.

A third man eyed us. "Hyperion? What are you doing here? And what do you mean Falkner's dead. How?" He was olive-skinned and slender in his navy raincoat, the shoulder lapels frayed.

"Hi, Jose." Hyperion stuck out a hand, and the two men shook. "I heard you were a client."

"Heard from whom?" Jose asked. "And what happened to Falkner?"

"How did he die?" Anna leaned forward, her dark brows drawn down, her brown eyes gleaming.

"I don't know how he died," Hyperion said. "but it was murder. The police came by our tea and Tarot room to question one of the customers."

Anna hissed an indrawn breath. She hugged her raincoat tighter. "Verbena? Or was it Katey?"

"Why would you think it was either?" I asked.

"Because neither are here," she said.

Fair enough. "Verbena," I said. "But Katey knows too. We spoke with her this afternoon. Did Katey have a motive to want Falkner dead?"

"No, of course not," Anna said quickly. "Katey wouldn't— She's not that sort of person."

"What sort of person is she?" Hyperion cocked his head.

Anna smiled faintly. "Diligent."

"And I repeat," Jose said, "who told you about me?"

"Verbena," Hyperion said. "She mentioned the meeting tonight. We thought we'd check it out."

"There's no meeting without Falkner," Tad said in an Australian accent. "And you should know that if he's dead. What are you really doing here? Come to pillage his course materials?" He stuck his hands in his trench coat's pockets.

Hyperion sneered. "As if."

It was a weak retort on Hyperion's part. My partner seemed to realize it, and his skin darkened.

"Did the police arrest Verbena?" Anna asked eagerly.

"No," I said, "but—"

"What did they say?" she asked.

I shifted. "Only that Falkner was dead."

"What did Verbena say?" she asked.

I rubbed the back of my neck. "That she had no idea what happened."

"Do you know anything more?" she asked.

"No," I said. "We hoped you might."

Anna shook her head, her voice dropping. "What a shame," she said. I didn't know if she regretted our lack of intel or the death of her coach. "But there's nothing we can do here." She moved toward one of the parked cars.

"Wait," I improvised. "We came to offer you the tearoom. For your meeting tonight."

"Yes," Hyperion said. "You should support each other in this time of, er... Verbena said you would be out a meeting place."

Tad lifted his chin. "What's in it for you?"

"Goodwill." I forced a smile. Being accused of having ulterior motives is super irritating—particularly when you *do* have ulterior motives. "We've got a tea and Tarot room, and I don't know enough of the people in the spiritual community in Santa Cruz."

Tad's eyes narrowed to slits.

"We also have leftover scones we can't do anything with," I continued. "And we'd like to build our business as an after-hours meeting space. We wouldn't charge for tonight, of course, but your feedback would be useful."

Tad grinned at me. "You had me at scones."

Chapter 6

OWNING A PRIVATE MEETING space has its advantages. Even if the chairs were upside down on the tables when we walked in, the tearoom was clean. Or at least it *was* clean until we trooped down the rear hallway and across the tearoom's freshly mopped floor.

Ugh. Resigning myself to another round of mopping, I grabbed an overturned chair and handed it to Jose.

"Uh, Abigail?" Hyperion pointed to the floor around the front door.

"I'll mop it when—" I sucked in a breath.

Water puddled on the laminate floor. I peered through a window. Water rivered down the sidewalk, hitting our sandbags and sheeting straight up, before pooling at the front door.

I cursed. Someone had moved the sandbags so that they formed a semi-circle around the door instead of Brik's barricade redirecting the flow into the street.

I opened the door. A gust of wind caught it, yanking me forward, and I staggered into the rain.

Water gushed into the tearoom. Hyperion's arm shot past my shoulder, and he grabbed the blue door. I waded into the deep puddle and tugged at a sandbag. Sodden with water, it was too heavy to move.

Gently, Hyperion pushed me aside. "I got it." With a grunt, he hefted a sandbag. "I don't know what idiot moved these," he gritted out, "but I *really* want to find out."

Leaving him to shift sandbags, I jogged to the kitchen for the mop and a white tablecloth. I tossed the latter to the newcomers. Jose caught it one handed. Anna removed her plastic rain cap and shook out her black hair.

In a few minutes, Hyperion had all the sandbags back where they belonged. I pushed the worst of the flood waters back onto the brick sidewalk.

Hyperion swept droplets of water off his dark hair. "If we hadn't returned tonight..."

"The flooding would have been a lot worse." I shuddered. Water damage was insidious. Mold. Mildew. Warped wood and flooring. There could have been serious expenses involved—expenses we couldn't afford.

Tad draped his trench coat over the back of a chair. "I think you said something about scones?" He pronounced the final word "skons."

"Give her a moment." Jose smiled at me. "She's been battling the elements."

"We *all* have," Tad groused.

"The coat tree is right *there*." Hyperion jerked his chin toward the tree near the hostess stand.

"How can I help?" Anna walked to the coat tree and unbuckled her pale blue raincoat, exposing a neat, black dress. Tad followed suit.

I pointed to the bar. "Go ahead and choose your tea from the selection behind the bar. You'll find the cups and hot water dispenser there too."

I strode to the kitchen. Anna was an apothecary. She could brew her own tea.

When I returned with the scones, jam, and lemon curd, everyone was around the table. Steaming teacups sat in front of them.

I set the tray on the table and passed out white plates. "How does your group coaching usually work?" I asked brightly.

"Falkner would start with a short lecture on a topic." Anna plucked a cherry-lemonade scone from the tray. "Then we'd ask questions about anything we had on our minds, and he'd give us advice."

"Just Falkner?" Hyperion asked.

"Sometimes we'd chip in from our own experience." Jose tugged on the worn collar of his sweater and reached for a scone.

"There's no reason not to do the same tonight," Hyperion said. "You're all here, you're together."

"Why *are* we here?" Tad folded his arms over his bulging stomach. The buttons on his plaid shirt threatened to pop. His gaze flicked to the scones.

"To coach each other, presumably," I said. "But before we leave you to get started, why don't you tell me more about your businesses?" I sat in the empty chair between Anna and Jose. "Maybe we can help each other."

"I own a small apothecary shop." Anna spread lemon curd on her scone. "It's got decent pedestrian traffic, but that drops in the winter. I'm trying to move to more online sales to smooth things out and increase my income."

"Hyperion's mostly online." I took a scone from the tray. "How's that working for you?" I asked him.

My partner shot me a look. He knew I knew *exactly* how it was going.

"My biggest surprise was that most of my sales don't come from my website," Hyperion said. "It comes from social media. The downside is, I have to spend several hours a week making videos and social posts. I don't have a system where I can just set it and forget it. Not yet, at least."

Jose braced his elbows on the table, rumpling the white cloth. "Where and how often are you posting?"

A lively and incredibly boring discussion ensued. They talked about the benefits of various social media platforms, still images vs. video, and podcasting. Tad argued between bites, downing two scones piled with lemon curd and cherry jam.

While the men argued about short vs. longform video, Anna leaned toward me. "Your tearoom is charming. I'm sorry I haven't stopped by sooner. I've heard of Beanblossom's, but when your tearoom is open, I'm busy working at my own shop."

"Trust me, I get it. If I didn't have staff, I'd be anchored to this place." I crumbled off a corner of the scone.

She sighed. "I'm on my own. I had a part-time assistant, but she quit a month ago." Her voice dropped. "What's it like having Hyperion for a partner?"

"It's made life a lot easier," I said, purposely vague. She was fishing for gossip, and I wasn't interested in giving it to her. Admittedly, this made me a hypocrite, since I wanted gossip from Anna about the coaching group.

"Where do you source your herbs?" she asked.

I gave Anna the name of my supplier, and she nodded. "That's one of my suppliers, too. Say, have you considered any cross-promotional opportunities?"

I straightened a little in my chair. "Such as?"

"Such as selling your Tarot teas in my apothecary, and me selling tinctures here?"

I considered that. Quality control was important to me. I controlled what I was selling at Beanblossom's because I made everything. If I started selling other people's products, they'd have to be good.

But I *had* sold scones from a nearby bakery when I'd started out. Selling other people's stuff wasn't out of the question. "Interesting idea. I'd love to learn more about your tinctures."

"Why don't you come to my shop?" Anna asked, and we arranged a time for a visit.

I slathered lemon curd on my piece of scone. "Have you done much cross-promotion?"

She set down her tea. "A little with Katey." She shook her head. "Falkner was working with us to get things started."

"Was he a good coach?" I popped the scone into my mouth. With the lemon curd, it was extra tangy. The chewy dried cherry had a little sour to it as well, and the chewiness was perfection.

She blinked rapidly and looked away. "Yes."

Would she say more in front of the others? I lowered my voice. "Anna—"

"Tad is right." Jose put his cup on his plate with a clatter and gave Hyperion a hard look. "You're asking too many questions about Falkner."

"I don't want to steal his stupid methods," Hyperion snapped. "I'm a Tarot reader, not a coach."

"Are you sure about that?" Jose asked.

Hyperion blinked. "I guess there is some coaching involved in my readings, but... I don't care about Falkner's business."

"Then why are you asking so much about it?" Tad asked.

"Because I'm nosy," Hyperion said. "Don't you want to know who killed your coach?"

"I expect when the police arrest someone," Jose said calmly, "we'll find out."

"But what if they don't?" Hyperion asked. "Crimes go unsolved all the time. And what if they arrest the wrong person?"

"That almost never happens," Tad said.

Hyperion snorted.

Anna looked thoughtful. "I find it interesting that the police questioned Verbena."

Tad rolled up the cuffs of his plaid shirt. "She obviously had the hots for Falkner, and he wasn't interested. Verbena is the Sheila scorned."

"No," Anna said. "That's not what I meant. I'm surprised the police didn't question *Katey*. We all heard them arguing last week."

"Anna..." Tad said warningly.

"Arguing about what?" I asked.

She glanced at Tad. "I couldn't hear the words," she said, "just the raised voices. And then she stormed off. Did any of you catch what it was about?"

"Some of us don't listen at keyholes," Tad said, and Anna's heart-shaped face flushed.

"I'd rather not gossip. It's bad for the soul." Jose rose. "But I admit, this discussion has been... enlightening. Perhaps it *would* be worthwhile to continue our coaching sessions?"

Tad scraped back his chair. "I'll think about it." He grabbed his trench coat off the coat tree, strode to the back of the tearoom, and vanished down the hallway. The metal door at the end of the hallway clanged.

"I guess that's it then." Anna stood as well and collected her raincoat. "Thanks for sharing your tearoom with us. I'll see you later."

"I'll be there," I said. And so would Hyperion.

She left as well. Jose hesitated. "I do want to know who killed Falkner. The world needs balance. It won't have it as long as his murderer is free."

"Can you think of anyone who might have wanted to kill him?" Hyperion asked.

"Falkner had no family. His life was his work. His consulting practice was nearly all online. He only worked with us in person because we're local, and because I think he liked to keep his hand in with live coaching. He'd sometimes test new presentations out on us before he posted them online. But... there were strange currents within our group."

"What sort of currents?" Hyperion asked.

Jose walked to the coat tree at the front of the room. "The energies were... off. Not just between Falkner and individuals within the group. Between nearly everyone. I thought of quitting because of it."

"But you suggested continuing the group just now," I said, my lips pressing flat.

"Yes." He shrugged into his navy raincoat. "I think... I want to see where this is going. Good night. I'm sure I'll see you both again." He walked to the rear of the room and vanished down the hallway as well. The heavy door banged shut.

"Do you believe him?" Hyperion asked.

I didn't believe any of them, and I shrugged. But I was cynical. It wasn't the first time I'd noticed the spiritual community could be less than enlightened.

My parents were as New Age as they came and both had a major spiritual deficit when it came to parental instincts.

I mopped up dirty footprints while Hyperion pretended to be busy with something in his office. Then I geared up in raincoat and galoshes, and the two of us left together.

Outside, I turned to lock the rear door. A gust of wind and rain buffeted me, and I blinked to see the keyhole.

There was a metallic creak, and I glanced around the dark parking lot. But my vision was limited by the storm and the dumpster, which had somehow rolled into the middle of the lot.

It rolled an inch, and I frowned. Could the wind have moved it? It *couldn't* be full.

"Hurry up," Hyperion bounced from one foot to the other, his long, charcoal coat flapping around his knees. "It's freezing."

The lock clicked. I clambered over the sandbags and followed him toward our cars, parked side by side.

Hyperion stopped short. "Hey!"

The dumpster rumbled toward us. I blinked, disbelieving. "You don't see that every day."

"Get in the game. We have to stop it before it hits my—one of our cars." He splashed toward the rumbling blue dumpster.

But it wasn't going to hit a car. The dumpster gathered speed, water arcing from its metal wheels.

The tendons in my neck tightened, and I shouted a curse. It was going to hit Hyperion.

Chapter 7

"Look out!" I lurched helplessly for Hyperion. Rain sheeted down, blinding.

The dumpster jounced and rattled, bearing down on my partner. He shouted and leapt sideways. Gripping his elbow, he pirouetted, vanishing behind the speeding dumpster.

"Hyperion!" I dodged the dumpster, my red galoshes splashing through the parking lot.

A flash of lightning illuminated Hyperion's lean form, bent double, one arm cradled to his chest. The hems of his long, dark coat billowed like a cloak.

CRASH.

"Are you okay?" Panting, I stopped beside him. My hand reached out to touch his back, and then I withdrew it.

He straightened and grimaced. "Yeah," he said tightly. "Just banged my elbow. I heard a crash. What did it hit?"

"What?" I turned, and my stomach bottomed. The dumpster pressed against the side of a small blue car—*my* small blue car. I slogged toward it and swore again.

I wouldn't be driving anywhere soon. The Mazda's tires bent at odd angles. The driver's side had been crushed. A lump hardened my throat. I *needed* that car.

Hyperion clapped my sagging shoulder. "Look on the bright side. My Jeep is fine."

My chest heaved. "Bright side for *you*. What were you thinking jumping in front of that thing?"

He rubbed his elbow and tried to look contrite. "I've never seen a dumpster move that fast."

"And across a lot covered in water," I said, thoughtful. The wind *could* have blown the dumpster, but that would have to mean its wheels were...

Hyperion bent to study the dumpster's wheels. "They're unlocked."

Dammit. "Why did it have to hit *my* car?" I wailed. And what idiot had unlocked the wheels?

"There are only half a dozen cars in the lot," my partner pointed out. "Odds are it would hit one of them. You were just unlucky."

I stomped my foot, sending up a satisfying spray of water. This seemed like more than bad luck. Could someone have been trying to target us? I scanned the parking lot. Aside from Hyperion and me, it was empty. And I was being paranoid.

Hyperion grasped my shoulders and steered me back to the tearoom's rear entrance. He unlocked it and bundled me inside the dark hallway. "May as well call the tow truck where it's dry."

Shedding my raincoat, I made the call from the tearoom kitchen while I heated water for tea. I brewed two cups of ginger tea and brought one to Hyperion, ensconced in his office.

The twinkle lights and timed electric candles gave the room a cozy feel. Hyperion's coat hung from the antler coat tree. He tugged the collar of his charcoal turtleneck higher.

Hyperion took a cup without looking and booted up his laptop on the red-clothed table. "What's this?"

"Ginger tea. It's good for reducing inflammation. How's your elbow?"

"Inflamed." He sipped the tea. "When's the tow truck getting here?"

"It's going to be over an hour," I said. "The rain's caused a lot of accidents."

"That's nice," Hyperion leaned forward in his thronelike chair.

"Accidents are nice?"

"What? Sorry. No. There's a newspaper article about Falkner's death."

"Finally," I grumped. Grabbing the other chair, I dragged it around the table to sit beside him.

Police Investigate After Person Found Dead in San Borromeo Home

January 20, 2025

The San Boromeo Police Department has launched a suspicious death investigation after business coach Falkner Fiore was found dead inside his San Borromeo home.

Police and emergency responders were called to Fiore's home at 3:30 PM Friday afternoon when a gardener spotted Mr. Fiore prone in his living room. When emergency responders arrived, they found Mr. Fiore deceased.

"It doesn't say much," I said. How had Falkner been killed?

"I should have known Falkner had a gardener," Hyperion said. "He wasn't the type to get his hands dirty."

I crossed my legs at the ankles, and my galoshes squeaked. "He missed out. Getting your hands dirty is half the fun."

My partner grinned. "Oh, totally. And I'll ignore the potential for inuendo you left me, because I know you're only trying to cheer me up."

"Thanks." My gaze flicked to the white ceiling. "Too bad the paper doesn't mention the gardener's name."

"I'm sure the police have interviewed him."

They'd likely interviewed him at the scene, since he'd discovered the body. "Which means we wouldn't be interfering in an investigation if we talked to him now. Are there any other articles?"

Hyperion shook his head. "There are, however, some fairly recent posts."

"What?"

"You know, that social media thing where people pontificate in under 280 characters?"

Augh. "I know what a post is. How recent?"

"They must have posted them on their way to the tearoom." He tsked. "Texting and driving? And in this weather?"

"Not very spiritually aware," I said.

He angled his laptop so I wouldn't have to lean into him to read.

Tad Trzaskalski - Psychic
@Trzaskalski269 · 1/22/25

Shocking news. Faulkner understood spirit. He'll be greatly missed.

💬   ♡ 15   ↗

Anna's Apothecary
@A_ApothecarySC · 1/22/25

Awful, awful, awful. I can't believe he's gone.

💬   ♡ 22   ↗

Tea Witch
@verbenapillbrow· 1/22/25

No sudden death is welcome. But Faulkner had guru pretensions. A dangerous man. And as he would have said, the universe has a plan.

💬   ♡   ↗

I sank my head in my hands. *Worst. Condolence post. Ever.* "Verbena... What was she thinking? She *knew* she was a suspect. The cops picked her up!"

"Hers is a couple hours old," Hyperion said. "And I suspect she was thinking that the universe has a plan, and Falkner's death was meant to be. And maybe it was, but the post was a singularly noxious bad idea and a totally Verbena thing to post online."

I rubbed the back of my neck. "Baranko's going to have a field day with this."

"I can't believe they aren't using pictures of themselves in their social media profiles," Hyperion muttered. "It's just bad marketing. People do business with people, especially in the spiritual world."

I raised a brow. "You're worried about this now?"

"I'm wondering why Fiore didn't tell them to change those lame graphics. He's supposed to be an expert."

"Maybe he did, and they didn't."

Hyperion snorted. "Or maybe Fiore didn't know what he was talking about."

It took nearly two hours before the tow driver came. Hyperion swore he didn't mind waiting with me, and he kept himself busy online. But I knew he would have rather been home. I promised myself I'd make him his favorite scones—birthday cake with rainbow sprinkles—as a thank you.

Hyperion drove me home. I slogged up the stairs of my yellow bungalow and let myself inside, locking the door behind me.

Bracing one hand on the cream-colored sofa by the door, I tugged out of my galoshes. They'd started getting sweaty. I should have taken them off in the tearoom, but galosh removal was a pain.

I slouched to the couch in front of the white brick fireplace and flopped onto its blue cushions. A gaming controller beside me jounced. On the mantel, my grandmother's collection of fortune-telling teacups lined up evenly on both sides of the TV.

My bungalow's walls were a soothing blue, but I didn't feel soothed. I leaned my head against a cushion. The rolling dumpster *must* have been an accident.

I tugged on my ear. But *had* it been an accident? If it wasn't, that meant someone had been watching and waiting in the parking lot. This seemed like a lot of work, considering the storm.

Unless it had been one of Fiore's clients who'd come to our tearoom for the meeting. One of them could have lingered. But his or her car would have been in the lot too. Unless he or she had moved it out of sight and returned for a quick dumpster attack?

I picked up my gaming controllers and set them down again on the couch. No. It had to have been the wind. Just the wind—

BANG, BANG, BANG!

The French windows at the end of the bungalow rattled, and I shrieked. A dark, masculine shape loomed behind the thin panes of glass.

Chapter 8

Heart banging, I rose, trembling, from the couch. All it would take was a rock through a windowpane, and he could reach through to unlock the doors. The figure behind the glass shifted.

My shoulders sagged with embarrassment. It was only Brik in a navy raincoat.

I hurried across the bamboo floor to let him inside. A gust of cold air whipped the curtains, and I shivered.

"Jumpy?" he asked.

I exhaled shakily and drew him further inside. "There's been a lot going on." I told him about Verbena and Falkner as he unbuttoned his raincoat.

"Why didn't you call me?" He shrugged out of his coat.

"I thought you were busy with the storm, and I wasn't sure if we were getting involved." Hyperion had taken more convincing than usual.

His blond brows slashed downward, and he frowned. "Of course, you're getting involved. It's one of the things I love about you." He folded his raincoat inside out and folded it over a dining chair.

I leaned one hip against the blue couch and smiled, a shadow lifting from my heart. There'd been a time when Brik wouldn't have been keen on me nosing about a murder investigation. We'd come a long way together. "Sorry. I wasn't trying to hide anything—"

In answer, he pulled me into a damp kiss. Brik was warm and solid, and danger was far away. My worries evaporated, my heart heating, and it was just him, his mouth on mine. Everything stopped—the wind, the rain—everything but the roaring in my ears. Brik was here, and he loved me, and joy cocooned the bungalow.

After a time, we untangled ourselves, and he was breathing as heavily as I was. I drew him to the couch and leaned my head on his chest.

"I'm sorry I won't be able to help right now," he said. "At least, not until the storm is over." Brik's arm came around me. He toyed with a lock of my hair, curling it around his finger. "What did Razzzor find?"

"Huh? Oh," I said, brought back to Earth.

"What's wrong?"

I laughed. "If your first thought went to Razzzor, maybe I'm relying on my ex-boss a little too much for clues."

"Nah. You're outsourcing."

"Right." I grinned up at him. "And no, I haven't heard from him yet."

"Let me know what he comes up with. Once this storm lets up, I want to help."

I burrowed closer. "Sure, but... What were you doing in my backyard?"

He motioned toward the French doors, their blue curtains tied back with gold cords. "There's a minor flood near the fence. It's coming into my yard. I went into yours to check it out. Turns out it's just a bad puddle. Nothing to worry about yet."

"Yet?" I squeaked, alarmed.

"I think we're fine. We're not on a hillside—"

I frowned. "We sort of are." Aside from a thin stretch of beach, all of San Borromeo was hillside.

"Not on the edge of one," he corrected. "Erosion won't hit us like other homes up and down the coast."

"Yeah," I said, uneasy. My grandfather's house perched on a hill. And he'd said it was fine.

"It's going to be a busy week," Brik rumbled. "I've gotten half a dozen calls already from my old clients, asking for help dealing with storm damage."

"Is it bad?" *Is it dangerous?*

He nodded. "But I won't be working nights. We still on for our date tomorrow?"

"We'd better be." I smiled.

"If we need to turn it into a murder investigation, that's cool with me."

"Nope. We're dining in tomorrow night, as planned."

Our parting embrace wasn't quite so damp. Brik left with a jaunty wave and his raincoat slung over one broad shoulder. I went to bed smiling and thinking of murder.

"When are you getting your car back? I can't be your limo service indefinitely." Hyperion squinted through his rain-blurred windscreen at Anna's apothecary shop. Tugging on the collar of his coffee-colored turtleneck, he unbuckled himself one handed from the yellow Jeep.

"No idea." I'd left two messages with Mike at the repair shop already. Leaving a third just seemed pushy.

Besides, it was only Monday afternoon. Mike would call me when he got the chance. Taking a deep breath, I opened the Jeep's door, plunged into the rain, and stumbled to a halt.

Katey's gray stucco bookstore stood on the opposite side of the apothecary shop's narrow parking lot. They were neighbors.

I smacked my forehead. Why hadn't I made that connection when I'd mapped out directions?

"This was too easy," Hyperion muttered, studying the empty lot. "A waste of my spiritual gifts."

My partner had a knack for finding the perfect parking spot. This one was beside a handicapped spot and closest to the brick building's glass front door. "Don't anger the parking gods with a lack of gratitude."

"Good point. You coming?" Hyperion turned to face me, his long brown coat flaring around his knees.

We dashed to the front of Anna's brick building. Hyperion held the door for me, and I jogged inside.

"Careful," Anna Ogawa shouted from behind the counter. "The floor's wet."

Sapphire bottles of varying sizes ranged along the shelves behind her. Her silk blouse matched the color of the glass.

"*Everything's* wet." Hyperion brushed droplets off the sleeve of his wool coat.

Long, wooden tables displayed more bottles and candles and baskets of loose quartz. The latter looked like the crystals in Katey's nearby bookshop.

"Oh." The apothecary's smile was slight. "It's you."

"In the flesh." Hyperion bowed with a flourish.

"Thanks for coming by," Anna said to me. "Why don't you look around and get a better idea of what I sell? If you see anything your customers might like, we can talk cross-promotion."

I nodded and ambled around the small, dark-wood room. On the wall opposite the counter, oversized jars filled with dried herbs lined the shelves. I stopped in front of the jars and read the labels.

Ashwagandha had become a popular herb for memory, reducing inflammation, and stress reduction. The root wasn't something I could grow easily, and I wasn't happy with my current source. Anna had a big bottle of the dried roots.

Hyperion wielded a stick of selenite crystal like a sword. "Nice," he purred.

Anna shot him a sideways glance and walked around the counter. "I didn't think you'd be coming as well. Is the Tarot business slow?"

"Not at all." He folded his arms over his chest. "Beanblossom's is mine too, and my customers are interested in herbalism. I took a course."

Anna walked to the front window and peered through the misty glass. "Did you? Are you still seeing that police detective? What's his name?"

Hyperion blinked. "You know about Tony?"

"Right." Anna leaned closer to the glass. "That's his name—Tony. He's not a police detective anymore though, is he?"

"He's a PI," he said slowly. "Did I, er, tell you about Tony?"

My forehead wrinkled. If Hyperion had told her, he wouldn't have brought up Tony's career switch. It was a sore point for the detective.

"I can't remember where I heard he was fired." The apothecary started. "Is that—?" She relaxed.

"Is that what?" I asked.

She turned to me. Her smile looked forced. "I thought I saw Katey cleaning up the parking lot again. I told her to wait until after the storm passed, and I'd help. But she's very determined."

"With all the rain, her business is probably slow today too," I said. The near-empty parking lot wasn't a good sign. "Not a bad time for neatening up."

Anna glanced toward a string of Tibetan flags hanging from the brick wall. "It's her choice to run outside every time the wind blows to sweep up leaves. She shouldn't expect me to drop everything to help."

"*Does* she expect you to?" Hyperion returned the wand to its wicker basket.

The apothecary store owner pressed her lips together. "She's parking-lot obsessed. So, what are your net sales, Abigail?"

I stiffened. That seemed a little personal. "Ah... Why do you ask?"

"If we're going to sell each other's products, I need to know if it's worth my while," she said, expression bland.

"My inventory turnover rate is ten and a half percent." My teas didn't stay on Beanblossom's shelves for long. "Will Falkner's death affect your business?" I asked, changing the subject.

"No. I'll lose out on my upfront fee, but that's not important in the grand scheme of things." Anna shook her head. "Falkner. What a horrible thing." She returned to her spot behind the wood and glass counter.

"Of course," I said. "No one could have expected he'd be killed."

"No," Anna said, drawing the word out.

Huh. Anna struck me as a gossip, but she was being strangely reticent now. Or she was trying to get me to ask her about Falkner more directly.

"Though you thought Verbena and Katey might have had something to do with his death," I said.

Her slender shoulders twitched beneath her blouse. "It was a stupid reaction. I don't know why I said that."

"Maybe your instincts were telling you something," Hyperion said, probing.

"No, it's not my instincts. It was never—" Anna shook her head, the overhead lamplight shimmering off her sleek, black hair. Her hands atop the counter clenched. "I was projecting."

"You didn't get on well with Falkner?" I asked.

Anna's laugh was low and uneven. "The opposite. We got on too well."

Hyperion braced his elbow on the counter. "You don't mean...?"

"I shouldn't say anything," she said in a rush. "But that policeman knows now, and... Even though he was a jerk about it, it felt good to tell *someone*." She closed her eyes. "We were having an affair."

Whoa. At least she'd already told Baranko. That let us off the hook—now we wouldn't have to. "But... You were both single," I said. "That would be more of a romance than an affair, wouldn't it?"

Anna shook her head. "Yes. No. Falkner asked me to keep it secret. Please don't say anything to the others. The only reason I brought it up was because it's the only way to explain my reaction. I had feelings for him, so a part of me believed everyone else did too. I was jealous of nothing. Like I said, my reaction was stupid and wrong. Verbena and Katey had no real reason to want him dead."

"Why did Falkner ask you to keep your relationship secret?" I asked.

"He thought it would make things weird with his other clients," she said.

"I totally get that," Hyperion said. "After our talk last night, I realize my work is a form of coaching too. Clients can get attached."

Her shoulders relaxed. "Exactly. Now, I thought I could sell some of your loose teas over there." She pointed toward more shelves built into the walls and lined with bottles. "Just a small selection—more for cross-marketing than anything else. But do you think your customers would be interested in my tinctures?"

"Definitely," I said, "and I know just where to display them. But where are you getting your ashwagandha?"

We discussed the details, and I got the name of her ashwagandha supplier. Hyperion bought the selenite wand, and the two of us emerged from the apothecary shop into gusting rain.

Hurrying to Hyperion's Jeep, we ducked inside. The wind slammed my door behind me, and I jumped.

Hyperion wiped droplets from his angular face. "What do you think of Anna's romantic confession?"

"I think she seemed a lot guiltier about it than she should have been. They were both single, consenting adults."

He started the Jeep. "Yeah. I think there's more than meets the eye there. Or maybe she was flat-out lying."

"I don't know. She seemed genuinely upset when she heard about Falkner's death."

He rolled his eyes and drove from the lot. "And we've never been taken in by good actors before?"

We had, and I sighed. "I know, but—" My phone rang in the depths of my oversized purse. I found it and checked the number. "It's the mechanic." I took the call. Two minutes later, I dropped the phone back in my purse.

"Lay it on me," Hyperion said. "How much longer am I going to have to taxi you around?"

I hugged my arms to my chest. "It's the steering system. And the suspension. And—"

"Not the transmission?"

I nodded, and he swore. "I'm never parking by a dumpster again."

We hadn't though. The dumpster had moved. "The good news is they've got a rental for me," I said.

"Will your insurance pay for it?"

"I hope so." I'd filed a claim online. So far I'd gotten three texts back asking for more information. Apparently, getting hit by a dumpster was somewhat unusual in the insurance world.

Hyperion pulled a swift U-turn. "Let's get that rental."

We drove to the repair shop. My mechanic, Mike, gave me the bad news again, and with more detail than I needed or wanted. But I nodded and took notes.

Mike rubbed his slender hands together. "The good news is, I've got the perfect car for you, if you're looking for a rental. Follow me."

"I am, and it doesn't need to be perfect." *Just cheap.* All I needed was something that could get me to work and back. We followed him into the rain.

"You know, I do work for the police too," Mike said over one shoulder.

"We don't work for the police," Hyperion said loftily. "We're amateur detectives. Big difference."

"Yeah," I said, "We're just nosy." Then, because I didn't want to sound dismissive, I asked, "What do you do for the police?"

"Vehicle forensics," the mechanic said proudly. "San Borromeo's too small to have their own team, so they outsource. I took classes in it and everything."

Mike led us to a metal carport. "Here it is." He rocked on his heels, hands in the pockets of his denim-blue coveralls.

I gaped at the white convertible. Duct tape striped its gray cloth top. A front bumper jutted out like Hercule Poirot's moustache. The tailfins were ridiculous. It was ginormous, decrepit, weird. And I needed to get Hyperion's old word-of-the-day calendar out of my head.

I winced. I couldn't drive this, whatever *this* was. But Mike looked so proud of it. And he was doing me a favor. Maybe it was a joke? "Ah..."

"Oh. My. God." Careless of the rain flattening his dark hair, Hyperion circled the battered convertible. "Is this...?"

"A 1968 Amphicar 770." The mechanic rocked back on his bootheels.

Hyperion whistled. "Where the devil did you get it?"

"A client owed me money. He paid with this."

"And it drives?" I rubbed the back of my neck.

Hyperion grasped my forearm. "Drives? This baby floats."

Ah... "What?"

"It's an *Amphicar*," Hyperion said. "Amphibious car. OMG, this is perfect. I want to drive it."

"Wait," I said. "A what?"

"There are only 200 of these left in the world," the mechanic said. "Lyndon B. Johnson owned one. Not that I'm a fan. He had JFK assassinated because Kennedy wanted out of 'Nam," he added as an aside.

"Uh, huh." I nodded. *Vietnam. Right.*

"But still," Mike said, "it was the most successful amphibious car of its time."

I frowned at the convertible. It might be seaworthy, but I didn't like the look of that duct tape. The top probably leaked like crazy.

"And you're renting the car to *Abigail*?" Hyperion's brows shot toward the leaden sky. "Sorry, Abs," he said to me, "but do you know what these babies go for?"

The mechanic's cheeks reddened. "This one's not worth much yet. I'm in the process of restoring it. It drives. And I think it floats—"

"*Think*?" Not that I planned to go yachting in it, but since he'd sold it as a floating car, now I wanted one.

"I've got a lady in Vegas who's going to sew me new red-leather seats," the mechanic continued proudly. "Custom made."

I peered inside the car. The interior was grayish. Stuffing leaked through a slash in the driver's seat. "How much?"

He named a daily rate. It was shockingly low, and I squinted at him.

"There's a leak in the roof," he admitted. "But the drip's in the back seat, so it shouldn't bother you. And it can't do any more damage to the interior, which I'm replacing anyway."

"And it *floats*," Hyperion said, gleeful.

"I haven't tested that yet," the mechanic cautioned. "Don't take it on the water. But it would be great if you could give me some feedback on how it drives."

"It's a stick shift," I said gloomily. I hated sticks, but I knew how to drive them.

"We'll take it," Hyperion said.

"There's no *we* here." I looked hard at my partner. "I'm the one who has to drive it."

"You can take my Jeep," Hyperion said, "and I'll—"

"Uh, no can do," the mechanic said. "Abigail has to drive it. Liability reasons. You understand."

In the end, I was the one to drive it off the lot. Hyperion tailgated me all the way home.

I had to admit, the Amphicar handled surprisingly well. The steering wheel took some muscle, but the drips in the back weren't as annoying as they might have been.

I let Hyperion drive the car up and down the block a few times, because he begged. And then I parked it in my drive and covered it with the tarp the mechanic had made me promise to use.

It was the least I could do. I was getting a deal with the car, and my faith in the insurance company paying for it was low.

Brik came over later that night, and we drove it around some more. When we returned to my bungalow, I stopped short in the kitchen.

A puddle of water had formed on the white tile floor. I looked up. Water dripped from the ceiling. I stuck a metal pot beneath it and called my landlord, Tomas.

My honorary uncle cursed. "I thought this might be the year," he said. "That roof wasn't going to last forever."

Brik held out his hand. "Let me talk to him."

I gave him the phone. A drip pinged off the bottom of the pot.

Shaking my head, I went to check my TV. There were no messages from Razzzor on his gaming platform, which was odd. He'd been hot enough on the case to follow Hyperion and me from the tearoom. I'd thought he would have had intel on our suspects by now.

Brik came up behind me on the blue couch and massaged my shoulders. "I'll take care of the roof once the rain stops." His hands explored the planes of my back. "Don't worry about it."

My muscles unknotted. "I'm not worried." I twisted on the couch to smile up at him. "There's no reason for this to—"

The phone rang in the rear pocket of Brik's jeans. He checked the screen and frowned.

I pulled up my legs and huddled deeper against the cushions. Rain drummed the roof, relentless.

"Sorry," he said, "I've got to take this. Your phone's in the kitchen." He moved toward the French windows.

Taking the hint, I returned to the kitchen. I got a pot of water boiling and smiled. *Spaghetti.* Simple comfort food on a rainy night.

Brik walked into the kitchen. "Uh... I'm sorry, I have to go."

My eyebrows drew together, a prickling heaviness weighing my chest. Brik could handle whatever the storm threw at him. But accidents happened to careful people too. "What's wrong?"

"My friend's sister is in trouble," he said shortly.

I rubbed my forehead. "Storm damage?"

He grimaced. "Sorry. It's a long and ugly story. Can I explain it to you tomorrow?"

Ugly story? "Sure." I walked him to the door. He gave me a brief kiss and disappeared into the rain.

Biting my lip, I shut the door. It was probably nothing.

But I *was* worried, now.

Chapter 9

A GUST OF WIND rattled the tearoom windows. The water flowing down the street outside rippled, and rain pebbled against the glass.

A tiny woman in a red rain slicker, her umbrella blown inside out, lurched against the front door. Pulling the blue door wide, she stumbled.

The white tablecloths rippled, ghostly. Tarot cards blew upward, scattering across the tearoom.

Archer looked up from his paper menu and yelped. "Close the damn door!"

I hurried from behind the hostess stand to help. Another gust pummeled the street.

The woman in the rain slicker flew into my arms, and the door slammed. We staggered against a table to a chorus of feminine shrieks.

So. Another Tuesday.

Maricel and a Tarot reader hurried to untangle us. "You okay?" Maricel asked, and I nodded.

"Oh," the woman panted, her wrinkled cheeks pink. "I'm so sorry." She wrenched down her red hood. Despite the storm, her curls remained perfectly coiffed.

At a table for two, Archer adjusted his cravat. I shot a glance at the older man. He didn't usually come into the tearoom so often. What was the gossip columnist up to?

"Late as usual, Mary Beth." He sniffed.

"Sorry," Mary Beth panted, and I helped her out of her raincoat.

"I'll just put this by the door," I murmured and hung it on the coat tree there. Customers helped gather fallen Tarot cards.

Mary Beth trotted to Archer's small table. "Did you find out anything about Oswald?"

He smiled. "I found out *everything* about Oswald. Now what did you hear about the cemetery?"

"It's true," she said in a low voice. "Kids have been mucking about in there."

Archer's eyes narrowed. "Hooligans. Probably waiting to see if any bodies float to the surface." He didn't look too disturbed by the idea.

Hyperion, elegant in a forest green vest with a purple satin lining and earthy brown slacks, ambled from the rear hallway. He stretched, scanned the room, and beelined for me at the hostess stand.

Bracing one elbow on it, he leaned in and whispered, "I've got something."

"Oh?" I asked.

"News." Hyperion glanced at Archer. Raising a brow, he cocked his head toward the hallway.

In other words, private news. I checked the reservation book. Everyone who had reservations was already here. It was unlikely we'd get much street traffic today. Anyone with any sense was staying home and out of the storm.

I followed Hyperion back to his office. He held the door for me, and I walked inside, dropping into one of his red velvet high-backed chairs. "What's up?" I asked.

He circled the table and sat in the matching chair opposite. Bastet dropped from the driftwood altar, stretched on the carpeted floor, and swaggered to the red-clothed table.

I bent to scratch behind the cat's ears. The tabby arched his back in pleasure.

"Razzzor called," Hyperion said.

"And?"

"Falkner was likely poisoned."

"Likely?" I asked, miffed that Razzzor hadn't called me. I checked my phone.

Oh. I'd accidentally turned off the ringer. There were three missed calls from my ex-boss.

Hyperion's smile was smug. "He said it was a preliminary finding. And who has the most likely access to poisonous herbs?"

"Anna the apothecary," I said. "Do we know if Falkner was poisoned with something natural?"

"Er, no." Hyperion shifted in his chair. "Only that it was likely poison. Razzzor didn't know what kind of poison yet."

I drummed my fingers on the arm of the chair. Now Hyperion would want to *go* to Anna's Alchemical Apothecary, and we should. But I hated going out in the storm, which seemed to be getting worse with every passing hour.

"What?" Hyperion asked. "What's the problem? I know this is vague, but at least—"

"It's something." It was more than something. It was huge news. "I just don't like the idea of driving in this storm."

His gaze turned shifty. "We could take the Amphicar."

I lowered my head to study him. Hyperion didn't fool me for a second. He wanted to drive my rental. "For liability reasons, I'm the only one who can drive it."

"Oh, come on." He folded his arms. "You know that's bogus. Insurance covers whoever's driving it And you let me drive it last night."

I also knew that Hyperion and his yellow Jeep had developed a reputation in tiny San Borromeo. The garage owner probably just didn't want *him* driving the vintage car. "That was different."

Hyperion's gaze flicked toward the white ceiling. "Fine. You drive." He rose. "Well?"

I scrambled to my feet. "*Now?* I can't go now. I'm working."

"Please. You're fully staffed. The next seating isn't until one-thirty. That gives us two whole hours of freedom. This is the point where you just stand around glad-handing the customers, and we've got the Tarot readers to do that."

I checked my watch. He had a point. And if it really was poison that had killed Falkner... "I'll get my coat."

I told Maricel what I was up to, geared up, and met Hyperion by the back door. He'd changed into his swanky, knee-length brown coat.

He rubbed his long hands together. "Who knows? With all this water, we might even be able to go amphibious."

I shot him what I hoped was a quelling look. Taking a deep breath, I opened the back door. A gust of wind thrust it back at me, and I staggered into Hyperion's arms.

"Allow me," he said in a bored tone. He opened the door easily, and we tottered into the storm. I got into the S.S. Amphicar, leaned across the dingy seat, and unlocked his door.

Dripping, he slid onto the wide seat beside me. He ran his hand along the grubby white dash. Rain drummed the convertible's grayish top. Water drip, drip, dripped on the back seat.

"I'm in a Bond movie," he whispered. "It's beautiful."

"Are you delusional?" It took some next-level magical thinking to see this wreck on wheels as beautiful.

"Enjoy the moment. You're driving an Amphicar in the rain. Who knows? We might get lucky and have to go boat-mode."

"No." I started the ignition. "You heard the mechanic. No boating."

"I said we might *have* to. There may be no choice."

"There's always a choice."

I checked the map app on my phone and bit back a groan. The 101 was solid red all the way into Santa Cruz. To avoid the jam-up, the app routed us up surface streets and along a hilly highway.

I handed the phone to my partner. "You can be navigator."

"Yay," he said, less enthusiastic. My phone rang in his hand. "Oooh, it's Brik."

"Don't—"

He touched a button. "Hey, Brik, you're on speaker. We're in an Amphicar."

"A what?"

"Never mind," I said.

"You okay, Abigail?" Brik asked.

I grimaced. "Fine," I said. I didn't want to ask what had happened with his friend's sister in front of Hyperion. Brik had said the story was ugly. That might make it private, too.

"Why wouldn't she be fine?" Hyperion asked.

"Because there are landslides up and down the coast," Brik said. "I'm sorry, Abigail, but clients have got me busy shoring up retaining walls and repairing broken windows today. Did you say you're in a car?"

"Yeah," I said, "I'm driving. Can I call you later?"

"Please." Brik hung up.

Hyperion's coffee eyes widened with faux-sincerity. "You know, I can take the wheel if you want to call Brik back."

"Gee, thanks, no." I followed a detour sign onto a residential street.

We weren't the only ones getting re-routed. A long line of cars followed us up a hill and onto a winding highway. On a clear day, it overlooked the Pacific. Now we were lost in a sea of white.

The clouds of mist and dense tree line were another, primeval world, a world to hide in, a world to get lost inside. Fog wrapped us like a blanket, cozy and terrifying. I scootched closer to the windshield to see better.

Hyperion twisted in his seat and waved to the Tesla behind us. "We're out glamming a Tesla in this car," he hooted. "They're totally jelly."

My mind automatically did a Hyperion to English translation. "Jealous?"

"Natch."

"Naturally."

"Don't make a stuffed bird laugh."

Now he was just making stuff up. My lips pressed tight. Muddy water streamed down the hillside and across the narrow road. I gripped the metal wheel tighter.

"It's Victorian slang," Hyperion said. "It means, don't be ridiculous, which doesn't quite fit the context of our conversation, but it *did* rhyme. I'm trying to expand beyond Lovecraft."

"Uh, huh." I nodded.

"There's some great slang from that era. Like *bricky*. That means brave. I told Brik he was bricky the other day. He didn't get it."

"What a shock." I was starting to miss his Lovecraft word-of-the-day calendar.

I rounded a bend. The highway narrowed, and I hugged closer to the slope on my right. Brown water trickled down the hill and across the road.

A low rumble was the only warning. I might have missed the sound if there hadn't been a sudden lull in the rain. Automatically, I braked, scanning the road.

Hyperion peered through the curving windshield. "What's—?"

Mud and boulders rumbled down the hillside. I gasped, standing on the brake.

Rocks crashed inches from our front bumper. They bounced and broke and tumbled down the hillside on our left. A torrent of water rushed across the road, sweeping away sheets of mud.

"Eeep," Hyperion said.

I gaped at the new waterway blocking our path. The brown water turned whitish, then ran clear. "Oh my God," I whispered. Behind us, a driver leaned on his car horn.

Most of the rocks had swept past and down the hillside. But a few had stopped in the road, making rapids in the flowing water. My fingers released on the steering wheel.

The driver behind us honked again. A black monster truck on the opposite side of the newly made river revved its engine.

Hyperion rolled his window down. He stuck one arm out and shook his fist at the Tesla in my rearview mirror. "Keep your pants on." Rain drenched his arm and spattered his face. Hastily, he returned inside and cranked up the window.

I breathed slowly, reminding myself I still *could* breathe. If I'd been driving a mile-per-hour faster, we would have been hit. If I had shaved a second off a stop sign, we'd have been hit. If we'd been hit, we might have been carried off the hillside, might have tumbled with the boulders down the steep slope.

Hyperion whistled, low and quiet. "Nice driving, Abs."

"Thanks," I squeaked. It had been luck. Sheer luck. But I wasn't going to mention that now.

I checked the rear-view mirror again. A string of cars wound down the highway behind ours. A line of cars going in the opposite direction bunched on the other side of the fast-running water.

"This is going to take forever to get out of," I grumbled. Now that the danger had passed, it was easier to complain than contemplate how close we'd come to death.

But *had* the danger passed? I glanced uneasily at the eroded hillside above. Boulders jutted from a fresh gash in the earth, water splashing over and around the gray stones.

My chest squeezed, my stomach churning. I wanted off this highway, off this hillside. *Now*.

But there wasn't enough space on the highway to turn around and go back. The stupid Tesla was right on my rear bumper.

Another car honked. I squinted at the monster truck opposite. It looked a lot like the one that had showered me with water outside the tearoom.

"Drive across," Hyperion said.

"Are you kidding me?" The water wasn't that high, but it was moving fast.

A chunk of earth broke from the hillside, cracked into pieces, and trickled onto the road. Electricity tingled through my arms.

"We've got an *Amphicar*," he said. "It's *made* for this."

"It was made for genteel motoring around Lyndon B. Johnson's private lake." I'd done some internet sleuthing when I'd gotten home last night. This car was a sedan. It wasn't made for traversing washouts.

"Pshaw. Where's your sense of adventure? During the storm of the century, you were given the gift of a car that drives in water. It would be a crime not to take advantage."

"The mechanic said it hadn't been tested in water yet."

"Look, if you're afraid, I'll drive." Hyperion reached for the wheel.

I slapped his hand away.

"Don't you want to get back to the tearoom in time for the next seating?" he asked.

I turned off the car and sat back in my seat, arms crossed. More horns honked.

"Oh," Hyperion said, "real mature."

SCREECH.

CRASH!

My shoulders bolted up to my ears. I turned, craning my neck to look out the rear window.

An SUV behind the Tesla seemed to have attempted a fast, tight turn. It had hit the car behind it, which had nosed into the opposite lane.

The SUV must have overcompensated, because now its front end pressed against a eucalyptus tree. The back end blocked the left side of the road.

"Augh." I banged the back of my head against the rest. We were truly stuck. I couldn't go back until the SUV moved. And the SUV wouldn't move until the other cars moved. Judging by all the honking, that wasn't happening anytime soon.

A rock the size of a teapot arced through the air, hit the road, and tumbled into the stream. My heart jumped, my muscles tightening. The landslide wasn't finished. And I'd be damned if I'd wait for it to finish on top of us.

"Uh, oh," Hyperion said.

Fumbling, I started the ignition. I put the car in gear.

Hyperion whooped. "YES! Amphicar! Screw you, modern life!"

I edged forward. Water sloshed around the car, and a chill zipped down my spine.

I wasn't worried about drowning the engine—this car was made for water, theoretically. I was worried about being swept down the hillside. But the Amphicar was heavy, built in an era when steel, rather than plastic, was the norm.

I crept forward. More rocks tumbled into the road, forcing the stream to widen. The SUV behind us tried to back up. Angry drivers honked.

I pounded one fist on the wheel. "Can't people see the road's blocked?"

"It's hard to see much of anything in all this fog and rain." Hyperion leaned forward in his seat.

The river's edge was only fifteen feet ahead. The tension in my hands relaxed, and I leaned closer to the wheel. Ten feet… It was working. We could do this.

The monster truck roared forward. A wave hit the side of the Amphicar, and we lurched sideways.

"What was that?" Hyperion asked.

The car's wheels lifted off the pavement. My stomach hardened, my hands clammy on the wheel.

We were floating. Toward the cliff.

Chapter 10

"Turn, turn," Hyperion yelled.

"I *am* turning the wheel." I twisted it frantically. The Amphicar continued its drift toward the edge of the mountain road.

Horns blared. The black monster truck skimmed past, arcing water from its oversized wheels. Its wake pushed us closer to the foggy edge.

My head whipped around, searching for something to anchor on. But no boulder lay in the car's path.

My breathing accelerated. What lay hidden in that sea of fog? Rocks? An abyss? A houseful of people, unsuspecting of what was about to come crashing down?

"Use the propellers. You have a motor." Hyperion pushed buttons and turned dials.

"How—?"

A different motor roared to life. Lacking any better ideas, I jammed my foot on the gas. The Amphicar leapt forward, speeding through the water until our tires touched pavement. I hit the gas to get out of the mess, then slowed, stopped.

I twisted in my seat. The gap in the hillside had deepened, a low pile of mud and earth blocking the roadside where our car had been.

Behind us, the monster truck cruised sedately down the opposite side of the road. Other cars had begun to back away, turn around. No one seemed hurt, and I swallowed, relieved.

"They're okay, and so are we." Hyperion gripped my shoulder. "You did the right thing getting us out of there."

I thought about the dangers that Brik might be facing, and my stomach burned. He'd said he was shoring things up, but what? Retaining walls? Hillsides? Falling trees? I clawed a hand through my hair.

Hyperion pushed another button, and the roar of the boat motor ceased. A new noise took its place. It sounded like an old-fashioned coffee percolator.

"Uh... What's that?" Hyperion asked.

"The sound of getting off this damn highway."

We inched down the winding two-lane road, my knuckles white on the wheel. Near the bottom of the hill, the road began to flatten.

I relaxed my grip. We'd made it. We'd actually made it a couple miles back, but I only let myself believe it now.

The engine fell silent. I sucked in a breath and wrestled with the stiff, pre-power steering wheel.

"Are you kidding me?" Hyperion shook his fist at the convertible's canvas roof. "What next?"

"At least we're off that hill," I said, the car still rolling. "If we can get to El Camino, we might actually get a tow truck driver in a reasonable amount of time."

But there was nothing reasonable about this storm. And I was starting to take it personally.

The steering wheel locked completely at the top of a blessedly straight road. We glided past neat Craftsman-style homes with flooded lawns.

My jaw tightened. From here it was a straight shot to El Camino. All we had to do was hope no one got in our way. My foot hovered over the brake pedal.

The Amphicar drifted right, toward a blue Victorian with white gingerbread trim and an emerald front lawn.

"What are you doing?" Hyperion asked.

"Parking."

"I thought you wanted to get to El Camino." He pointed through the front windshield. "It's right down there."

"The car wants to go *this* way," I gritted out. "The wheel's locked." Rain hammered the convertible roof.

"You're just having trouble because you're frail and elfin. It's normally totally charming, but—" He reached across me and grabbed the wheel, blocking my view.

"No, wait—"

The car bumped over a sidewalk, and I slammed on the brakes. We lurched against our lap belts. The car came to rest on a lawn.

"Huh." Hyperion let go of the wheel and sat back, his face faintly flushed. "The wheel really *was* locked."

I turned off the ignition and glared. "Really?"

"Whoops." My partner shrugged, expression penitent.

The Victorian's white door opened. A burly man in a Use Magic Responsibly tee and baggy jeans emerged on the front porch. He shouted something I couldn't distinguish.

"Sorry. Car trouble," I hollered before realizing he couldn't hear me through the rain and the closed window. I reached for the window crank.

Hyperion bolted forward in his seat. "Is that…?"

I squinted through the rain washing down the windshield. My stomach crashed. "Baranko." I'd never figured the detective for living in a Victorian. I'd pictured him in something more brutalist or industrial.

"Start the car," Hyperion urged. "Start the car."

One of us whimpered. I can't swear to it, but it *may* have been me. I twisted the key in the ignition. The car sputtered hopefully.

"Don't flood it," Hyperion shouted.

"You're not helping," I ground out.

Baranko jogged down the porch steps and stormed toward us. I twisted the key again with similar results. Baranko slipped on the grass. His legs flew upward, and he splashed onto the lawn.

Hyperion groaned. "We are so dead."

"Only if he catches us." My lips pressed together, and I turned the key again. The Amphicar roared to life.

I backed from the lawn. The car lurched into the street, and I looked over my shoulder. We'd left two ugly, muddy tire tracks in the lawn. I swore again. "We have to stay. Look at the damage—"

Hyperion reached one long leg across mine and stepped on the gas. The Amphicar roared forward. A horn honked behind us.

"Too late now." Cautiously, Hyperion lifted his foot off the gas and retracted his leg. "We've officially fled the scene of a crime. If we get caught, he'll run us in for sure."

"And whose idea was—?" I cut off the retort. It didn't matter. I'd wanted to run too. My shoulders slumped. "We are so dead."

───*ℓℓ*───

We reached the apothecary shop without further incident. The shared parking lot was empty, but instead of the spot near the door, I parked in front of Anna's brick wall. Beside it, water beaded on narrow-leaved, pink oleander bushes.

"Are you *trying* to get me wet?" Hyperion asked. "You can get closer."

"I need to make a call." I dialed the mechanic who'd lent me the car.

"I told you, I didn't mean to hit you with all that water in the kitchen last week," Hyperion said. "I didn't think your spray hose would have the range. Forgive and forget, why doncha?"

"I don't forget getting a face full of water because I don't—"

"Yeah?" the mechanic answered.

The water beat a rhythm on the car roof. I stuck a finger in my other ear to hear better. "This is Abigail. With the Amphicar?"

"Oh, yeah," Mike said eagerly. "How's it running? Oh, sorry. Your car still isn't ready."

"I know. The Amphicar stalled out on me today." I winced. And who had decided to use it for a boat? *Oh, yeah. Me.* "I got it going again, but I thought—"

"Yeah, it does that sometimes. Other than that, how's it going?"

I tipped my head to one side. *Really?* That was it? "Um, fine, but should I bring it in?"

"No, no. If you can't get it started again the next time, let me know."

"Okay," I said, doubtful. "But—"

"Gotta go." Mike disconnected.

"So?" Hyperion asked.

"He said it's no big thing."

He shrugged. "Whatevs. The Amphicar got us off that hillside. Let's do this."

We dashed around the front of the brick building and inside the dark-wood shop.

Anna, in a ruby red silk blouse, looked up from behind the counter. "Oh, hi. Did you come to a decision about cross-selling our products?"

Oh. That. I shifted my weight on the linoleum floor. I hadn't thought about our sales deal since we'd met yesterday. "Yes. Let's do it," I said recklessly. "We can do a trial run—no harm, no foul if the sales aren't what we expect."

She smiled and smoothed her long, dark hair. "Sounds good to me. I have an agreement like that with Jose."

"Jose?" I asked. "The, er—"

"Healer," she said. "Why don't I email a copy to you to look over, and we can modify it to suit?"

"Perfect." That way I wouldn't have to dig one up. "Mind if I look over your herb collection?"

"Not at all."

Hyperion braced an elbow on the wood and glass counter. "How are you doing?" he asked her in a low voice. "After Falkner's death, I mean?"

I wandered to shelves lined with jars of dried herbs and gnawed my bottom lip. If she was a poisoner, she wouldn't leave anything incriminating out in the open.

I turned to a wooden table displaying glass dropper jars and metal tins. Idly, I picked up a tin and studied the label. *Belladonna Flying Ointment.* I studied the instructions.

Rub on the inside of wrists. Do NOT ingest.

Ingredients:

atropa belladona, balsam poplar buds, sunflower oil, pure filtered beeswax.

I grimaced. *So much for nothing poisonous out in the open.* Atropa belladonna could be deadly.

"And Falkner was poisoned," Hyperion murmured.

Something crashed on the other side of the store. My shoulders jerked at the sound, and I turned.

Anna ducked behind the counter. "Sorry. Dropped a bottle. Poison?" her voice floated up to us. "Falkner was poisoned? Are you sure? How awful, awful, awful," she continued before Hyperion could answer. "Who could do such a thing?"

"An irate client?" he asked.

A bulky silhouette passed outside the misted front window.

Anna stood, fragments of broken blue glass cradled loosely in one hand. "But *why*? I can't imagine he could have a customer that unhappy. Falkner was *good* at what he did."

"Hm." Hyperion said. "What about—?"

The wooden front door opened. I glanced over my shoulder and froze. No, *no, no.*

Baranko's meaty hands fisted in the wide collar of his stained brown coat. His legs were planted wide. His nostrils flared. "You."

Chapter 11

Baranko glowered, his broad face darkening, and he stepped into the apothecary shop. Rain splashed through the slowly closing door, darkened the shoulders of his trench coat, and dashed against the front windows.

Hyperion cleared his throat. "We were—"

"My daughter gave me that shirt," the detective said.

I blinked. *Shirt?* He'd changed into a blue button-up, I noticed. "That's... ah..."

"*Use Magic Responsibly,*" Baranko continued. "She thought it was funny."

Silence fell—a silence of squirming, hot embarrassment which I knew only too well. But this time, it was on Baranko's account instead of my own. The *fremdschämen* was a nice change.

"*Use Magic Responsibly* is a, uh, cool slogan," Hyperion choked out.

"I liked it," I agreed.

The detective gave Hyperion the side eye. "What are you two doing here?" he growled.

"Abigail and I are signing an agreement to sell each other's wares in each other's shops," Anna piped up from behind the counter. "How can I help you?"

Baranko stared hard at my partner. The detective's mouth firmed. He jerked his head toward the door. "Beat it. This is a private conversation."

My partner raised his hands in a warding gesture. "We were just leaving."

"I know," Baranko growled.

I smiled and sidled out the door. When Hyperion didn't immediately follow, I splashed through the parking lot to the Amphicar. A few moments later, Hyperion got into the passenger side and shook his wet hair like a dog.

"Well?" I asked. "What happened?"

"Just a casual threat exchange."

I was almost sorry I'd missed that. But as they say, ignorance is bliss.

I turned the key. The Amphicar rumbled to life, and my shoulders loosened. Maybe the earlier stall really *had* been no big thing.

"I want a cross promotional opportunity," Hyperion said.

"I only did it so we could have reason to talk to her more."

"Yeah, but I could have done it."

I turned in the wide, faded-to-gray seat to study him. "Have you got something in mind?"

He rubbed his chin. "Katey Molina *does* have a metaphysical bookstore. Which means she sells metaphysical books. And I happen to have my own book on Tarot. It has been selling okay online, and flogging it in Beanblossom's has been a natural fit—"

"Have you heard from your friend, Tom?" Tom had helped edit Hyperion's book on Tarot. But after a family tragedy, he'd sort of disappeared.

"Not since I got that postcard. I'm sure he's fine. It's not the first time he's gone hermit. But *as I was saying*, more sales couldn't hurt." He angled his damp head toward the bookstore on the other side of the lot and bobbled his eyebrows.

"And maybe Katey sells on consignment?"

"I *am* a prestigious local author."

I turned off the ignition. "And what can you offer her in return?"

"Aside from a cut of the sales?"

"Aside from that, yes." I wasn't being a jerk. I wanted Hyperion's book to sell. But he didn't always think things through.

"I could do an author reading at her store. Maybe throw in some free Tarot readings too, promote the event online and elsewhere. Video's getting big. We need to do some for Beanblossom's."

I sighed. Video had been big for years. I just didn't want to go on camera. I checked my watch. "I need to get back to the tearoom."

"Oh, come on. Maricel's there. In this weather, she'll understand if you're late."

"Except the weather won't be what's making me late." But we were here already. It seemed a shame not to take advantage. We got out of the car and sloshed to the bookstore on the other side of the parking lot.

It was as deserted as the apothecary shop had been, though damp footprints on the thin gray carpet indicated someone had been in and out recently. I hoped they were Baranko's, because that meant he wouldn't be returning soon.

Katey sat behind the glass counter reading a hardback. Head propped on her fist, she twirled a pen between her long fingers. She looked up as we approached, and her smile faded. "Oh, I thought you might be customers."

"I come bearing business opportunities," Hyperion said.

She straightened on her high stool, her stripey blue caftan rippling. Her silver hair was done up in a bun held in place by a stick with a crystal on the top. "Oh?"

"As you know," he said, "I have written a book on Tarot."

Her expression turned wary. "Oh?"

"I thought it would be fun to do a signing here. You could sell *The Mysteries of Tarot*, and I could promote the event online and to my customers."

Her gray eyes narrowed. "I would have thought you sold your books to your customers directly?"

"Well, yes," he said, "but if I'm doing free Tarot readings here, it will bring them into your shop. And I'd like more visibility beyond San Borromeo. Santa Cruz is a bigger market."

"It might." Katey nodded. "All right. I suppose I could keep some of your books here before and after the event. Sold on consignment."

"I would expect nothing less. Or more." He shook his head. "Whatever."

Katey rose. "I'll get an agreement from the back." She strode through the shelves to the back of the store. A door clicked open.

Hyperion leaned on the glass counter and turned the hardback there to face him. "Hm." He opened the book. A breeze gusted through the store, fluttering the pages.

I glanced at the front door. It was still shut. "What's she reading?"

"She wasn't. She was writing."

I hissed an indrawn breath. "Is that her journal?"

"Yep."

My shoulders jerked upward. "You can't read that. It's private."

"Damn right it is. Did you know she was sleeping with Falkner too? What *was* it with this guy?"

"What?" I slid the journal from beneath his fingers and read. Heat flushed my face. We shouldn't be reading something so intimate.

A door closed in the back of the store. Hastily, I shut the book and thrust it into Hyperion's outstretched hands. He dropped it. The book thudded softly.

I hurried to intercept the bookstore owner. Rounding a corner, I nearly crashed into her in a narrow hallway. Katey jerked backward and dropped a handful of papers beneath a framed, black and white photo of a garage.

"Um, is that your father's business?" I guessed.

"It was." She stooped, kaftan billowing around her knees, and retrieved them from the thin gray carpet. "I told you I'd bring the papers."

"Sorry." I trailed after her into the main room.

Katey strode behind the counter, her caftan fluttering. Her gaze fell on the journal. She took it from the glass and slipped it beneath the counter, sliding the pages she'd brought toward Hyperion. "Here's the standard form. Look it over."

Hyperion scanned the sheets, whipped a pen from the inside pocket of his green vest, and signed. "Done."

She took the paper and reviewed it. "You missed one." She pointed to a signature line.

"Whoops." He signed the form. "*Now* it's done."

"All right," she said. "Are you free on Friday?"

Hyperion took an involuntary step away from the counter. "That, uh, doesn't give us much time to promote. Besides, with all this rain, who would come?"

"Next Friday then," she said.

"I suppose that will work," he said slowly. "We can do some live videos—"

"I don't do videos," she said.

Right on. I lifted my fist in the air. "I'm with you."

A twenty-something woman hurried into the bookstore. She shook off her umbrella.

"There's an umbrella stand by the door," Katey called out. "Feel free to use it." The bookstore owner gave me a brief smile. "If you'll excuse me?" She walked to greet the customer.

Dismissed, Hyperion and I left the bookstore and returned to the Amphicar. A small piece of yellow paper was stuck beneath its windshield wiper. My stomach seized. A *ticket*? But I was in a private parking lot.

I peeled the sheet off the windscreen. Blue ink dribbled down the page.

"What is it?" Hyperion asked.

"I don't know. The ink ran." I tilted my head. I tilted the sodden paper. Was the first letter a B? "At least it isn't a ticket."

He plucked the soggy sheet from my hand and dropped it in a nearby garbage bin. "It's either a complaint about your driving—"

"What?" My driving was *fine*.

"Or someone wants to buy your car."

"Too bad. I don't own it, so I can't sell it." I got inside the car and reached for my phone to call Brik, then shook my head. He'd told me he was busy with landslides. After our road experience earlier, I didn't want to bother him while he was working. I just wanted him safe.

"Do you think Anna knew Katey was also seeing Falkner?" I started the ignition.

"You think we've got a murderous love triangle on our hands?"

"Now we know why Falkner asked Anna to keep their relationship secret," I said dryly.

"Yeah, he didn't want Katey to know he was stepping out on her."

I pulled onto the street. "I'm starting to see why you didn't like Falkner much."

"Mm. What next?" Hyperion asked.

"Work." I aimed the car toward Beanblossom's.

The rest of the afternoon was slow. We had a couple cancellations for our next seating due to the rain. There were no walk-ins. Hyperion left on an unknown errand.

Studying the empty tables, I wiped down the white quartz counter, my mouth dry. I hadn't seen the tearoom this empty on a Tuesday since we'd first opened.

Maricel came to stand beside me. "Slow day."

"We've been lucky," I said. "I can't believe we have as many people as we do with all this rain." Beanblossom's had come a long way and had a loyal clientele.

I *was* lucky. I had the business of my dreams, a great partner, and terrific staff. Not to mention a terrific boyfriend. And I noticed that when I focused on what I was grateful for, I didn't stress as much about what might happen. Like going out of business.

"The storm's really messing up the traffic," Maricel agreed. "Your friend Archer stayed for the second seating though."

"Oh?" I smoothed my apron. "Was he on his own?"

"No, he met some guy here."

Great. Archer was turning Beanblossom's into his private office. I liked the older man, and he was a good tipper. Normally, I wouldn't mind him hanging around. But I suspected he was staking us out for more "hot goss" on the murder.

And yes, I was again being a hypocrite, because I wanted more *hot goss* on the murder too. I liked to think our snooping was in the service of good. But a part of me just enjoyed untangling problems, helping to set the world right again in my own small way.

I shuffled my feet. "Maricel... Would you mind if I bugged out for another hour or so? I'll be back in time for closing."

"Sure. We got this."

"Thanks," I said guiltily. Just because I was the boss, didn't mean I could take off whenever I wanted. But murder made for an urgent excuse.

I grabbed my coat and drove up the hill toward Falkner's house. Instead of turning into his long driveway, I turned into his neighbor's long driveway.

The muddy road wound past stands of redwoods to a pale green ranch house. Water gushed from its roof spouts. I splashed through a puddle to the concrete steps, rang the bell, and waited.

An elderly man with a shock of white hair opened the door and peered out. "Yes?" He wore a baggy green cardigan, matching pants, and spectacles.

"Hi. I'm sorry to bother you, but I'm looking for the gardener who worked at your neighbor's house." I pointed toward Falkner's lot, hidden behind a faded redwood fence and a stand of eucalyptus trees.

He adjusted his spectacles. "Why?"

"Er, for gardening."

"And you needed to ask *now*? You're not going to be able to get much work done in this rain."

I shifted my weight. A hanging fern brushed my cheek. "I believe in planning ahead."

"You should do your own gardening. It's good for the soul."

I scrubbed my hand over my face. I *did* do my own gardening, and it *was* good for the soul. But did he know the name of the gardener or not?

"It's for my mother," I lied. "She's gotten a little infirm and needs help." The last I'd heard, my mother was on a beach in Monaco.

"And *you* can't help her?"

"I have a job." Guilt scorched my chest for abandoning my mythical invalid mother. Which was more than my real mother had ever felt for abandoning me.

His eyes narrowed. "And yet... you're here, mid-afternoon."

Terrific. Now he thought I was lazy *and* a terrible daughter.

The man leaned sideways, peering past me. "Good Lord. Is that an Amphicar?"

"Ah, yes. But—"

"Where on earth did you get that?"

"Would you believe it's a loaner?"

He studied me. His mouth pinched. "I believe I might." He shook his head. "An Amphicar. I never thought I'd see one outside of a James Bond movie."

"Look, the gardener may have information about the murder next door. Do you know his name or not?"

He burst out laughing. "Now that makes more sense. I don't know her name, but her truck said *Green Thumbs Up*. I suppose you can find her online."

"I suppose I can. Thanks." I hesitated. "Want a quick spin in the Amphicar?"

He grinned. "Indeed, I do."

Chapter 12

SLEEP IS ONE OF my favorite pastimes. So one of the many nice things about running a tearoom is work doesn't start at the crack of dawn. I had time for some quick snooping before baking scones and collating finger sandwiches this Wednesday morning.

I had to be back by ten though, so I'd made an appointment before charging out to meet with *Green Thumbs Up*. The owner and sole employee met me at a local nursery on the coast south of San Borromeo.

We slogged through the aisles, rain drumming on my umbrella. Dezdenea wore a dark green rain slicker and matching hat. Beneath it, her longish brown hair was tied back in a neat ponytail. She was an attractive woman, roughly my age, with slender, callused hands.

"Yeah, I found Falkner." She picked up a plant in a plastic bucket, squinted at it, and returned it to the plywood table. "Why?"

"Because it looks like he was murdered." I tugged my pink trench coat tighter.

"Of course he was murdered." Dezdenea picked up another plant and stuck it in her red wagon.

My brows lifted. "Of course?"

"He'd been vomiting. Looked like some sort of plant-based poison to me. Some furniture was knocked over too, like he'd been staggering around."

"Why plant based?"

She shrugged, her rain slicker squeaking. "Intuition."

"The overturned stuff—it didn't look like there'd been a fight?"

"Not to me."

Dezdenea was the ideal witness for an amateur detective. She hadn't questioned my nosiness and was happy to talk. I probably should have been suspicious, but I was too pleased with myself for finding her.

"Did you know Falkner well?" I asked.

Dezdenea faced me and grinned. "The cheapskate wanted to swap services. Gardening for coaching. I told him I didn't need a coach. He took it well enough. Can't blame a guy for trying, but I'm a cash-only sort of gal."

I found myself liking her. "Did you see anything else that looked odd or out of place?"

"Aside from Falkner's body?" She shook her head and wheeled the wagonful of plants down the aisle. "His back door—the glass sliding one—was unlocked, but it usually was. At least when I came around. I'd stick my head inside and say hi. And remind him when his bill was due."

"Did he pay on time?"

"Yeah. He was cheap, but he paid."

"Where was Falkner when you found him?"

"He was right there in the living room on that fancy Persian rug. I could see him through the glass door. I went inside to try and help. When it was obvious I couldn't, I called the cops."

She kept walking. I stopped.

"It was raining when you discovered Falkner," I said.

Dezdenea halted at another table and examined a potted oleander bush. "So?"

"I'm surprised you were able to get much gardening done," I said, thinking of Falkner's elderly neighbor.

She returned the plant to the makeshift table. "I couldn't do a damn thing."

"Then why were you there?" I rubbed my cheek. "To collect your check?"

"Nope."

Rain hammered my umbrella. It sent up splashes in the muddy puddles on the aisle.

"Then why?" I asked.

Dezdenea turned to face me. "Well, we were sleeping together."

I started. Falkner was having an affair with the gardener, too? This was getting ridiculous. "That night?" I asked in a strangled voice.

"Of course not. If we'd been together that night, I could have gotten him help. I just thought I'd... you know. Stop by and see how he was doing."

The gardener's laugh had a bitter edge. "It was no big thing," she continued. "He wasn't serious about it, and neither was I. It's just... Some nights get lonely, you know? Some mornings too."

I frowned. I should have been able to cheerfully deny any lonely nights—not that I ever would out loud. That would be rubbing it in. But I hadn't seen Brik since our date had gotten interrupted by that phone call.

Dezdenea looked toward a greenhouse. "It was hard though, seeing him lying there." She swallowed.

I shook myself. "Did Falkner ever confide in you? Was he worried about anything?"

"No, he didn't, so I don't know if anything worried him."

"Do you know if he was, er, seeing anyone else?"

"A couple of his clients, I think."

My eyebrows rocketed upward. "And he told you that?"

"He told me we weren't exclusive. I sort of figured out he was seeing some of his clients. Don't ask me how," Dezdenea said before I could ask. And I really wanted to ask, too.

"Do you have any idea who could have wanted him dead?"

"Not a clue," she said.

I made it back to Beanblossom's in time to brush the mud off my brown slacks and start baking the scones. I'd made them so often, it was the perfect automatic task for thinking. But I didn't think about murder.

There's a cost to digging up bones, and it's not always what you'd expect. The worms and dirt you turn over are often your own.

There was no way I could be in an open relationship like Dezdenea and Falkner. I needed more. That need sometimes scared me.

Not because it was wrong. There was nothing wrong with wanting a true meeting of minds, with wanting real love and commitment. But after a childhood of loneliness, I couldn't completely trust my craving for the opposite.

I worked at the kitchen's long, metal table making birthday-cake scones. Cuffs of my pink blouse rolled high, I lightly kneaded scone dough. (You never want to over-mix or over-knead scones. It makes them tough).

A white chocolate chip tumbled out of the dough dotted with colorful sprinkles. I jammed it back in and smiled.

Time to call Brik. I slid the scones in the oven, peeled off my work gloves, and pulled my phone from the pocket of my apron.

The kitchen door swung open hard enough to bang against the opposite wall. Verbena strode inside, her long brown hair swinging. Water dripped from her clear rain poncho. The hems of her forest-green leggings were dark with damp.

My neck stiffened. "What—?" I pressed my mouth into a hard line. "You can't be in the kitchen."

"One of your waitstaff let me in. Oh my God. Are you using *American* flour? It's full of pesticides."

"You don't have a hairnet." I pointed at the hair cascading over her skinny shoulders. The collar of her coffee-colored knit top was dampened by the rain.

"You need to tell me what's going on with the murder investigation. And why aren't you using Italian flour? It's much healthier."

Pocketing my phone, I strode into the hallway. As I'd hoped, she followed.

"Well?" Verbena crossed her arms.

"I thought you were in denial about being a suspect?" I asked.

Her narrow face spasmed. "It's not denial. I'm just not a very good suspect. There's no reason why someone should think I had anything to do with Falkner's death—"

"Except you posted online that he was a dangerous man with guru pretensions."

Verbena flipped back her hair. "It was the *truth*. Besides, I posted that after he died."

"What does that—?" I shook my head. *Never mind.* "Why was he dangerous?"

"I told you. Because he had guru pretensions."

Augh. "Could you be more specific?" I gritted out.

Verbena huffed a breath. "Falkner didn't have clients. He had disciples. He didn't want any of us getting outside coaching aside from him. *And* he hit on me once."

"Really?" I pursed my lips. Tad had said Verbena had been hot for Falkner, but *he'd* turned *her* down.

"It was gross. He was my *coach*."

"But you kept working with him."

"Yes," she said, "but that incident made me suspicious. I started to question what he told us, and that made him angry. Also, he had Rasputin eyes. And hair. So what have you found out?"

"Why do you think I've found anything out?"

Verbena cocked her head and gave me a disgusted look. "Come on. Everyone knows you've been snooping. You're always snooping. You know everything that goes on in this town."

Sure I was a snoop, but only when it came to murder. "I wouldn't say that."

A door snicked open down the hall.

"I just *did* say that," she said. "Now, what did you learn?"

"Ah..." I couldn't tell her about Falkner's affairs, because I couldn't trust her not to blab. "It looks like he might have been poisoned." That should be safe enough, and it should satisfy her.

Verbena sucked in a breath. "Anna."

Archer, dressed like a pudgy Cary Grant, strode down the hallway toward us. "Your bathroom needs more TP."

Dammit. Had he heard us? The gossip columnist sailed past the open kitchen door and toward the tearoom.

"It had to be Anna," Verbena said. "*She* killed Falkner."

Archer's shoulders twitched.

I massaged my forehead. He'd definitely heard *that*.

"No," I said, "there's no—"

"She's an apothecary," Verbena said. "She knows all about poisons."

"She knows about healing and—"

"I *knew* it. Well, if she thinks she's going to get away with this, she's got another think coming." Verbena stormed down the hallway to the rear door.

Aghast, I stared after her. That... hadn't gone the way I'd planned.

Chapter 13

"Verbena, wait." I hurried down the tearoom hallway after the tea witch. The inset overhead lights flickered, and I glanced up anxiously.

Were we going to lose power? Because I didn't have a generator. It was one of those big but necessary expenses I'd kept putting off.

"I'm done with waiting." She shoved open the rear, metal door. A gust of rain blasted into the hallway, rustling her plastic rain poncho and splashing the laminate floor.

"We can't tip Anna off." I grabbed the mop leaning against the wall. Whenever someone opened that door, the rain created a slip-and-fall hazard.

She released the door. It clanged shut. "You have a plan?"

Uh... "Yes," I lied. *A plan. A plan to keep her busy and out of my hair...*

Maricel walked past Archer into the hallway. She hesitated outside the kitchen door. Archer pretended to read a text on his phone.

Verbena folded her arms. "What is it?"

I hurried to the tea witch and dragged the mop over the faux-wood. "If we let Anna know she's a suspect before we have any evidence—"

"She's an apothecary, and Falkner was poisoned." Verbena's nostrils quivered. "That's evidence."

"That only demonstrates a possible means," I said, glancing at Maricel. She was obviously waiting for me, but I had to make sure Verbena didn't do anything crazy.

"Means of what?" Verbena asked.

"Means of murder. You know, a killer needs means, motive, and opportunity. But we don't know yet if she had opportunity—"

"The whole point of poisoning someone is you can stick it in their sugar bowl and wait for them to take it when you're away."

"Yeah, that's, ah, yes." All our suspects seemed to have had access to Falkner's house. They held their meetings there. This was going to be tough to logic out.

Maricel smoothed the apron over her black, *Dark and Stormy Night* tee. My manager frowned. Archer shifted his weight.

"But the police will need more than that," I said.

"And you plan on getting that information how?" Verbena arched a brow.

Oh, come on. Hyperion and I couldn't do everything at once. "We need to gather more evidence before accusing anyone of murder." The overhead lights flickered again, and I scowled at them.

"How?" Verbena asked.

"First, by talking to other people who knew them, like... Jose."

"Fine." Verbena shoved open the metal door. "Let's go."

Wait. What? "I can't go now."

"You don't have to," Verbena said. "I'll go by myself."

Oh, hell no. She'd say something to make Jose mad, and then Hyperion and I would never get a decent crack at him. "We're prepping for our first seating." I motioned toward Maricel. "People have reservations."

Maricel coughed. "About that..."

"What's wrong?" I asked her.

Maricel grimaced. "The 101 is flooded. Over half our guests have canceled. And since the rain's supposed to get worse..."

My stomach sank. This was not going to be a good day for the tearoom. Not that I wanted our customers to risk their necks getting here. But this storm was getting expensive.

"What about the staff?" I asked.

"Everyone's here who's supposed to be here," Maricel said.

I wrinkled my nose in frustration. If everyone was here, we were now overstaffed. I blew out my breath. "In that case, I guess I can go with you to see Jose."

Verbena's smile was triumphant. "We'll take your car."

"Is this seatbelt even legal?" Verbena tugged the Amphicar's lap belt, cinching her clear poncho tight. "It can't be legal."

"The car's vintage." I rounded a corner, windshield wipers slapping.

Fortunately, since we couldn't take the freeway, Jose's shop wasn't as far north as Santa Cruz. We crawled along El Camino with all the other freeway refugees.

Verbena sniffed. "The gas mileage on this tank must be awful. This car is a crime against nature."

"At least we won't drown."

"What does this button do?" She pushed a button, and the boat's motor roared to life.

I switched it off. "Don't—"

She pushed another button. Another motor groaned.

I switched that off too. "That button's for the roof, which won't retract since I didn't unsnap it." Also, it was still raining like crazy.

"Oh." Verbena sank back against the stripey gray seat. She pointed at a craftsman-style bungalow with a cheerful purple sign on the lawn. *The Wizard of Santa Cruz.* "There's his place."

I trawled for parking and finally found a spot three blocks away. What was attracting customers to this area? Because the storm hadn't deterred them like it had Beanblossom's customers.

I got out of the car and unfurled my umbrella. "Too bad Jose doesn't have his own parking lot."

"It's not all bad," Verbena said. "At least he doesn't have to deal with parking lot wars like Anna and Katey."

"Oh?" I straightened.

"Those two share a lot, and neither likes sharing. Didn't you notice?"

"I noticed the shared lot, but—"

"You should see how packed it gets in the summer. People aren't supposed to park there for the beach, but they do. And neither Katey nor Anna can be sure if the car belongs to one of the other's customers or not, so towing isn't really an option."

Footsteps splashed behind us, and I glanced over my shoulder. A figure in a long raincoat and umbrella turned down an alley and vanished behind a high wooden fence.

"Can't they coordinate?" I asked.

She smirked. "Those two hate each other. I heard them last August shrieking about their customers hogging the lot. You should have heard Falkner's lecture on resource sharing."

"But Katey sells Anna's stuff." You don't enter into a business agreement with someone you despise. At least, I wouldn't.

"That was just a coaching exercise of Falkner's. He basically forced them to do it, but it made no sense. A customer can walk across the parking lot to see all of Anna's wares."

"But if they don't like each other—"

"We know Anna killed Falkner. What do you care if Anna and Katey have a beef?" Verbena asked.

I hopped around a puddle. "I don't know, but it's interesting." And I wondered if the tension between the women was really over a parking lot or if there was something deeper. Jealousy over Falkner?

The back of my neck prickled, and I glanced over my shoulder. The person with the raincoat walked about a hundred feet behind us, black umbrella blocking his or her face. *Weird*.

Verbena heaved a sigh, and I tore my attention back to her. "The only reason Katey was working with Falkner was because Anna was. She was too competitive to let Anna have an edge. And once they were in, they had to take his recommendations. They were paying him enough. We all were," she grumbled.

We turned down the concrete walk to Jose's two-story purple bungalow. The person with the umbrella continued past, and I relaxed. I really was getting paranoid.

On the covered porch, we shook off our dripping clothes. I raised my hand to knock.

Verbena opened the door and strolled inside. A bell tinkled.

Frowning, I dropped my hand and followed her into the small entryway. A painted tin sacred heart decorated the wall beside an entry to a sitting room.

Jose walked into the foyer. The hems of his gray slacks were slightly frayed. He adjusted the collar of his simple checked, button-up shirt. "Verbena? How can I help you?" He smiled at me.

"You know how backstabby Anna is?" Verbena asked. "Well, she's a murderer too. She poisoned Falkner, but we can't prove it. So tell us what you know. After what she did to you, there's no reason *not* to tell."

Heat crawled up my neck. I smothered a groan. Why had I thought my presence would moderate Verbena? And what had Anna done to Jose?

The healer blinked. "I— What?"

"Falkner was poisoned." I shot Verbena a quelling look but didn't have much hope of it working. Verbena was unquellable. "We don't know who did it."

"I have nothing against Anna," he told Verbena in a gentle tone. "She didn't do anything to me that mattered."

"Oh, please," Verbena scoffed. "Anna told everyone your healing amulets were worthless junk."

"And she had every right to believe what she believes," he said, "and to say what she wanted."

But her saying it couldn't have helped his business. My neck stiffened. And why hadn't Verbena mentioned this before? "Healing amulets?"

Jose walked into a sitting room, and we followed. Plants hung in macrame hangers near the windows overlooking the street. Comfortably worn leather chairs grouped around a low table. A deck of Tarot cards lay fanned neatly across the round table.

He motioned me toward a plain but old-looking glass-fronted cabinet. Inside, pendants made of gemstones and spiral coils of copper wire were displayed. Anna's blue bottled tinctures lined the bottom shelf.

"They're for energetic healing—both physical and emotional," he said. "Though we seem solid, everything that exists, including our bodies, are over 99 percent energy. Yet when we try to heal our bodies, we focus on the less than one percent of matter that makes us up. If we can change our energetic state, we can improve our health."

"And these pendants do that?" I asked.

"They can be an aid to healing," he said, "yes."

"My favorite is the trauma healing pendant," Verbena pointed at a pendant made of blue and black stones beneath the glass.

"Emotional trauma," Jose corrected. "Our emotions create energies. We remember something that hurt us, our body responds with a cascade of chemicals and hormones, and we feel a feeling. And then that feeling solidifies the painful memory, and we get stuck in it. Instead of moving forward or even just being in the present, we find ourselves living in the past. Sometimes, we need a little help to break the pattern."

Verbena huffed, and I glanced at the tea witch. What trauma had made Verbena who she was today? Was a part of me still stuck in the past?

No. I wasn't that hurt kid anymore. But I understood how difficult and long it could take to get past those wounds. I needed to be more patient with Verbena.

I stepped away from the glass cabinet and cleared my throat. "What's with all the traffic?" I nodded toward the windows. "With the 101 flooded, San Borromeo is dead."

"A local furniture store's going out of business."

I nodded, depressed by the thought. A lot of small businesses were going under. And a good bargain would be enough to drive people into the storm.

"Have you thought of anyone who might have wanted to hurt Falkner?" I asked.

"I've been asking myself that question since I learned of his murder," Jose said. "Falkner had a talent for drawing people in, for making them not only want to change, but to believe that they could. But not all his clients did change."

"There were failures?" I asked.

"I wouldn't call them failures. It's not enough to believe. You have to do the work. Not everyone wants to take that step. We want quick solutions."

I lifted one corner of my mouth. "Like a healing amulet?"

"If wearing an amulet is all you do," he said, "it's not enough. It can help with the work, and it can help realign the energies. But a help is all it is. Ultimately, we're responsible for our lives."

Verbena grunted. "Americans are so lazy."

His brown eyes twinkled. "We all tend toward laziness. But that doesn't mean we have to *be* lazy. One good thing about the group, I met Katey. She puts us all to shame. That woman hustles." The doorbell rang, and he turned. "Will you excuse me for a moment?"

He left us for more than a moment. Verbena wandered to the case and studied the amulets.

I walked to the window. An orange traffic cone lay on its side beside a flooding storm drain. I gnawed the inside of my cheek. The weather report said we'd have five more days of this, but the rain was starting to seem unending.

Jose cleared his throat. I started and turned from the window.

His dark hair and the shoulders of his button-up shirt were damp. "Sorry about that. The deliveryman was at the wrong house. I had to direct him to my neighbor's. What were we talking about?"

"Did Falkner have any dissatisfied clients who made their displeasure known?" I walked to a leather chair and braced one hand on its back.

Jose hesitated. "Tad," he finally said. "He wanted a quick fix. But the process of building a business—any business—is slow. Sometimes people and businesses seem to shoot onto the scene out of nowhere, but that's only because we don't see all the work that's gone before."

"Tad complained?" I asked.

"Not in so many words. He had an intense sense of...dissatisfaction about him. Sometimes he was sharp with Falkner over things that seemed trivial."

"Can you give us an example?" I asked.

He shook his head. "I didn't dwell on it, though I did notice it."

"I didn't notice any of your amulets at Katey's bookstore," I said.

"No," Jose said. "I need to explain their usage and work with the customer before selling an amulet. They aren't toys. They aren't lucky charms. And they won't work properly unless you use them properly."

"And yet you admire her hustle," I said dryly.

"I confess, some of the things Falkner asked me to do I resisted as not right for my business. Katey does all the things. She's got *heart*."

"Did you like Falkner?" I asked him abruptly.

"He was an excellent business coach."

I knew an evasion when I heard one. And I'd heard several from Jose today. I folded my arms. "But did you like him?" I persisted.

"I didn't dislike him. We were very different people, that's all."

I asked Jose a few more questions. He gave me more vague responses.

Normally, this would have irritated me. But it was hard to be annoyed with Jose. His Zen demeanor was the ultimate deflector. Which made me wonder how Anna could have been so vocal about his pendants, especially since he was selling her tinctures.

Jose checked his watch. The leather band was worn and discolored. "Sorry, I have to go."

"Where?" Verbena asked.

"None of your business." Jose's smile eased the sting of his words. "And Anna doesn't hate me. She apologized about the amulets. She even said she'd give me a good review online."

"That's... quite a turn around," I said.

He shook his head. "You never know with people. At any rate, she can't get a tow-truck out there until tomorrow in this storm, so I told her I'd give her a lift to visit one of her elderly clients."

He saw us to the front door and opened it. "You should know I do shamanic and herbal healing," he told me.

"Er..." I cocked my head. "Herbal?"

Jose's olive skin flushed. "Ah. You're thinking of the poison. I have knowledge of some locally grown deadly herbs, but that isn't why I brought up my work."

"Why did you bring it up?" Verbena asked. "Since I already knew what you did?"

"I thought you might be interested someday." His gaze met mine. "Childhood wounds often cut the deepest. They can influence our behavior in unexpected ways."

A chill struck my core. How could he know about the abandonment? Had Hyperion...? I shook my head. No. He would never do that. "I'm sure they do," I said and walked out the door.

Verbena followed me to the sidewalk. "Of *course* he had to end with some vague pronouncement to make himself look mysterious and knowing. Everyone has childhood wounds. It's not like you're special." Heedless of the puddles, she strode past me.

"Yeah," I said. "Everyone." And for the first time, I was glad Verbena was around. She might be a pest and a know-it-all, but her bluntness could be refreshing.

"Though your so-called tearoom is a cry for help if I've ever seen one." She told me everything that was wrong with it on the way back to the car.

Chapter 14

THE AMPHICAR WHEEZED. "COME on. Come on." I twisted the key a third time, and its motor sputtered to life.

Verbena tugged down the cuffs of her knit, forest-green sleeves. "Finally," she shouted over the rain thudding on the canvas top. "Tad's office is on the south side of San Borromeo."

"And?" Water dripped steadily onto the back seat.

"And obviously we need to talk to him. He can't stand Anna either."

I started the car. "Why not?"

She tightened her lap belt over her clear poncho. "Probably because she's in everyone else's business." She angled her head and squinted at the windshield. "The woman's a gossip, in case you haven't noticed. It's gross."

Huh. I pulled from my spot, and we splashed down the waterlogged streets toward Santa Cruz. I turned right at an orange detour sign.

Verbena sighed and propped her elbow on the car door, her head on her fist. "This trip is going to take forever." She turned on the radio and fiddled with the dial.

"...battered by high waves. The San Borromeo and Santa Cruz piers are closed until further notice, and a temporary evacuation order is in place for beachside homes and businesses. If you can evacuate safely, do so immediately. If you are unable to evacuate, shelter in place and move away from ocean-facing windows. If you're in imminent danger due to structural damage or wave intrusion, call 911."

My stomach fluttered unpleasantly. Beanblossom's wasn't far from the beach. The tearoom was on a hill, but it wasn't a very big one. I pulled over.

A horn blared, and I winced. A black monster truck zoomed past, sheeting the car with water. The dripping in the back seat became a steady stream.

My mouth firmed. *Stupid truck.* Who needed a truck that big in Silicon Valley? It *had* to be the same one that had gotten me before.

"Why are you stopping?" Verbena asked. "We're not there yet."

"I'm calling the tearoom."

"Now?"

"Now." I phoned Maricel.

She answered on the third ring. "Sorry. I was with a customer."

"Have you heard about the evacuation order?"

"It's all everyone's talking about. But we're a block outside the evacuation zone."

"What about the wait staff? Are any of their homes—"

"No, we're all good. None of us can afford beach views."

But Hyperion's boyfriend Tony had a beach-view condo. "Okay, I've got one more errand to run, and then I'll be back." I adjusted my trench coat's collar.

"We've got everything handled. Take your time." Maricel disconnected.

I called Hyperion.

"Your timing is impeccable," he said without preamble.

"I just heard about the evacuation order. Tony—"

"Has moved into my apartment."

I fell silent. Tony was a germaphobe. I'd been to his condo a few times, and it had always been hospital-level immaculate. Hyperion lived in chaos. "How's that going?" I asked carefully.

"He's sanitizing my kitchen counter for the third time. It's the grout. It's hard to get it looking really clean. Beanblossom's is out of the evacuation zone for now, but—"

"For now?" I yelped. "Beanblossom's must be fifty feet above sea level on that hill. Or at least thirty."

"We're twenty-five feet above sea level," he said. "But if the storm surge gets bad enough— Hey! Gimme."

"Storm surge is complicated," Tony said, by which I assumed he'd commandeered Hyperion's phone. "If the storm hits perpendicular to the coast, it's going to create a bigger surge. Add to that San Borromeo's concave coastline—"

"You mean the bay?"

"Plus, you've got water pushing up into the estuary," he continued. His voice seemed distant. I guessed he was holding the phone away from his face to avoid microbes. "Beanblossom's isn't going to get washed away, but there could be flooding."

"I'm sorry you had to evacuate."

"So am I." The PI disconnected.

I dropped the phone into my purse on the frayed seat beside me.

"Can we go now?" Verbena asked.

"Yeah." I launched the HMS Fuel Tank from its spot and navigated more blocked and flooded roads to Tad's place of business, a tiny blue stucco building jammed up against a flooded lawn. A neon palm lit one of the windows.

Verbena and I picked our way through the water, and I was glad for my waterproof boots. We climbed the concrete steps to his sunshine yellow door.

We knocked. We waited. We rang the bell and waited some more. I knocked again.

Verbena tapped the window and gave me a scathing look. "The *Open* sign isn't lit."

"Then I guess he's not here."

Verbena scowled. "Why didn't you call Tad first?"

"Why didn't *you*?"

Tad yanked open the door. His sandy hair was plastered to his head, and rain darkened the cuffs of his loose khakis. "Let me guess," he said in his Australian twang. He pressed a pudgy finger to one temple and closed his eyes. "You're here to grill me about Falkner's murder."

"Psychic intuition?" I asked.

"Jose called." He scanned the flooded yard. "Is Hyperion with you?"

"No," I said.

"Then you may as well come in." He turned his back on us and walked inside.

Verbena strode in after him. I followed more slowly into a room decorated like a gypsy caravan. Long strips of deep purple fabric swagged the walls. Turkish stained-glass lamps stood on the small tables and dark wood bookcases. Cut crystals hung in the windows.

I wandered to a small shelf with framed photos. There were a couple portraits of Tad with a few minor celebrities, some NASCAR drivers (I knew by the outfits), and shots of Tad working in a pit crew.

"You were in NASCAR?" I asked.

"Pit crew. Most exciting thing I ever did in my life. I love America." Tad's smile faded.

The psychic dropped into a thronelike chair with gilt arms and glowered at us from across the low, round table. The chair looked disturbingly like Hyperion's. Though Hyperion didn't force his clients to sit lower than him on stupid poofs. Hyperion's clients got matching thrones.

"You asked about Hyperion." I perched on a purple poof opposite. "Was there something you wanted from him?"

His mouth curled in a sneer. "Are you kidding me? What would I need from that dog's breakfast? He's no psychic."

Annoyed, I sucked in my cheeks. "He's never claimed to be. Hyperion reads the cards, that's all."

"That's never all," he said.

Verbena claimed a lime green poof and sat. "Why do you think Anna killed Falkner?"

I glared. "That's not—" That was totally leading the witness. You were supposed to start with open questions, see where they led, and follow up with more probing questions. "We don't think Anna killed Falkner."

"I do," Verbena said. "She's an apothecary. She has access to poisons."

"We don't *know* that," I objected.

"And Tad thinks she did it. Don't you, Tad?"

"She *did* accuse Falkner of cheating her out of five grand." Tad drummed his fingers on the gilt armrest.

"Cheating her how?" I asked.

"By manipulating her into signing onto his coaching program."

"*Did* he manipulate her?" I shifted on the poof. The rough fabric made a scraping sound against my pink trench coat.

"He manipulated everyone," Verbena said.

Tad raised his bushy eyebrows. "That's not true. Falkner's a good salesman—*was* a good salesman, I mean. He told her the benefits of his coaching services, and she decided to sign on. That's all."

"That's *not* all," Verbena said.

He shrugged. "There was some time pressure, of course," he admitted. "But people need to be pushed to make decisions."

"And Anna felt he hadn't followed through?" I guessed.

"She was threatening to sue for breach of promise or something," Tad said.

"Okay," I said. "So that would have probably gone to small claims court given the amount, and worst case, he'd have to give back the money—"

"You think *that's* the worst case?" Tad crossed his legs. "This is a reputation business, darling. We're *all* in reputation businesses. A public lawsuit would have been more trouble than losing some money."

"Which would have given Falkner a reason to kill Anna," I said, "not the reverse. Though I'd think it would be easier for him to just refund the money and keep it out of the public eye."

"Exactly." Tad leaned forward in his chair as if I'd just said something significant.

I blew out a noisy breath. *Exactly what?* "You mean... What do you mean?"

His look was scathing. He relaxed in his high-backed chair. "Obviously, he was blackmailing her with something."

"Wait. What?" How was that obvious?

"Duh," Verbena said.

"Blackmailing her over what?" I asked, exasperated. This wasn't how you conducted an investigation. We were speculating. And wildly.

Tad looked around, as if expecting a gypsy spy to pop from behind one of the purple curtains. "I heard... One of Anna's clients *died*."

"Where did you hear this?" I asked.

"From Falkner."

I folded my arms. "What exactly did Falkner tell you?"

"That before Anna moved to San Borromeo, one of her clients died. It was why she moved here. To start over."

My breath caught. *Died?* "Moved from where?"

"Sacramento," Tad said, smoothing his khaki shirt. "There was a wrongful death lawsuit. It ruined her. Now she's trying to rebuild her business here."

"I use one of Anna's tinctures," Verbena whispered and touched her throat. "I could have died."

"But you haven't," I said, "so you're probably okay."

"If it got out that Anna had killed a customer," Verbena said, "it would have ruined her. Plus, *everyone* hates blackmailers. No wonder she killed Falkner. Who can blame her?"

"The police, for starters," I said.

A black cat prowled into the sitting room. He wound between the legs of Tad's gilt chair.

Verbena rolled her eyes. "Oh, the police. What do they know?"

More than we did. It would be nice to know what Falkner had been poisoned with.

The cat rubbed against my leg, depositing black hair on my brown slacks. I bent to pet him.

"Why would Falkner tell you about Anna's legal problems?" I asked Tad.

One corner of his mouth lifted in a smile. "Falkner told me all sorts of things."

Absently, I stroked the cat's silky fur. "Why?" What made Tad special? It wasn't as if...

I exhaled slowly. Briefly, I closed my eyes. "Tad, were you having an affair with Falkner by any chance?"

"Yes, but don't tell anyone. Falkner wanted it kept secret."

"I'll bet he did," I said dryly.

"He didn't want anyone to think he was playing favorites."

Verbena's eyes widened. "But Falkner was—"

I leapt to my feet, and the cat started away. Grabbing her elbow, I hauled her off the poof beside me. *Do not tell him about the other affairs, Verbena.* "Thanks, Tad. We'll keep in touch." I maneuvered a sputtering Verbena outside.

"Why did you drag me out of there?" Verbena demanded. "Falkner was playing favorites if he was telling Tad his coaching clients' secrets."

Warmth raced from my neck into my face. *Oh. Right.* Verbena hadn't been there when we'd learned Anna and Katey had both been having secret affairs with Falkner.

"Ah... We don't want to antagonize Tad," I improvised. "He might remember something important later."

"Who cares if he's antagonized? This is murder."

"Right. Right."

We returned to my car. A slip of paper in a sandwich bag was snagged beneath one of the windshield wipers. I pulled it free. Carefully opening the plastic bag, I extracted the letter.

Verbena stuck her head out the passenger window of the Amphicar. "OMG. We have places to go. What is your problem?"

"I want to read this," I shouted over the noise of the rain on the car's convertible top. And I didn't want Verbena reading over my shoulder.

"Do you really have to do whatever it is you're doing standing out in the rain? Were you born in a barn?"

Okay, that was... a good point. I roughly squished the damp baggie into the pocket of my raincoat, closed my umbrella, and got inside.

Angling my body so she couldn't see, I opened the letter. The writing on the sheet of torn paper was legible this time.

BACK OFF.

Huh. I shivered. So the first letter on the other note *had* been a B.

Chapter 15

Hyperion dropped the plastic bag with the note inside on his office table. Leaning back in his thronelike chair, he steepled his fingers.

Bastet bounded after the note and his paws skidded on the crimson tablecloth. The tabby regained his balance, looked around as if making sure no one had noticed, and casually licked a paw.

"I dunno," he said. "It doesn't really point to someone who plans ahead."

"Like a poisoner?" I sat in the velvety chair opposite.

My partner adjusted the cuffs of his charcoal fisherman's sweater. "I'm just saying, any idiot should know not to leave a letter out in the rain."

"I'm not sure it takes a genius to poison someone. Maybe the killer is high anxiety. He killed Falkner, and now he's panicking." And the letter writer had learned, putting it in a baggie this time.

"Or she." He angled his head toward the white box on the table. "Thanks for the scones, by the way. They're my fav."

"You're welcome. The point is, it's rare to make good decisions when you're in a state of panic."

"Which either makes the killer more dangerous or easier to catch. It's possible this letter has nothing to do with Falkner's murder."

I lowered my head to stare. "Really?" It wasn't like I got threatening notes on a regular basis.

Hyperion sighed. "We need to consider the possibility the note and the murders are two separate incidents."

It was possible, but it didn't seem likely. "Where were you all day?"

"Cleaning my apartment," Hyperion said, waspish.

"I would have thought Tony—"

"He offered to do it himself. But I know where everything goes. I couldn't turn him loose on the place. He might throw out something I *need*."

I nodded wisely.

"Don't give me that look," he said. "You try moving in with Brik and see how that goes."

I gripped the arms of my chair and leaned forward. "What's that supposed to mean?"

"I mean when two people move in together, there's a lot of stuff to deal with." His coffee-colored eyes narrowed. "What did you think it meant?"

I sucked in my cheeks. "I didn't know. That's why I asked."

"Trouble in paradise?"

"No," I said, surprised. "Brik's doing emergency construction out in the storm. I'm worried. And I've been trying not to bug him, because I don't want him answering the phone when he's driving, or getting interrupted in the middle of something dangerous."

My stomach tightened. The storm was worsening, and Brik was still out in it. I'd tried calling him after I'd dropped Verbena at her apartment. My call had gone straight to voicemail.

Bastet batted the plastic bag on the table. The tabby rolled onto his back and stretched, claws extended.

"Brik can handle himself," Hyperion said. "Let's talk about *us*. Have we reached a roadblock in our investigation?"

"Not quite." I reached into my apron pocket and pulled out my phone.

"What are you doing?"

"Calling Razzzor."

My ex-boss picked up on the first ring. "Hey, Abs. Problem?"

"No problem. I was wondering what you found in your deep research?"

"Uh... I told you about the poison, right?"

"You told Hyperion, and he told me."

"Right."

I waited. I crossed my ankle on my knee.

"It's just... I kind of got distracted," Razzzor said. "With work."

I frowned. *Work? A distraction?* This was *Razzzor*. He could manage multiple software companies and still find time for a *Zombie Nazis in Space* marathon.

But he didn't owe me research. It had been a favor... A favor I'd thought he'd been keen on, since he'd followed us all the way to Falkner's house.

"Okay," I said.

Hyperion mouthed, "*What?*"

"Okay?" Razzzor said. "Wait. Are you just saying it's okay? Because it's okay to feel your feelings and to express them."

I rolled my eyes. "I know, but you were doing me a favor. And the intel on the poison was gold."

Silence met me on the other end of the line. "You're mad I didn't get more, aren't you?"

Bastet sniffed the legs of my slacks. The orange cat shot me a suspicious look. I crossed my legs, wary.

"Nope," I said. "It's all good. Hyperion and I probably should be doing this on our own anyway. I can hardly drag you—"

"What else do you need?"

Ha!

Wait. Was I being manipulative? I sank lower in my chair. Yes, I *was* being manipulative, dammit. *Stop being selfish.* "What's going on at work?"

"What?" he asked.

"You said you had a work problem."

"Maddox isn't a problem. He's a low-talent, narcissistic irritant."

"Ah..." *Okay.* "Who's Maddox?"

"*Maddoxxx*, three x's, two d's. It's ridiculous. Who needs that many consonants?"

Says a man named Razzzor. But even I'd heard of Maddoxxx. He was the hot new thing in Silicon Valley.

He'd done the opposite of every other big shot and stayed behind a keyboard. No one knew what he looked like. The mystery made him more intriguing. "What's he got to do with you?" I asked.

"Nothing, except he's been trying to poach my staff."

That *was* uncool. "Trying? Hold on. Was that why you were asking if anything unusual had happened to me? You thought he'd made me a job offer?"

"Uh, yeah. I thought he might go after you."

"And that I'd give up my tearoom for him instead of you?" I asked, insulted. "What kind of a friend do you take me for?"

"Sorry. Sorry. I know you wouldn't knife me in the back."

"Has anyone taken him up on his offer?"

"No. They like me better," Razzzor said smugly. "So, what do you need?"

"If you have time, that background info on our suspects," I said. "And on Falkner Fiore."

"Sure. No problem."

I rattled off the list of suspects, just in case he'd forgotten. We disconnected.

"Well?" Hyperion asked.

"He said he'll get on it."

"Wait. You mean to tell me he wasn't *already* on it?" Hyperion rose from his chair and walked to me, his hands extended as if feeling his way in the darkness. "You've... lost your power over Razzzor? Something is very wrong."

"I don't have any power over Razzzor," I snapped. "We're friends."

"Riiiight. Friends. Like *that* can happen."

"What are you talking about?"

"Please, girl. As if you don't know he has a major crush on you. He's not interested in investigating murders. He's interested in you."

My face heated. "That's ridiculous. He loves digging up stuff on the web."

"For *you*." He waved his hands above my head.

"That's not—" I sputtered. "What are you doing?"

"An aura check. Brik's dissing you, Razzzor's dissing you. Something's off."

I scooted the velvet chair back and stood. "Please stop talking."

"Seriously, have you pissed off a witch?"

"Have *you*?"

He waggled his head side to side. "I might have. The magical community can get tense, as you should know from our current imbroglio."

It was hard to stay mad at a guy who used words like *imbroglio*. "All right. What's next?"

"I think you should call Brik."

"I meant, what's next for our investigation?"

"Oh. That. Well, if, as you say, someone followed you to Katey and Tad's places of business, that lets out Katey and Tad."

"Not... necessarily. Verbena and I had to wait a while for Tad to answer the door. And he looked like he'd just come in from out of the rain."

"It lets Verbena out though."

"Yeah," I agreed, morose. It's not that I wanted her in jail. But I was starting to regret helping the tea witch.

"We've missed something," he said. "But we won't figure it out now. I'm fried, you're frazzled. Let's sleep on it."

It seemed as good an idea as any. I drove home. Brik's deep blue house next door was dark. I ate leftover sandwiches from Beanblossom's and thought of calling Brik but didn't. I didn't want to seem needy.

Near midnight, Brik's truck pulled into his driveway. No, I hadn't been watching for him. His pickup has a distinctive rumble. I could hear it from my bedroom over the drumming of the rain.

My doorbell chimed. And though I wasn't at his beck and call, I jumped out of bed, heart jittering, and hurried to answer.

Brik stood on the step. "Sorry I didn't call."

"Come in out of the rain."

He did. His hoodie was cold and damp, and I hugged him tightly anyway. "How have you been?"

"Busy."

"There's that much storm damage?" I walked into the kitchen, and he followed.

Brik peeled off his navy hoodie. "That, plus my friend's sister, Jude. It's never a quick fix with her. I don't mind the couple hundred bucks a month I have to dish out to pay for her hotel when she runs out of money—"

"You're paying for her hotel?" I bent to fill the kettle with water so he wouldn't see the concern on my face. Setting it on the stove, I turned on the heat.

"She's homeless. Jude travels around the country trying to prove she's the victim of a criminal conspiracy. Every time she calls for a hotel room, there's a problem, and I spend an hour on the phone paying for her room... It would be quicker if I just went to the hotel myself, but I'm too damn busy."

I leaned against the gray granite counter. "Tell me about her."

Briefly, he closed his eyes. "I was her brother's friend. There was a hiking accident. He died, she was in a coma for a month or so. When she came out of it, she wasn't right. Paranoid. She can't stay in one place."

The poor woman. "And you're the only one who can help her?"

"No. She's got another brother who won't answer her calls anymore. There's also a cousin who's handling her trust. She says he's been withholding money from her."

"Has he?"

His laugh was hollow. "Who knows? She makes the perfect victim. Who would believe her? She spends hundreds of dollars a week printing off screeds to the FBI and then sending them off certified mail."

"Hundreds?"

He raked a hand through his damp hair. "They're long letters. I haven't read them—she won't let me—but I've seen the pages." The phone rang in the pocket of his jeans, and he pulled it out. His tipped his head backward. "It's her."

The phone rang again.

"Aren't you going to answer?"

"No."

I lightly bit my bottom lip. "In this weather—"

Brik's mouth compressed, and he gave a quick shake of his head. He answered the phone. "Hello?" He was silent a long time. A woman's voice echoed faintly from the receiver. "Fine," he said shortly and hung up.

"What's wrong?"

"There's a problem at her hotel. I have to go over there to sort it out."

"Now?"

"No." He pulled me into his arms. "Jude can wait."

We held each other a long time, saying nothing. I didn't tell him he was a good man for helping her. I didn't tell him sometimes he let his chivalry take him too far. Both were true.

And God help me, I loved him for it. I loved him for caring. I loved him for his sense of right. I loved him for all of him, even the parts that sparked my own anxieties. But tonight, those felt far off.

He kissed me and kissed me and kissed me. And then, he left.

I went to bed. Love warring with dissatisfaction, I tried to get to sleep.

Eventually, I did sleep. I awoke the next morning bleary eyed and staggered to the kitchen, where I reheated an extra birthday cake scone and made Empress Tea. I took both to the French windows and looked out over my redwood deck.

Rain blurred the glass. I still had the fantasy of living closer to the beach, or at least on a hillside that overlooked the ocean. But this morning, with landslides threatening, I was glad I lived on a viewless but stable street.

I studied my raised garden. At least my plants were getting watered. I glanced at the six-foot fence separating my bungalow from Brik's and bit back a curse. The fence, covered in jasmine, leaned inward. *So much for stable ground.*

A gust of wind slapped at the windows. Something flapped beside the leaning fence.

I squinted, pressing my nose closer to the glass. Huddled in a mass of fallen jasmine was a dark mass—of fabric? A line of prickling ants marched from the nape of my neck to my scalp.

I slipped into my tennis shoes, tugged on a raincoat. At the French doors, I hesitated, then opened them and stepped onto the deck.

Wind and rain lashed me, and I hugged my raincoat tighter. Blinking against the rain, I trotted down the redwood steps and to the tanbark path lined with lavender. I jogged to the fence and sucked in a breath.

Anna Ogawa lay curled against the collapsing fence, her face turned upward, water streaming across her unseeing eyes. My shovel lay beside her.

Chapter 16

Police officers milled between my garden's raised beds, rain beading on their navy raincoats. The dogwood tree drooped in the rain, its buds small and hard and dripping in the morning chill.

Brik draped an arm over my shoulder and squeezed. I leaned against his warmth.

"What was she doing in *your* yard?" Detective Baranko growled.

I turned from the French doors to face the big detective, half-sitting on the back of my blue sofa. "I don't know," I said.

Before the police arrived, I'd had time to change into jeans and a slouchy gray sweatshirt with the word LOVE printed on it in red. You don't want to face the police without a bra on. Trust me on this.

Brik pulled me tighter. "You don't have to say anything."

"But I don't know," I said wildly, pressing closer against the hard planes of his chest. "I have no idea why she's here. I don't even know how she knows where I live. Knew where I live," I corrected.

"You two were business partners," Baranko said. "Why didn't she know where you lived?" The front legs of the sofa lifted an inch off the bamboo floor.

"What?" I blinked rapidly. "No we weren't."

"You were signing an agreement in her shop," he said. The couch dropped with a thud. "I saw you."

I closed my eyes. I'd put my home address on our agreement. That must have been how Anna had found my house.

"The agreement was to do some cross sales," I said. "I'd sell Anna's tinctures in my tearoom, and she'd sell my teas in her apothecary shop.

It was a temporary agreement. If it worked out, we'd continue. If it didn't, we'd stop."

"And the shovel?"

I blinked rapidly and looked away. "It's mine. I use it for gardening. I kept it in that little open shed along the side of the house, by the walkway." Anyone could have taken it. A killer had.

"What time did she arrive?"

I clawed a hand through my hair. "I don't know! I got home around eight last night, but I didn't look in the backyard until this morning. It was dark and raining—"

"Abigail!" Tomas pushed through the cluster of policemen at the front door. "Abigail?" His leathery face was pale.

"Here," I said.

Relief creased the older man's face. His shoulders sagged beneath his rain darkened orange and black windbreaker. "*Dios mio*, Abigail. I thought—"

"What's he doing here?" Baranko bellowed loud enough to rattle the teacups on the mantel.

"He said he's the homeowner," a younger policeman replied.

"He is," I said. "I rent the bungalow from Tomas."

The older man pushed forward. "Are you talking to the cops? Stop talking to the cops. Brik, you should know better than letting her talk to the cops."

Brik shrugged, the fabric of his soft t-shirt shifting against my cheek. "I tried to tell her—"

"But I don't *know* anything," I said.

"Then shut it," Tomas snapped.

"All right," Baranko said. "We'll go down to the station and talk."

"Not without a lawyer," Tomas said. Slowly, I nodded.

The detective gripped my upper arm. Brik growled, and Baranko hastily released me. "After you." The detective gestured sarcastically toward my front door.

"But... the tearoom," I said. "It's Thursday. I have to work."

"Not today, you don't," Baranko said.

Brik drove me to the station in his pickup. Tomas followed in his Buick.

I called Maricel along the way and explained the situation. And then I spent the next three hours getting grilled by Baranko and saying nothing in return. Okay, I did get in a few more *I-don't-knows*. It was important he believed I really *didn't* know.

Nausea swam in my gut, my muscles jumping. What *had* Anna been doing in my garden? Why had she come? Why had she gone around back instead of to the front door?

Why? I stared at my hands on the metal table. Studying the freckles and burn marks from the oven beat staring into the mirror, with its hidden watchers. It also beat staring at the clock, which I'd swear ticked backwards for every thirty seconds it went forward.

Baranko cold and steely was worse than Baranko red-faced and raging. He asked the same questions, testing for changes in my answers. But I had none to give.

The metal door clicked open. A forty-something, straight-backed blond man in a very expensive suit strode into the cinderblock interrogation room. Baranko's eyes narrowed.

The newcomer set his briefcase on the table. "Ms. Beanblossom has nothing more to say."

Baranko swore, pushing back his chair and rising.

After some back-and-forthing between Baranko and the man, who apparently was obviously my new lawyer, the detective released me. I stumbled, dazed, into the station's dingy waiting area.

Razzzor leapt from a plastic visitor's chair. "About time." He glanced at the lawyer. "Thanks, Pete."

Pete nodded in response. "Not a problem." He walked to Tomas, who rose creakily from his chair. His orange and black windbreaker brushed against a wilted palm, and its fronds rustled. The two men traded grips.

"Where's Brik?" I scanned the damp and motley crew filling seats in the reception area. My throat tightened.

"He had an emergency," Tomas said. "He didn't want to leave, but I told him he could. There was nothing he could do here."

My heart plummeted. No, there was nothing Brik could do. There was no sense in him ruining his morning too.

The man in the expensive suit conferred with Razzzor. My ex-boss and current gaming partner clapped the lawyer on the shoulder. "Great. We'll let you handle everything."

"Thanks," I said, "but—"

"Don't interact with the police," the lawyer told me. "If any come by or ask for information, call me." He handed me a business card that read: *Pete Shapiro, Attorney at Law*.

I pocketed the card, but I wouldn't be calling him. I didn't know how I'd pay for his bill as it stood. But I'd pay Razzzor back somehow.

The lawyer strode through the station's arched, wooden door, and I turned to Tomas. "Did Brik say what kind of emergency it was?" I asked.

"It sounded like something medical."

My chest clenched. *Brik's mother*. She was in a retirement village, and... I pulled out my cellphone and called.

He answered on the first ring. "Abigail? Are you out?"

"Yes. What's going on? Tomas said there was some sort of medical emergency?"

"I'm sorry I left you there. It's my friend's sister, the one I told you about... I got a call at the station that Jude overdosed. I think she's going to be okay, but I'm at the hospital now."

My muscles loosened. "That's a relief. I thought... I don't know what I was thinking." I'd been panicking and feeling sorry for myself—a terrible combo at the best of times, and a shameful instinct at the worst.

Anna was dead. My throat hardened, my eyes burning.

Brik laughed hollowly. "Is it? This has been going on for years. I'm amazed she isn't dead yet."

I pushed my hair out of my face. If this had been going on for years, why was this the first I'd heard of it? "Okay, but—"

"Sorry, the doctor's here. Can I call you back?"

"Of course."

"I really am sorry about this," he said in a lower voice. "I've been trying to... Sorry. I've got to—I'll talk to you later." He disconnected.

Slowly, I returned the phone to the rear pocket of my jeans. My insides quivered sickeningly. Why did everything feel like it was unraveling? Like I was unraveling?

Get a grip. I drew a slow breath and released it. It didn't make me feel better.

"Everything okay?" Razzzor asked anxiously.

Everything was *not* okay. There was a body in my garden... Okay, it was probably out of my garden by now, but I'd *known* Anna. She'd been a real person. She'd been *alive*.

"No, everything is *not* okay," Tomas said, and I started at the echo of my thoughts. "I nearly had a heart attack when my cop friend told me there was a dead body at my bungalow. *Your* bungalow. I thought..." He scrubbed a gnarled hand over his face.

"You didn't tell Gramps, did you?" I asked, alarmed.

"Of course I didn't tell your grandfather," he snapped. "What kind of fool do you take me for?"

"Sorry," I said meekly.

"Oh, hey," Razzzor said. "I got that, er, research for you."

Tomas shot him a black look. "Not here." Grasping my elbow, he steered me from the police station.

Rain sheeted down, obscuring the candy shop across the street. Water rippled down its wavy, shingled roof and made a curtain in front of its half-timbering and smooth, white stucco.

I loved the fairytale style. But the insides of the homes and businesses never matched the outsides' enchanted look.

But that was life. We put up false fronts to be sociable or to just fit in, and we never really knew what was going on inside others. Sometimes we didn't really know what was going on inside ourselves.

My jaw firmed. No more self-pity. It wouldn't help Anna. And I wasn't going to worry about Brik and his friend's sister. He'd been dealing with her for years, and I chose to trust him.

Not to trust him meant I was still that little girl who'd been abandoned at an airport. And I wasn't that wounded child anymore.

Though we could have walked to the tearoom, we drove. Tomas and Razzzor's cars were at the station, and the weather was still awful.

We parked behind the tearoom and hurried inside. Pulling off my pink raincoat, I strode into the kitchen. "How's—?"

"Fine," Maricel said from behind the long, metal table. She loaded scones and sandwiches onto a plate. "The good news is, everything's under control. The bad news is, that's because we've had more cancellations."

"Does that mean you've got food going to waste?" Tomas asked hopefully from behind me. "Because I'd hate to see food go to waste."

"Abigail?" Hyperion strode into the kitchen. "Why didn't you call me? I had to hear about your arrest from Maricel." He glanced at her. "No offense, Maricel."

My partner swiped at a fleck of flour that had landed on his charcoal turtleneck sweater. Its color exactly matched his skinny slacks.

"No offense taken." Maricel picked up the plates and bustled from the kitchen.

"She wasn't arrested," Tomas said. "Get your facts straight."

"Was Anna really dead in your garden?" Hyperion said. "That makes zero sense."

"She was." My voice cracked, and I busied myself plating a scone and a chicken salad sandwich for Tomas. "I don't understand it either."

Hyperion glanced at Tomas. "Let's sit down and hash this out." He jerked his dark head toward the kitchen door. "My office."

We crossed the hallway to his open door. Its twinkle lights flashed erratically.

Inside his office, Hyperion motioned me to the high-backed chair he usually sat in. I hesitated before realizing why he was giving up his usual seat. Tomas wouldn't sit unless I did, and there were only two chairs at the table.

I sat. Hyperion motioned Tomas toward the guest chair.

"No," Tomas said. "You take it."

"I've been sitting all day." Hyperion braced an arm on the top of the chair I'd taken.

"And I need to pace," Razzzor said, doing just that. "Nervous energy. Maddoxxx is up to something. He hasn't been in his office lately."

"Are you spying on him?" I handed Tomas the plate and a white-cloth napkin.

"Thanks," he said. "And who's Maddoxxx?" Tomas sank into the other red-velvet chair with a groan. "This is nice." He looked around.

"Maddoxxx is a competitor," I said. "And how would you know he's not in his office?"

Razzzor's gaze turned shifty. "I hear things."

Huh. But I didn't press the issue. The more I considered it, the more I realized I really didn't want to know.

Bastet dropped from the driftwood altar. The tabby sniffed Tomas's shoes. He lowered the scone plate, and the cat sniffed at that too, then curled beneath Tomas's chair.

"You said you found something on Anna?" I asked Razzzor.

"Yeah, she was involved in a wrongful death lawsuit."

I sat forward. "Having to do with her herbalism?"

"Uh, no." Razzzor adjusted his glasses. They glinted beneath the dim, overhead lights. "It was a car accident. Her insurance paid out."

"So, it had nothing to do with Falkner's murder." Hyperion hunched his shoulders, disappointment sketched across his expressive face.

"I don't see how it could," Razzzor said. "I couldn't find a connection between the accident victim and Falkner or anyone else in that coaching group."

"Which brings us back to why that poor woman was in your garden." Tomas took a bite of the sandwich.

I lifted my hands and let them fall. "Honestly, I have no idea." My stomach twisted, because that was a lie. I *did* have an idea, that Anna's death was my fault. She'd come to my home, after all. "I'm assuming she was coming to see me—"

"Why?" Tomas asked.

"We'd talked about Falkner and his death. Maybe… she wanted to tell me something? Or ask me something?"

"Why not go to the police?" Tomas blotted one corner of his mouth with the napkin. "Why go to you? Why sneak around your backyard?"

I glanced up at Hyperion and looked quickly away, my chest tightening. By sticking our noses into Falkner's murder, had we led Anna to believe that she should come to us instead of the police? *Were* we to blame for Anna's death?

Chapter 17

When in doubt, bake.

And I had a lot of doubts to bake out of my system. About Anna, about myself.

I told myself the only person responsible for Anna's murder was her killer. I told myself if she'd made a bad decision, then that was on her, not me. I told myself this wasn't our fault.

But I didn't buy any of it.

I needed to get out of my head. Though it was well past our time to bake scones, with so few customers in the tearoom, it was the perfect time to experiment.

I jammed up the sleeves of my loose sweatshirt. Spring was on its way. I'd been planning to try matcha as an ingredient.

Don't think about Anna. Matcha is basically ground up green tea leaves. They're special green tea leaves, hence the "basically" qualifier.

Don't think about the rain beading on her face. My hands fumbled the bag of matcha.

I mixed the dry ingredients, hesitated, then added more matcha. These needed to be spring green. *Green like the jasmine leaves coiling around Anna's shoulders.*

I gripped the edges of the metal worktable and breathed deeply. My throat ached. *Pull it together.*

Maricel bustled into the kitchen. I straightened and added slivered almonds to the metal bowl, both for contrast and because I had an intuition that they might work well with the bite of matcha.

I cut the dough into haphazard triangles and slid the scones into the oven. Now... what to pair them with?

Murder?

I shook myself. *Stop it.*

I was already putting lemon glaze on the scones. Lemon curd seemed like overkill. What to pair them with? Strawberry jam?

Maricel plated miniature scones and sandwiches. "You're trying the matcha thing?"

I nodded. "No time like the present."

"Sounds great." My manager nodded. "What spread goes with matcha?"

"I could make a matcha murder— I mean spread." Matcha *spread*. Spreads were easy enough.

"Would that be too much matcha?" she asked.

Probably. "Maybe berry jam then."

"Ooh!" She braced her hands on her hips, rumpling her apron. "What about that anise plum jam?"

Thunder boomed. The kitchen door swung open, and Verbena strode inside, her long hair drifting over one shoulder in a ponytail.

"Verbena, hair net!" I barked.

She made a face. "Oh, come on. It's not—"

"Hair net." I pointed to the bag on the metal rack by the door.

Reluctantly, she pulled out a net and tucked her long, brown ponytail inside. "Happy?"

Not by a longshot. "What are you doing here?"

Maricel's full lips pursed. With a quick shake of her head, she left the kitchen, plate in hand.

"I have evidence," Verbena said.

"Then take it to the police." I hesitated. Dammit. How could I *not* ask? "What sort of evidence?"

"From Anna's Apothecary."

Ice hardened in my gut. "You were at Anna's? When?"

"Last night, of course. When else was I supposed to break in?"

My head spun. "You broke into... Verbena, Anna's *dead*."

"I know that *now*. It's all over the internet."

"You can't go around breaking into people's businesses," I said, exasperated and more than a little afraid. Not because I thought Verbena had run into Anna, killed her, and dumped her in my garden. Though the thought had flitted across my mind. But because she might have tampered with evidence.

"Look what I found." She slapped a beaded green pendant on the central counter. Its coppery chain curled around its metal coils. The chain was broken.

I hissed a breath. It was one of Jose's amulets. "You took that from her shop?"

"It was on the floor in the back room. She told everyone that his amulets didn't work. But she had one in her *office*."

And presumably around her neck at some point... and ripped from her neck. She'd tampered with evidence. Suddenly, I had a hard time swallowing. "Verbena—"

Maricel trotted into the kitchen, Detective Baranko at her heels. "Abigail, I'm sorry. He insisted—"

"You're under arrest," he said in a flat voice.

My stomach lurched. "For what?" I stepped backward, my hip clipping the kitchen's long, metal worktable. "You just released me—"

"Not you. Verbena Pillbrow, you're under arrest."

She lifted her pointy chin. "For what?"

"For breaking and entering. You were seen at Anna's Apothecary last night, and we found your prints all over the place."

My shoulders dropped. I slumped against the flour-dusted table. Maricel clapped her hands to her mouth.

"Give me a break," Verbena huffed. "You're not going to arrest me. Abigail does this sort of thing all the time."

He grasped her wrist. Twisting it behind her, he slapped on cuffs.

"Ow!" She glared at him. "Stop it."

"You see what you've started," Baranko snarled at me.

Heat flushed my face. "I didn't know she'd—"

"Of course you didn't know," he said. "You're an amateur. You have the right to remain silent," he told Verbena and led her from the kitchen.

"Oops, sorry," Archer said in the hallway. "Just headed to the gents."

"Watch it." Baranko snarled at him. "Anything you say can and will be used against you..."

Archer stuck his head into the kitchen. I narrowed my eyes. "Sorry," he said, "this isn't the gents." Hastily, he ducked into the hallway.

"Oh, no," Maricel whispered. "Should we... Should we do something?"

I swallowed. Even if I could afford a lawyer for Verbena, I didn't trust her not to stick me with the bill. And after Anna's death... Maybe she'd be safer in jail?

"She's an adult," I said. "She made her choice." But guilt wormed inside me. Had I led Verbena down the garden path to prison?

***

"This isn't our fault." In his high-backed chair, Hyperion made a quick negating motion with his head.

"Isn't it?" I leaned against his closed office door and scraped flour from beneath a fingernail. "Because I can't help *feeling* that it is."

"I'm just glad Baranko didn't arrest *you*."

"I thought he was going to," I mumbled and dropped my hands to my sides. And a part of me thought I deserved being arrested.

"*Could* Verbena have done it?"

"I don't know." I straightened off the door and paced. "She doesn't seem murderous. Irritating beyond belief, but not murderous."

"Yeah." Hyperion slouched lower in his chair. "I don't think Verbena did it either. If only we knew what Falkner was poisoned *with*."

"Hold that thought." I called Razzzor.

"Has Maddoxxx contacted you?" he asked. Laser sounds blasted in the background.

"No," I said patiently. "And I told you, it wouldn't matter if he did."

"It would matter to me," he growled.

"Were you able to find out what exactly killed Falkner?" I asked.

"Oh, yeah. Didn't I tell you?"

I squeezed my eyes shut. He was doing us a favor. If I was annoyed, that was on me. "No. What was it?"

"Oleander."

"Oleander?" I echoed. There was oleander growing next to Anna's Apothecary. But it was also a common roadside barrier, seen along most every California freeway.

"Yeah," he said. "Does that help?"

"Maybe."

"Oh, and I found another weird death."

"Another?" My flesh pebbled. "What do you mean?"

"Katey's dad died under mysterious circumstances. Carbon monoxide poisoning. Hose through the window of his car, closed garage, the works. It was ruled a suicide. His garage was going under, and he couldn't face it."

I cupped my hand to my mouth. *How awful.* My parents had deserted me, but at least they were still around. Suicide seemed the ultimate desertion. What a horrible thing for Katey to live with. "Thanks," I said heavily, and we disconnected.

"Oleander?" Hyperion asked. "What did he say?"

"That's the murder weapon. You know, that big bush with pink flowers we saw growing outside Anna's Apothecary?"

Thunder rumbled outside. We glanced at the white ceiling.

"Oh," he said. "That's poisonous?"

"There's a story about Southern Belles brewing oleander tea to poison Union soldiers." Gramps had taken me as a child on a cross-country road trip to visit historic sites. The tea trivia had made an impression.

"Nice." Hyperion rubbed his neck. "But those bushes are everywhere. Anyone could have used it. The fact that it grows in Anna's parking lot—"

"And Katey's," I reminded him.

"Doesn't mean they were the only ones with access. Did Razzzor tell you anything else?"

I told him about the suicide of Katey's father. "And then there's this..." Avoiding his gaze, I held out the broken pendant Verbena had brought, wrapped in a sandwich bag. I'd been careful not to touch the pendant with my fingers.

"I didn't get a chance to give the pendant she'd stolen from Anna's to Baranko," I said. And I hadn't realized she'd left it until after she and Baranko had gone. In fairness, there'd been a lot going on.

"It's on a chain," he said.

"And the chain is broken."

Hyperion pushed back his red-velvet chair and stood. "Let's talk to Jose."

"Again?"

"Just because you went behind my back with Verbena to visit him—"

"I told you everything he told us, and you know I only did it to keep her from harassing Anna. Besides, it's after seven o'clock. His office will be closed." Beanblossom's already was. With so few clients, we'd cleaned it up in record time.

But none of that was the reason for my reluctance. Jose had gotten too close to an uncomfortable truth about my past. I didn't want to go there again. The past should stay where it was—done and gone.

"Jose lives in that office," Hyperion said. "Well, above it."

"But..." I tugged on my bottom lip. "What if we're making things worse? Verbena's—"

"Bunk and bunkum. You know Verbena. She was going to do something stupid whether we encouraged her or not. And we didn't encourage her."

"I might have—"

"Don't go there." Hyperion plucked his forest-green trench coat off the antler coat rack—a gift from Tony. He slithered into it. "Are you coming or not?"

Dammit. "I'm coming." Jogging to the kitchen, I grabbed my own raincoat.

I followed Hyperion's Jeep. I had to admit, I was getting used to the Amphicar. It might be as big as a cruise liner, but at least I didn't have to worry about high puddles. And there were lots of high puddles on the way to Jose's office.

Hyperion found a spot out front. I had to circle the block before I could find a space long enough to park my rental. By the time I returned to the two-story purple bungalow, Hyperion was standing beneath the covered porch talking to Jose, both men framed in the door's rectangle of light.

A woman in a red raincoat and hat picked her way down Jose's concrete steps and hobbled down the path toward the sidewalk. Her sleeve brushed mine. She skidded, her rain boots rippling the puddle. I grasped her arm, steadying her.

Her gnarled face looked up at me. Her black eyes twinkled. "My new protection amulet must be working already." She touched her raincoat at chest height.

"Good to know," I said lightly and smiled. "Maybe I should get one."

"Maybe you should." The white-haired woman turned, her gaze searching the darkened street. "It's a bad storm. I'm afraid worse is coming."

My stomach tightened. I was afraid of that too.

She tottered down the sidewalk to a 1970s Corvette. Its engine revved, its headlights flashing. The Corvette roared down the street, water flaring from its wheels.

Smiling, I jammed my hands in the pockets of my raincoat. I hurried to join the men on the porch.

"You two may as well come in." Jose turned and walked into the sitting room.

"He knows why we're here," Hyperion said and followed.

I closed the door, wiped my sneakers on the mat, and extracted myself from my dripping pink coat. I followed the two men into the sitting room.

"Tea?" Jose asked. "It's a nasty night."

"No, thanks." I sat on the sofa beside Hyperion and braced my elbows on the thighs of my jeans.

"Then I hope you don't mind if I have some." He walked to a side table with an electric kettle and poured water into a mug then dunked a teabag into it. "Because I'm going to do it anyway."

"Tell me about this amulet." I pulled the plastic bag from my purse and laid it on the coffee table between us.

He glanced at it and added sugar to his mug. "It's a grounding amulet for protection."

"Protection from what?" Hyperion asked.

"From evil, from stress, from EMF radiation. Everything Mother Earth can protect us from."

"How does it work?" Hyperion asked.

"The neodymium magnets are placed to increase the energy from the copper coil and charge the clear quartz stones."

Yeah, that... didn't help at all. "Did Anna need protection from evil?" I asked.

"She's dead, isn't she?" he replied sharply.

My muscles hardened. "Yes," I said, tone even. "Anna's dead."

"Sorry." Jose grimaced. "I didn't mean to be... I still can't believe she's gone.."

"Did she say anything to you?" I asked. "Anything that might have indicated she thought she needed protection from evil?"

"No," Jose said. "Though someone had been messing with her car. They put sugar in her gas tank a month or so ago. Maybe that's why she bought the amulet."

"When did she buy the charm?" Hyperion asked.

"Two weeks ago," he said.

"Well *after* she'd announced to the group that your amulets didn't work?" I asked.

Jose nodded.

"I don't suppose she ever issued a retraction," Hyperion said dryly.

"She said she would," he said. "I didn't push her. Besides, what goes on between my customers and me is confidential."

"You didn't tell people that she'd bought one?" I brushed a bit of stubborn flour off the sleeve of my gray sweatshirt.

"No," Jose said. "What my customers do is private. Telling would go against my values."

"Did you ever see Anna wear the amulet?" I asked.

"Yes." Jose sipped from his mug. "She wore it beneath her top. I don't think the amulet was her style."

"And she said *nothing* to you when she bought it?" I asked. She must have had a reason, something... Something that meant it wasn't my fault, that her death warrant had been signed before we'd met. "Nothing that might have indicated she was under some stress or threat?"

Jose angled his head. "She did say something odd. She asked me if it could protect her from fear."

"What did you tell her?" Hyperion asked.

"I said it could protect her from her own fears, but not the fears of others."

I looked toward the windows. The plants in their macrame hangers swayed lightly in the blasts from the floor heaters.

I'd have to take the amulet to Baranko tonight. But that wasn't what caused the tension in my gut. Jose's client with the Corvette was right. The storm was getting worse. Two people were dead. And I had a bad feeling it wasn't the end.

Chapter 18

BRIK'S HOUSE WAS A beacon in the storm. Literally. The narrow, two-story home towered over its neighbors like a lighthouse, light beaming through its windows. *All* its windows.

I pulled the Amphicar into my driveway and turned off the headlights. Rain sheeted down the windshield.

Gathering my things, I took a deep breath and raced from the car to Brik's front step. Though we were in the *mi-casa-es-su-casa* stage of our relationship, I rang the bell.

No one answered. I crammed closer beneath the overhang and pressed the bell again. Baranko hadn't been happy when I'd brought him the amulet Verbena had taken, but he hadn't arrested me either.

After a minute, a woman's voice called, "Who is it?"

I stiffened. "It's Abigail."

"Abigail who?"

"Abigail Beanblossom." A hardness crept into my voice, and I grimaced. I was not going to act like a jealous girlfriend. "From next door."

The door opened. A tall woman with long, ebony hair stood in Brik's bathrobe. She was stick thin, her cheekbones sharp enough to slice an artery on. Her eyes were deep blue, soulful pools. Her tan looked unhealthy, her skin damaged by the sun. And did I mention she was wearing Brik's bathrobe?

"Oh, *you're* Abigail!" She grabbed my wrist before I could protest and pulled me inside. "Brik's told me so much about you. He *loves* you." She shut the door and bolted it. "I thought you were the *other* one."

Unmollified, I studied her. "The other one?"

"I'm Jude."

"Jude," I said flatly. I'd guessed as much.

His dead friend's sister was a beautiful woman, even with sun-damaged skin. Brik never could say *no* to a damsel in distress.

"Yes, I'm not like my brother." Jude's face fell. "Before they killed him, of course. Would you like some coffee? Oh! You're a tea person, aren't you? Brik brought me scones from your tearoom. I love dried cherries and lemons." She turned and walked through the living area to the open kitchen.

Before they killed him? My palms went damp, and not from the rain. I wasn't entirely surprised by her fractured speech. Brik had said she'd had a brain injury. But seeing and hearing it was a far cry from merely hearing *about* it.

I hesitated then trailed after her to the kitchen. But instead of going inside it, I stayed on the far side of the white granite counter.

I loved Brik's new open kitchen, its luminous wood cupboards, its modern pendant lights, its tile floor that looked like hardwood. I didn't love this woman inside it who was taking up his time and energy when he was already stretched by the storm.

Behind her, rain blurred the glass doors, obscuring Brik's backyard. The thrashing shrubs and small trees distorted to indistinct shapes, and for a moment, they looked like people staring inside, an enraged mob.

"I think he keeps the tea in here." She opened a cupboard, frowned, and opened another. "Here it is. Something herbal for sleep?" She pulled out a tin of my *Sleep Well* tea from Beanblossom's. "It's not a good idea to sleep too well. They come at night, you know."

"Who comes?" I shifted uneasily. Rain drummed on the roof, an insistent beat.

"I don't know who, exactly," Jude said. "They come at night to poison me while I sleep. They work for my cousin, I think. Or maybe my other brother, now that he's out of jail." Jude pulled a blue mug from the cupboard and filled it with water.

Jail? Brik hadn't mentioned that. Or was this part of her delusion too?

My chest squeezed with sympathy and shame. What would it be like not to know fiction from reality? And I'd been annoyed with the inconvenience she was causing. "I'm sorry," I said.

"It's not your fault. It's all the money. They've stolen it from me. I've written letters to the FBI and the police, but they own people in those departments. It's no good." She clutched the mug to her chest. "Why are you asking all these questions?"

"Brik told me there'd been an accident, and he was trying to help you. But that was all he said." I braced my elbows on the kitchen's counter. "I'm just... curious."

Jude's shoulders relaxed beneath the white robe. She opened the microwave and stuck the mug inside. "Oh. I suppose that makes sense. I told him not to tell anyone. It would only put them in danger. I thought the other one was the poisoner, but the other one was here for *her*."

My scalp prickled. "Here for her?"

"The dead woman in your yard." She filled a tea strainer with the loose tea.

"You know about—?" I lifted my elbows off the counter and straightened. "Did you see someone here last night?" Had she seen Anna's killer? Or had Brik told her about the body?

"I can't stay anywhere long," Jude said. "They find me, and they poison everything. They leave food out, but I'm not stupid. Brik brings me clean food."

My pulse quickened. "Did you see the dead woman arrive at my house last night, or early this morning?"

"I saw the woman last night. I think it was around ten."

At *last*. "What exactly did you see?"

The microwave pinged, and my muscles twitched in response. She turned to retrieve the mug. "They work for my cousin. He manages my trust, but he keeps all the money for himself. Brik's going to help me."

"But the woman you mentioned last night—did you see her do anything? Did you see anyone else?"

"You have to be careful at night. They use the dark to hide."

"Did you see anyone else, or just that woman?" I persisted. She'd seen Anna. If she'd seen more...

"Everyone hides," she said dreamily.

I rubbed the back of my neck. *Dammit*. Had she seen Anna or someone else? Even if she had seen someone, Jude wasn't exactly a reliable witness. And maybe I shouldn't be pushing someone who was mentally unstable.

Ease off. Maybe Brik could get more from her later. She seemed to trust him. "Where *is* Brik?" I sipped the tea. It was lukewarm.

"Getting dinner. Do you want to eat with us? He always brings too much food. He's been wonderful since the accident."

I set the mug on the counter too hard, and the ceramic clanked against the white stone. "The accident?"

"It wasn't really an accident though. They did something to the trail to make us fall. I hit my head. I was in a coma for a month. My brother died. My parents never liked me after that. And then they died."

I swallowed. It was probably all a delusion. But one of her brothers *had* been killed on that trail. "I should go. Would you tell Brik I stopped by?"

"Yes, of course. Brik's been wonderful. He's the only person I can count on." Jude followed me to the door.

I reached for it, and Jude scuttled in front of me. "Wait." She peered through the peep hole. Then she unbolted the door and stuck her head out. "I don't see the other one. I think it's safe, but go quickly." She stepped away from the door.

Feeling suddenly too hot, I walked into the rain. "Who—"

She shut the door in my face.

I rubbed my eyes. "Thanks anyway," I said, backing from the closed door.

I jogged through my side yard to the lean-to where I'd stored the tarp, then pulled it over the Amphicar. I didn't do a very good job of it. My movements were jerky, and I wanted inside. Not because of the rain. Because of my growing anxiety.

When I was certain the tarp wouldn't blow off, I hurried up the wooden steps to my bungalow and inside. I flipped on the light and exhaled slowly, my back against the door.

My gaming controller lay snarled on the blue couch in front of the TV. My grandmother's fortune telling teacups lined the mantel. The blue tablecloth brightened the dining table with my open laptop.

I was alone.

But I checked my bedroom, the kitchen, the bathrooms and closets. No one was hiding inside.

I was being foolish. Jude's paranoia had spooked me—that and the murder in my backyard. I paced in front of the French windows. My figure reflected in their blackness, and my flesh crawled.

There was a murder scene outside that I should investigate. *Right outside.* In the dark and rain of my backyard.

I grabbed a lasagna from the freezer and drove to my grandfather's house.

His two-story home stood at the end of a short cul-de-sac. Rain rampaged down its rippling shingled roof and splashed over its ivy-covered walls. Lights glowed from the downstairs room in the turret of the white stucco house.

I walked to the arched front door and rang the bell. After a moment, my grandfather opened the door. His sweater vest bulged where he'd put the wrong button in the hole.

"Abigail?" Gramps smoothed wisps of white hair over his head. "What are you doing here?"

His duck, Peking, waddled to check who was at the door. Seeing it was me, the mallard quacked.

"I brought lasagna." I raised the cold dish, covered in foil. I made it in big batches with spicy Italian sausage, which he loved, then froze the extra.

"It's not lasagna night." Gramps cocked his head. "You shouldn't have come in this weather."

One corner of my mouth tilted upward. "Too late."

He smiled in response. "I won't say 'no' to lasagna. I'll turn on the oven."

I followed him into the country kitsch kitchen, and Peking followed me. Gramps set the temperature on the ancient oven and straightened. "You look worried."

Avoiding his gaze, I put the lasagna on the wide, tile counter that separated the living room from the kitchen. On the wall separating the counter from the oven, a row of souvenir spoons nestled in a display case fashioned like an Alpine hut. Its peaked roof was dusty.

"Verbena was arrested," I said.

"That tea witch who's been bothering you? Is she guilty?"

A row of my grandmother's Hummel figurines smiled down at me from a shelf above the sink. "I don't know," I said. "I don't think so. But she's been behaving..."

I rubbed my thumb along the grooves of the white kitchen tiles. Could Verbena have used us to try and cover up her crime? Or at least to keep abreast of the investigation? She was arrogant enough to think she'd get away with that sort of thing. But...

"I don't think so," I repeated. The mallard pecked at my damp sneaker. "She broke into Anna's Apothecary. Someone saw her do it. The police think she may have been involved in Anna and Falkner's deaths."

"And how's that your problem?"

I leaned against the counter and folded my arms over my sweatshirt. "I agreed to do some amateur investigating. That might have encouraged her."

"Did you ever tell her to break in?" he asked.

"No, but—"

"Did she ever see you break into someone's place of business?"

"No, but—"

"She's a grown woman, not a child. If she broke into that apothecary shop, that's on her."

"Things have gotten so complicated. I'm worried about Brik."

"Because of his work? He knows what he's doing."

"Because he's helping a friend who's homeless and delusional," I said.

"Of course he is. You wouldn't like him much if he didn't." Although the oven wasn't anywhere near temperature, he opened its door and slid the lasagna inside.

"It's a long-term thing," I said. "He's been helping her for years."

He straightened. "And you think he's taking advantage?"

"She, and Jude's *definitely* taking advantage. But if she's mentally ill, she probably doesn't see it that way. I'm not sure I see it that way."

"If?"

"Sorry, there's no *if*. Jude's got a brain injury."

"You've met this Jude person?" He folded his arms over his expanse of stomach.

"She's staying at his house tonight."

Peking quacked and fluttered onto the counter.

Gramps shot me a sheepish look. "I told you, duck, the counters are off limits." He shooed the mallard onto the new laminate floor, made to look like wood like the tearoom's. Unsnapping the plastic top off a container of blueberries, he tossed a berry to Peking.

The duck waddled after the berry. He snatched it up before it could roll beneath the refrigerator.

"Are you asking me if you can trust Brik?" Gramps asked.

"No, of course not. I'm just venting. I feel guilty about Verbena. I feel guilty about Anna's death. And I haven't been much help to Brik with Jude either."

My grandfather's mouth puckered. His gaze fell to his tasseled loafers. "Have you ever wondered why your mother is the way she is?"

"Why she's a narcissist who abandoned me at the airport so she could live her best life? Yeah." *Like every other day.*

"And did you come to any conclusions?"

I hadn't, and I fell silent. My grandparents had given me a wonderful childhood.

Even after my grandmother had died, when I was still pretty young, my grandfather had soldiered on and made me feel loved. How had two such wonderful people raised a narcissist?

"Maybe the why doesn't matter," he said. "Maybe the why is just something we ask ourselves to keep from letting go."

"Maybe," I said. "But letting go of what?"

"Of wanting things to be different."

"Well, I do want things to be different. I want Anna alive, and Verbena—God help me—out of jail, and for Jude to be well." But we couldn't change the past. We could only move forward in the present.

"What your parents did," he said, ignoring the comment, "abandoning you. That was on them, not you."

My throat thickened, and for a moment, I couldn't speak. "I know that."

"Sure you do."

But the event had marked me. I'd moved through it, but it hadn't been erased.

"Want some wine?" Gramps ambled to the other counter and reached above the cabinet where he kept his cheap wine.

"Sure."

We drank a glass. And then we drank another with our lasagna. They were small glasses though. I didn't feel affected when I drove home, thinking hard about what my grandfather had revealed over that wine.

It wasn't the wine that dulled my awareness. It wasn't the wine that kept my mind spinning as I stepped from the car. It wasn't the wine that kept me oblivious until I'd finished tying the tarp over the Amphicar.

I stopped, one hand on the wet rope. It was only my racing thoughts that had blocked out the cold, crawling sensation of being watched.

Chapter 19

THE HAIR ON THE back of my neck stood at attention. Rain slanted down. It rattled down the drainpipes, plunked off the Amphicar's tarp, splatted on the driveway.

And someone was there, watching. I couldn't see the person, but I felt their regard, dark and malignant.

I froze, a terrified rabbit. Across the street, silhouettes of eucalyptus trees lashed in the wind. Brik's house was dark. Faint lights gleamed from the house on the other side of mine and were absorbed by the rain.

Maybe some mysteries aren't meant to be explored. Especially when you're a woman alone in a dark, narrow driveway. Forcing my feet to move, I hurried up the wooden steps to my bungalow's front door.

It should have been physically impossible to keep my back to the door and fit my key in the lock. I managed it anyway and slithered inside.

Heart thumping, I shut the door, locked it, and flipped on the light switch. I leaned against the door. Everything seemed as I'd left it. Gaming controllers on the couch. Laptop on the dining table. French windows shut.

Paranoid. I was being paranoid, scaring myself. It was easy to conjure up an uneasy, prickling feeling with the rain hammering on the roof and water curtaining the windows and—

THUMP.

The door shuddered beneath me, and I yelped. I flipped off the lights. It was instinct that made me do it. It was only a fraction of a second later that I realized with the lights on and the drapes open, I was visible to anyone lurking outside.

The drapes. Moving jerkily, I lurched for the curtain string.

CRASH.

The window exploded inward. I ducked, sucking in a sharp breath that may have been a cry, hands covering my head.

Wind and rain whipped the blue curtains. I wobbled, my knee hitting the floor, and slapped my palm down to brace myself. Something sharp and hot sliced my skin. I shrieked a curse in the dark and yanked my hand away.

The room roared, spinning. I shook my head. The roaring wasn't the room, wasn't the storm. It was the blood in my ears, pulsing to the beat of my anger.

This was the second time someone had thrown a rock through that window since I'd lived here. This was my *home.* Clenching my teeth, I rose and flung open the door. I strode onto the front steps. My hands fisted and unbunched.

"Come out!" I shouted.

A figure crept along the fence separating my property from Brik's, and I tensed. Jude rose, her shoulders hunched defensively, one hand on the wooden gate post. Her other hand she raised to her lips. She pointed.

I tracked her gesture to the street. A car sped off. In the glare of its taillights the water fanning from beneath its tires glowed red. In the darkness, all I could tell was it was a mid-sized car, shaped like every other mid-sized car these days.

I looked again toward the fence. Jude had vanished.

My adrenaline rush collapsed, and my shoulders folded inward. Even a paranoiac like Jude knew when it was time to turn tail. Hands trembling, I backed into my bungalow, shut and locked the door.

Things got busy after that. I called the cops. I called Brik. I called my landlord, Tomas.

Tomas arrived first, with plywood and a sheet of heavy plastic, my grandfather, and a toolkit. The older men didn't ask questions after their first, *were you hurt?* Once they realized I was okay, they got busy covering the window.

Two community safety officers arrived next to take my statement. It was depressing that vandalism no longer warranted a real police response. But what were the cops going to do? I didn't have a license plate or a description of the attacker.

At least a police report might be handy for insurance purposes. Though this was the second time in two years that window had been broken.

Fortunately, the last time it had been replaced with safety glass. Now pebbles of it littered my living room. It was a step-up from shards, but it could still cut you. I glanced at my bandaged palm.

"I'm sorry, Tomas." Leaning against the gaming couch, I gripped my upper arms and shivered. I'd removed the cushions from the couch in front of the window. Gramps dug for pebbles of glass between the couch's back and the pullout bed.

Tomas winked, toolchest in hand. "At least you're making the right sort of enemies." He smoothed back his wet hair. His Giants windbreaker was dark with rain.

"The sort that throws a rock through her window?" My grandfather straightened and extended his gloved hand. Chunks of glass glittered on the thick leather. "I suppose it could be worse, but I don't like this trend."

"Neither do I," Baranko growled from the open front door. Lightning flashed behind him, which seemed appropriate in an old-movie sort of way. "You've been poking around in my investigation. I don't like it when people poke around in my investigations."

"I don't like it when the cops take thirty minutes to get to a crime scene," my grandfather snarled, his hand closing on the glass.

"We have better things to do than chase petty vandals," Baranko said. "We've got bigger cases to solve."

And yet, the detective was here. My neck tensed. This couldn't be good.

Tomas's eyes narrowed. He set the tool chest on a blue and green throw rug. "The police *used* to be able to walk and chew gum at the same time. Doesn't look like they're doing much of either anymore."

Baranko's jaw firmed. "Witnesses?" he asked the community service officers standing inside my living room.

They shook their heads. I opened my mouth to speak, then shut it.

I hadn't mentioned Jude to the community service officers, because in the chaos, I'd forgotten. Now that I'd remembered, I wasn't going to inflict Baranko on the woman. Jude was traumatized enough.

The wind rattled the plywood covering the window, a draft stirring the mail on the dining table. I set my laptop computer on top of the envelopes. "I saw a mid-sized car driving away," I said. "But I couldn't identify the make or model in this rain."

Baranko's fleshy lip curled. "Of course you can't."

I straightened my spine. What the hell did he expect? It was dark and had happened fast.

Brik strode into my bungalow. "Are you okay? I was at a site. I—"

I hurtled into his arms, silencing him. "I'm fine." His arms came around me, and I breathed, listening to the pounding of his heart.

Tomas picked up his toolbox. "You would have been a good man to have around earlier."

Sheepish, I pulled away from Brik. I'd never played damsel in distress before, and he already had one of those in his life—Jude.

Finally, everyone left but Brik. I turned and pressed my face against his broad chest. His arms encircled me, one hand at the small of my back, locking against my spine. I relaxed into the embrace and listened to the steady beat of his heart.

"I haven't been around for you as much as I should have," he said.

"What—?"

"Jude may have seen the person who did it." I motioned with one hand toward the plywood on the window.

He stilled. "Did she come over here?"

"No. I thought you were home and knocked on the door. She told me you were helping her."

His face spasmed, his arctic eyes widening. "She was inside my—?" His muscular arms tightened around me. "I got her another hotel room. I didn't know she'd found my new house."

"Found?"

"Or figured out a way inside," he said in a strangled voice. "Did you tell the cops—?"

"No," I said quickly. "It didn't seem like a good idea."

"I'll talk to her, see what I can get, and get her back to her hotel. But don't expect much."

I stepped away from him. "She seems a lot more... disturbed than..." I struggled for an ending. *Than what?* Than he'd implied? He'd told me she had mental problems. I walked to the French doors. Loosening their ties, I tugged the blue curtains shut.

He exhaled slowly. "I'm sorry. I hoped you two would never meet. I've never seen her do anything violent, but she can get fixated on ideas and people. I didn't want her fixated on you. I didn't want her bothering you."

I turned to face him. "FYI, she was wearing your robe. It looked like she'd just gotten out of the shower."

He growled low in his throat and closed his eyes, the picture of a frustrated Viking. "Abigail, she isn't—"

"I believe you," I said quickly. My chest tightened. I shouldn't have brought up the stupid robe. "What else can you tell me about her?"

"After the accident, Jude would call me every now and again, and we'd talk. But the last few years she's gotten worse. She calls every couple months when she runs out of cash, and I pay for her hotel room until she can sort something out. She's so awkward around cops, that whenever they interact she gets arrested."

"And then you get called." And he *would* help, because he was chivalrous, and because you don't walk away from a person in distress when it's inconvenient.

He raked both hands through his hair. "Sometimes, if it happens nearby. Sometimes she just stays in jail until they figure out she's harmless and let her go."

Lightly, I touched his arm. I couldn't imagine the fear and confusion that must be her daily companions. "Shouldn't she be somewhere she can get help?"

"Yes, but I can't put her there, and the system won't. Honestly, I don't know why she's not dead, the way she's been living."

I wished Brik had told me all this earlier. From the sounds of it, she'd been in his life for years. It was a burden we could have shared.

But he hadn't shared it. There'd already been so much drama in our lives, I imagined he hadn't wanted to add to it. At least, I hoped that was the case. I hoped he hadn't thought I was too busy, or too selfish, to handle it.

The next morning, I did what I'd been avoiding. Huddled beneath my umbrella, I examined the crime scene in my own backyard.

Police tape fluttered from the posts of my collapsed redwood fence. It looped around stakes marking out the puddled imprint of a small body. I stared down at the sad impression in the earth. My boots sank deeper into the mud.

I shuddered and dug my free hand deeper into the pockets of my pink trench coat. Its cheerful color seemed horribly inappropriate now.

The convenience of having a crime scene behind my house was dwarfed by its dreadfulness. A killer had been in my yard, steps away from my deck and its vulnerable French doors.

I had serious bolts on those French doors. Experience had taught me not to mess around when it came to home safety. But one rock through a windowpane would gain an intruder entry.

I glanced up at those doors, my gaze clouding. Why hadn't Anna come to my *front* door? "What were you doing back here?" I muttered. She must have come for me, but why?

My raincoat was suddenly too hot. Feeling sticky inside it, I undid its brown buttons and squatted beside that dismaying puddle. Any evidence would have been removed by the police, so now I was just being morbid.

At the thought, I straightened, ashamed. I widened my search, walking along the brick paths between my raised beds. Then I returned to my side yard.

I found nothing in the jasmine climbing the redwood fence. There were no weapons beneath the hose, coiled like a snake on a hook against my yellow home. No signs of blood darkened the gardening tools in their lean-to beside the wheelbarrow...

I straightened. But why was I looking here? The presumed murder weapon, my shovel, had been right beside her...

And I hadn't seen blood on that either. I'd checked for that before the police had arrived. It had looked clean—to the naked eye, at least. I'd kept the shovel in the lean-to, where it would stay dry, and where a killer could have easily taken it.

I supposed the blood could have washed off in the rain. Naturally, the police had taken my shovel for evidence. They suspected it was the murder weapon.

Which meant Anna had been killed here. My neck corded, bile rising in my throat.

A woman's life had been taken in my backyard. And I hadn't even noticed.

Chapter 20

No one answered Brik's door when I knocked the next morning. That was both a relief and an annoyance. Relief because Jude wasn't there. Annoyance because neither was Brik.

But I was more annoyed at my motivation for showing up without calling that wet morning. I'd wanted to see for myself if Jude was still in his house.

I yanked the tarp off the Amphicar and stowed it in my lean-to in the side yard. Ducking inside the car, I called Brik. Rain drummed on the car's canvas top.

"Hey," he answered. "Sorry I didn't call. I had to leave early for a job site. I thought you might still be sleeping."

"More storm damage?" I wrinkled my forehead.

"A section of cliff we were working on collapsed last night."

Briefly, I closed my eyes. Thank God it had collapsed last night instead of yesterday, when he'd been on it. "Was anyone hurt?" I started the car.

"No, but we've got some salvage work to do."

I shivered and turned on the heater. "Will this rain *ever* stop?" I enjoy a good storm, since we have so few big ones in California. But there was something sinister in the relentlessness of the wind and rain.

"Not for another five days, according to my weather app. I talked to Jude."

My breath caught. "What did she say?"

"She's convinced the person who threw that rock through your window was coming for her and got the houses confused."

Steam blurred the windshield, turning the eucalyptus trees lining the roads to shifting giants. I turned on the defroster.

"Does she have good reason to think someone might be after her?" I asked, knowing it was a fruitless question. She was mentally ill. She didn't need a good reason.

"Money. Her family had a lot of it. The threat could be all in her head, or part of it could be real. No one's poisoning her. As to the rest, I don't know."

"That's... Wow."

"Her trustee is in Santa Cruz. I've spoken with him. He told me he gives her the required monthly allowance, and beyond that, it was none of my damn business. And it's not. I'm just a friend. I don't have any legal standing."

I exhaled slowly. I'd learned about financial elder abuse from my grandfather, a retired CPA. It happened too often, because when people got old and forgetful, they made easy victims. Why believe someone who was doddering?

The same would be true in Jude's case, and the front of my skull heated with frustration. Her fractured speech made her sound insane. Who would believe her story? On the other hand, she *was* insane. There was no reason to believe her. "Well. Damn."

Brik's laugh was sardonic. "Exactly. She needs help. But... I seem to be the only friend she has, and I don't think I'm a very good one. I'm getting tired of being her personal bank and travel agent."

The defroster hummed, clearing two arch-shaped spaces on the windshield.

"What exactly did she see when that rock came through my window?" I asked.

"She saw someone in a raincoat," Brik said. "She says it was a man, but she's obsessed with her brother and her cousin. It could have been a woman."

"I guess..." I picked at the stuffing escaping the seat's frayed seams. "There's no sense in telling the police what Jude saw." That was some relief. I didn't like withholding evidence.

"I'm not even sure she saw *anyone*. The people she sees aren't always there. She thinks people sneak in at night to poison her food. And FYI, she let herself into my house. She found the spare key under the flowerpot. I've taken it back from her."

I leaned my head against the rest and exhaled slowly. "Where is she now?"

"That hotel by the San Borromeo freeway exit."

I straightened and nodded, though he couldn't see me. I knew that hotel. San Borromeo had only one. "What does her brother look like? The ex-con, I mean?"

"Like her. Dark hair. A couple inches shorter than me. Slim."

"Jude wouldn't have been able to tell hair color that night in the storm."

"No," he said.

"So, she may or may not have seen somebody. But someone *was* out there. The rock through my front window is proof."

"Yeah," he said unhappily.

We said our goodbyes and disconnected. I waited another minute for the defroster to do its job. Then, navigating flooded streets and fallen branches, I made my way to Beanblossom's.

I sloshed through the parking lot to the rear, metal door. The water washed the remains of my garden mud from my scarlet rainboots. It swirled in brownish coils toward an overburdened drain.

Was I imagining the water was higher? My gaze darted around the parking lot, as I gauged the water level vs. the car tires.

I stepped over the barricade of sandbags and unlocked the door. Inside the tearoom hallway, I eyed the extra sandbags Brik had stacked there.

Even more reservations had been canceled today than Thursday. At noon, I sent two of the waitstaff home. I hated cutting their hours, but they seemed relieved to leave early.

Archer was the only one who turned up for our final seating of the day. And when his "friend" didn't show, he sniffed and rose. "Canceled," he grumbled. "And at the last minute. What happened to manners?"

"The storm *is* pretty rough," I said.

He adjusted his cravat. "It's not the storm. No one has any respect these days. Have you heard? Grave robbers were spotted in the cemetery yesterday. Can you believe it? We've regressed to the days of grave robbing. What next? Are we going to start using human teeth as currency? *'I'll trade you one molar for a scone, my good woman.'* What a time to be alive."

"I heard kids had vandalized the place," I said. It was still all sorts of wrong, but it was a massive step up from robbing the dead.

"I heard that too. Little monsters." He studied his reflection in a butter knife and brushed back his silvery hair with one hand. "Mark my words, soon we'll be cannibalizing each other. Everything started going downhill in the sixties with those unwashed hippies. Standards matter. *Have* long hair, *wear* prayer beads—what do I care? But take a bath."

I finally got Archer out of the tearoom. We closed early, and I let the rest of the staff leave while I cleaned up. With so few customers, it was depressingly easy.

"This bites." In a brown jacket and herringbone vest, Hyperion lounged against the open kitchen door like a high-fashion country squire. The skinny jeans were all California though.

I closed the reach-in refrigerator door. With the back of my wrist, I brushed back a wisp of hair. "Five more days of rain, according to Brik." I tossed the sponge into the big metal sink and peeled off my yellow work gloves.

"Didn't you hear? The forecast has changed."

"Really?" I brightened. "How many days are left now?"

"Seven."

I swore.

"The pier's closed," Hyperion said. "They've evacuated it."

"I heard." It was still hard to believe it was in any danger. The San Borromeo pier was massive. You could drive two trucks down it in parallel. A fish restaurant sat at its end. The town held a farmer's market on it every weekend.

"I hate this." My partner straightened off the doorframe. "I hate being at the mercy of the elements. Let's do something. Let's snoop."

I hesitated. It wasn't like I had anything better to do. But Anna... Verbena... My stomach rolled uncomfortably. If we'd left it alone, would Anna still be alive?

"We can take the Amphicar," Hyperion wheedled. "I'll even let you drive."

"*Let me?* It's my rental. I have to drive."

"Don't rub it in. It's unattractive."

I scraped my teeth over my bottom lip. "I don't know if now's the right time for snooping."

His expression flattened. "We have to see this through," he said, playful tone gone. "Whatever happened, whatever the cause, if it was on us or not, we have to see it through."

I blinked rapidly. He was right. We'd come too far now. "Only if we take the car to Anna's shop first."

"Why? It'll be closed. There's nothing to see."

"I want to see it anyway."

Hyperion nodded slowly. "And we can hit Katey's bookstore too."

"Agreed."

"I'll get my coat." He vanished into the hallway.

I collected my red jacket and belted it over my sensible brown slacks—sensible because water stains weren't as obvious on them. Then I tugged my rain boots over my shoes and grabbed my umbrella.

Hyperion met me at the door. We stepped over the sandbags and slogged through the dark parking lot.

My gaze darted around the lot, then back to the tearoom's rear door. "Is the water getting higher?"

"No. We already have enough problems. Don't add to them."

Roughly, I motioned toward the buildings opposite. "I'm only wondering if we should add more sandbags."

"They're fine. Leave 'em."

Right. I had to be imagining the water was rising. *Paranoid.*

Unlocking his door, I walked around the Amphicar to open my own. I tossed the umbrella into the back seat, got inside, and started the ignition.

The car purred to life, and I pulled from the lot. Belatedly, I remembered I had to turn on the headlights manually.

I edged onto the street. "So," I said casually, "someone threw a rock through my front window last night."

"And you're only telling me this now? What time? That gives us one more question to ask Katey."

"Eight forty-seven," I said, "after I got home." I'd checked.

He grunted. "It was pretty dark then."

"Which is why I didn't see anyone," I said guiltily. But Jude was Brik's secret to tell, not mine.

Though roads were flooded, we managed to make decent time. Most people were staying put, so traffic was light this Friday evening.

To my surprise, a few cars had parked in the shared lot between Katey's bookstore and Anna's Apothecary. The lights of the latter were dark.

My heart pinched. Anna had been a business owner, like me. She'd worked hard, chased her dreams. Now it was all over. *She* was over, and I hated it. It wasn't right, or just, or fair.

We splashed through the parking lot to the bookstore. Light streamed through its dingy windows. Hyperion held the door for me, and I walked inside.

Shelves had been moved aside to make way for five short rows of metal folding chairs. Half a dozen people filled them. Katey, in a sapphire blue caftan, leaned against the counter and frowned.

At the front, a harried-looking author stood behind a podium and read from her book. "Faith is a tricky thing. Too much, and you can be made a fool of. Too little, and you can't form meaningful bonds with others. The same is true of faith in magic. You need faith in the magic for it to work. But blind faith can make you credulous."

Hyperion and I glanced at each other and found seats. The author continued on. She was a good speaker. I found myself paying attention.

"True faith isn't blind or close-minded," the writer continued. "It's a decision to act with trust. Like love, faith is a practice, and it takes courage. But faith and hope and love also give us the courage to keep going and to stay in the game. And faith in something higher than us gives us humility—it keeps us from developing God complexes, a real threat to people with magic and other forms of power. So have faith that life has meaning, and that we're all a part of that meaning.' She closed her book. "Thank you."

I sat back with a sigh. *Faith.* Was that my problem? Had I lost faith in myself? Or had I only really had faith when times were good?

An iron-haired woman in the front row raised her hand. "But how do you *read* the cards?"

The author launched into a lecture on different card readings, intuition, and finding cards that pointed in the same direction. Hyperion sat forward in his chair and draped his long arms across the back of the empty metal chair in front of him.

The Q&A petered out fifteen minutes later. I was surprised it had gone on that long, but one of the audience members was persistent. The audience rose, chairs scraping back, and shuffled to the counter.

"Damn," Hyperion muttered. "We're going to have to buy something, aren't we?"

"That poor author," I whispered. "There are only eight people here including ourselves."

"How much of that is due to the rain and how much to poor marketing?" Hyperion asked. "Okay. I'll buy her cards. You buy the book."

"Cards?"

His dark brows slashed downward. "She was reading from her oracle deck book, which means there's a deck around here somewhere."

"Damn." I hoped the book was worth it.

"Tell me about it," he said. "*Everybody's* making decks. I should make one, but they're expensive to print unless you go to China. And everyone knows as soon as you do, your deck gets pirated and slapped up online by the pirates at a cut-rate price and quality. But American printers cost so much they'll price you out of the market."

I tilted my head. "You really have been thinking about this."

"Like I said, *everyone's* doing it."

Dutifully, I picked up a book and got in the blessedly short line. The author signed it, and I paid. Hyperion bought his deck. We lingered at the counter while Katey consoled the author.

"It's the storm," the bookstore owner said. "Let's do it again in a few months. There will be more people when the weather's better."

Finally, the author and the others left. Katey touched the bulky necklace around her throat. "You're here about Anna."

"I'm sorry for your loss," Hyperion said.

Katey looked toward the windows. The night had turned them to obsidian mirrors. "We didn't get along that well," she admitted and swallowed. "But now that she's gone…" She lowered her head. "I shouldn't have let my fear and ego get the best of me."

"What do you mean?" I asked.

"Oh, that stupid parking lot!" She gestured roughly toward the front windows. "Parking wasn't my problem. It's my marketing. I need to do better."

"Jose told me you were doing all the right things," I said.

"Am I?" The skin bunched around her eyes, her hands clenching. "Tonight was a disaster."

I shook my head. "This weather is—"

"The problems started before the storm." Katey exhaled unevenly. "Thanks for coming by though. I appreciate your support."

"Did you see Anna leave the apothecary on Wednesday night?" I asked.

"No." She strode to the front door and flipped the sign in its glass to *Closed*. "I didn't notice her. I wish I had. I wish I'd had the chance to say something to her before… Do the police know when she was killed? That detective interrogated me, but he didn't tell me anything." She walked toward the back of the bookstore.

"I don't know," I said, raising my voice. "I guess some time Wednesday night or early Thursday morning."

But somehow, Wednesday night seemed more logical. That she'd come to my house that night to… *what? Talk to me? Why?* I studied the thin gray carpet.

"Where were you Wednesday and Thursday nights?" Hyperion asked loudly.

The lights in the bookstore went off. Footsteps came toward us. "None of your business."

"I know it's not," I said, "but—"

"I'm closing now." Her form emerged from an aisle. She wore a heavy coat over her kaftan and carried an oversized black umbrella.

We scuttled outside and watched while Katey locked the front door. She turned and grasped my wrist. "Is that...? Is someone watching?"

A tall silhouette stood on the other side of the parking lot, beside Anna's Apothecary, and I tensed. The figure pivoted and vanished into the shadows.

Chapter 21

No way. Uh, uh. *Done.* I was not pursuing anyone in the rain and dark. I folded my arms over my red jacket. Not every creaking floorboard was a ghost, and I was sick of jumping at shadows.

The figure in the parking lot could have been anyone, could have been there for perfectly innocent reasons. I opened my mouth to tell Katey so.

Hyperion bolted forward. His body jerked oddly. He stumbled over a curb stop, spun like a top, and landed face first in a puddle. My jaw sagged in horror.

I hurried to him. "Are you okay?" If he'd aimed for the puddle, he couldn't have hit it more dead center. Though in fairness, it was hard to miss. The entire parking lot had become a dark, rippling, raindrop-studded lake.

Hyperion sat up and pointed an accusing finger at Katey. "You tripped me," he howled.

I exhaled through pursed lips. He was okay.

Levering himself to standing, my partner brushed off the front of his jacket and herringbone vest. "Seriously. What was *that* about?"

"I'm... I'm sorry," Katey stammered. She pulled her dark coat closer. "I was just raising my umbrella... I didn't mean to."

Hyperion growled, and I bit back a laugh. Usually *I'm* the butt of the pratfalls. My partner glared, and I smoothed my expression.

"Honestly," I said. "Haven't you come to expect a Three Stooges-style disaster at this point? Whoever it was, he was probably just some guy taking a shortcut home in the rain." I peered at the dark window of the apothecary shop on the other side of the lot.

"I don't know," Katey said uncertainly. "I'd swear I'd seen him around before."

"Are you sure it was a him?" Hyperion asked. "It was too dark to see much of anything."

Katey gnawed her bottom lip. "If it's the same person I saw earlier, it was definitely a him. I *think*. Do... do you think I'm being stalked?" Her voice went up an octave. "Is someone trying to kill us all?"

Hyperion brushed muck from the front of his trousers. "By *us all*, I assume you mean all of Falkner's clients?"

"How many clients *did* he have?" I asked.

"For group coaching, I think just our bunch right now," she said. "He had thousands of people signed up for his online classes though. Or at least hundreds."

Hyperion's mouth pinched. His online students numbered in the dozens, and he worked his tail off to get them.

But after what had happened to Anna... *Maybe we should follow Katey home.* "Katey, do you want—?"

The phone rang in my oversized purse. I pulled it from the pocket where it belonged and answered without checking the number. "Hello?"

"Abigail, there's a problem at your grandfather's," Tomas said.

My breath stopped. I stumbled to a halt, rain pummeling my umbrella. "What's happened?"

"A tree fell in the front yard."

I relaxed a little. "Oh, no, was the house...?"

"Not on the house, on your grandfather's Lincoln. He was inside the car at the time. He called me for help. I'm headed over there now. I thought you should know."

My heart stopped. "I'm on my way." I disconnected and dropped the phone in my purse. "Sorry, Katey, I have to go." I jogged to the big red and white car.

"What's wrong?" Hyperion asked.

I unlocked the front door. "A tree fell on my grandfather's car. He was inside."

Hyperion grasped the Amphicar's passenger door handle and yanked on it futilely. I slid inside and across the seat to let him in.

"How bad is it?" He got into the car and slammed the door.

"I don't know." I started the ignition. "Gramps phoned Tomas. Tomas is on his way over there now."

"Did Tomas call the fire department?"

"I don't know," I said, too loud and too fast. I exhaled a short, hard breath. "Sorry."

"Want me to drive?"

I hesitated. "No." I drove as fast as I dared to my grandfather's house. His cul-de-sac was dark. No emergency vehicles cluttered the street, no emergency lights lit the houses.

The Amphicar screeched to the base of the driveway, its headlights illuminating rain and a fallen pine. My heart rabbited. Branches draped across my grandfather's Lincoln.

Putting my rental in park, I leapt from it and raced to his car. "Gramps?"

I stopped, sickened and swaying, beside the tangle of pine branches. The top of the sedan was crushed. Peking waddled around the sedan, as if the duck were looking for a way in.

Tomas's head popped up from behind the pine. "Frank's okay. He's just stuck."

My mouth slackened. "Are you sure?" *How could he possibly be okay?*

Water streamed down the driveway and over chunks of broken glass. Using my phone's light, I peered through what was left of the driver's window.

My grandfather lay stretched across the seats, his arms close to his sides. Miraculously, his cabby hat was still on his head. Glass glittered on the camel-colored leather seat. "Hey, Abigail. I'm fine."

"You're not..." I grimaced. *Don't make things worse.* "Did you call the fire department?"

My grandfather rolled his eyes. "Of course I called the fire department. They were the first people I called. Since it's not an emergency, they said it would be an hour."

"Not an emergency?" I said, outraged. Peking quacked, indignant.

Hyperion put his hand on my elbow. "He's okay."

"He's trapped in a car," I snapped. "He is not okay."

"At least the heater's running," my grandfather said cheerfully.

"He's right," Tomas said. "It could be worse."

I shuddered. It could have been a *lot* worse. Peking pecked at my boot.

"Um, guys?" Hyperion said. "This might not be the safest place—"

I shook off his elbow. "Maybe we can get you out."

Tomas shook his head. "Not without a jaws of life. We'll have to cut this tin can open."

"We could try a Sawzall," I said. "They have metal cutting attachments. Gramps has a full set."

"Yeah," Gramps said. "Try that."

"I don't think Sawzall's are meant for cars." Tomas lifted his baseball cap and rubbed the top of his head.

"Not the old cars," I said, "but they're not making cars of steel anymore. It's all fiberglass and stuff."

"Uh, Abigail?" Hyperion nudged me. "I don't like the look of—"

"Maybe we can cut through the door," I said.

"I think it's better if we just slide some hot coffee and blankets through to keep him warm until the fire department comes," Tomas said.

It wasn't a bad idea. It was, in fact, a more sensible idea than mine. I just hated it.

"Look out!" Hyperion wrenched me backward.

CRACK. There was a groaning sound. A shadow moved swiftly toward us, and a second pine crashed on top of the Lincoln.

Chapter 22

I SCREAMED. HYPERION YANKED me against his chest. The mallard fluttered into the air, quacking.

"Tomas!" Gramps bellowed from inside the crushed car.

Tomas. My stomach plummeted. The Amphicar's headlights spotlighted his absence. He'd disappeared behind the Lincoln and the second, smaller pine now atop it.

I couldn't breathe. Couldn't speak. Couldn't move.

And then Hyperion and I were running through the rain, racing around the car and fallen trees. "Tomas?"

The older man sat on the streaming driveway and rubbed his head. My knees wobbled. I braced my hand on the wet hood of the car for support.

"Where are you hurt?" Hyperion knelt beside him.

Tomas slapped his Giants baseball hat back on. "My pride, mostly. Also my elbow."

Hyperion straightened and extended a hand. Tomas let him haul him to standing.

"How is he?" Gramps shouted.

"Fine," Tomas snapped. He turned to me. "We need to get him out of there before any more trees come down."

"I'm calling Brik." I fished my phone from the pocket of my red jacket and called.

Twenty minutes later, Brik arrived in his pickup with a burly man in the passenger seat. A second battered pickup followed behind them. Three more men hopped out of it.

I've always appreciated efficiency. But watching those men leap to work, no arguments, no discussion, my heart swelled with warmth. Toxic masculinity might be a thing, but so is old-fashioned masculinity. I'd never appreciated the latter more.

They cut the trees off the car and towed the logs and branches onto the lawn and out of harm's way. Three of the men attacked the car with crowbars and other equipment. Thirty minutes later, they pulled Gramps feet first from the Lincoln.

I held my umbrella over my grandfather. A fire truck silently trundled up the court, its red and yellow lights flashing.

"Nice timing." Tomas harrumphed and folded his arms over his orange and black Giants windbreaker. It was soaked through.

Brik clapped his shoulder. "They can check his injuries."

"I'm fine." Leaning against what was left of his car, Gramps rubbed his forehead where a purple mark blossomed. "Better than you. At least I'm dry."

"Let's go inside," I said.

"But the firetruck..." Gramps waved a hand toward the truck. It parked, brakes groaning, at the end of his driveway. Three men in thick yellow raincoats jumped out.

"They can check you out inside," Hyperion said, shifting from side to side and hugging his arms. "I'm freezing."

Everyone went inside the house. The firemen and construction workers looked around the fairytale home curiously.

Brik drew me into the kitchen. "You okay?"

"I am now." Eyes hot, I put my arms around him. "Thank you. You really are my hero." I looked away, toward the sliding glass doors that led to my grandfather's side yard.

After years of would-we-wouldn't-we, our relationship was solid. Comfortable. Safe. And none of that was boring, like Verbena had implied. It was bliss.

"Thank the guys," Brik said. "We were finishing up at the site when you called. They all volunteered." He pulled me closer, heedless of our damp rain gear.

"That's— you were working this late?"

"We had to salvage what we could."

My eyebrows drew together. "How bad is it?"

"Our client's insured, and so are we."

In other words... Bad.

"Did you hear they closed the pier?" he asked.

I nodded, stomach churning.

We never had really destructive storms in California. Fires and earthquakes, yes, hurricanes and tornados, no. Closing the pier had to be an overabundance of caution. Didn't it?

It took twice as long to reach Beanblossom's the next morning as it would usually have done. And when I arrived, soaking wet, I almost wondered why I'd bothered. Most of our reservations had canceled.

But the water *was* rising in the rear lot. It wasn't my imagination. I sent everyone home who wanted to go and left the remaining staff to run the tearoom while I stacked more sandbags.

Digging my hands deeper into the pockets of my pink trench coat, I studied the parking lot. I hadn't paid much attention to its slight bowl-shape before. The tearoom sat on the side of a hill. The first developers had gouged a piece out of it for the buildings and lot.

That had been decades ago. Either the parking lot had sunk in the intervening years, or the storm was doing a real number on the asphalt. Gnawing my bottom lip, I adjusted a sandbag and returned inside the tearoom.

In the kitchen, I called Verbena. She didn't answer. Was she still at the police station? If they'd *really* arrested her...

My mouth compressed. That was denial speaking. Baranko didn't put people in handcuffs willy-nilly. Once the cuffs came out, there was paperwork involved. I shuddered. No one wanted that.

Maricel bustled into the kitchen and plated an Empress tea. It was our biggest and most expensive meal.

"We have a new customer?" I asked, pleased and surprised.

"A walk-in. He says he knows you? Australian accent? Name's Tad?"

I stiffened. *Tad the psychic?* "Let me take this out to him. Tip's all yours."

"Sure, boss." She handed me the three-tiered white plate, filled with scones and cakes and finger sandwiches.

I walked into the tearoom. Two iron-haired women sat at one of its tables. Archer had claimed a white-clothed corner table. The society columnist sat typing on his laptop, a multi-tiered Empress tea in front of him.

I smothered a sigh. I hadn't wanted Beanblossom's to turn into a coffeeshop/workspace—or a source of intel for Archer's website. But at least the gossip columnist was buying the most expensive teas on the menu.

The rest of the tables were empty. Tad sat at the bar, one booted foot tapping its reclaimed-wood base.

I walked behind the counter and set the tiered plate in front of him.

"Thanks." He sipped from his white mug.

"You're welcome," I automatically replied. I picked up a cleaning cloth from its bin beneath the counter and wiped down the white quartz. "I hope you're hungry."

"I have a weakness for scones," he said, and I had to smile at the word in his Australian accent. His fleshy lips quirked. "Suspicious about me turning up on a day like this?"

I glanced at Archer, his torso angled toward us. "I assumed you were here to learn what I knew about Anna's death. And for the scones."

The corners of Tad's mouth slipped downward. "Anna. Tragedy, that."

My chest hardened.

"Tragedy implies it was something inevitable and random. This was murder."

"You sure about that?"

"She didn't wind up in my garden by accident," I said hotly, and Tad smiled. Annoyed with myself, I counted to ten. He'd wanted a reaction, and I'd given him one.

"I *heard* she was found at your place," Tad said. "What was she doing there?"

"You're the psychic. You tell me."

He cocked his head. "I think she wanted something from you."

That much was obvious. "Like what?"

"Absolution?" Tad plucked a matcha and white chocolate scone from his plate and squinted at it.

"You're saying she was involved in Falkner's death?"

He took a bite of the scone. "No," he mumbled. "I'm suggesting she may have known something she didn't tell the police, but maybe she wanted to tell you."

"Why me? Why not the cops?"

The psychic swallowed. "Probably for the same reason she came to see me the day she died."

I started. "She came to see you? Why? What did she say?"

"Anna asked about the ethics of karma."

"Excuse me?"

Tad broke the green scone in two and took a bite of one half. He swallowed. "Were we required to serve up justice, or would we be putting a thumb on the karmic scales if we did? Was it better to just let karma play out, or to be a part of that play?"

That was... suggestive. I wiped my palms on my apron. "What did you tell her?"

"I told her if she knew something about the murder, she should tell the cops."

"And how did she react?" I asked.

"Guiltily. She didn't seem to like my answer. How did she find your house?"

I shifted my weight. "Easy. It was on an agreement we'd signed."

"An agreement?"

When I didn't explain further, he continued, "There's more trouble coming." He raised his mug in my direction. "Mark my words."

"It doesn't take a psychic to know that." I jerked my head toward the rain-streaked windows.

He grinned.

"Abigail?" Maricel said sharply from the hallway.

"Excuse me," I told Tad and strode to her. "What's wrong?"

"There's water coming in the back door."

Cutting short a curse, I hurried past her into the hallway. Water seeped beneath the rear metal door. The overhead lights flickered. Grabbing a sandbag, I braced it on one hip and opened the door. A gust of wind nearly pushed me back into the tearoom.

Water from the parking lot streamed over the sandbags. Insides jittering, I dropped the bag on top of the miniature dam and hurried into the hallway to grab more.

I had to put my shoulder into it to get the rear door open. Outside, wind battered the Amphicar, shaking the vehicle.

Marciel mopped the hallway while I worked. I dropped the final bag on the pile and retreated inside.

"It has to stop soon." Leaning on the mop, she swept a strand of black hair from her cheek. "Doesn't it?"

Hyperion raced into the hallway from the tearoom. "The pier's going," he said.

"What?" I asked blankly.

He strode toward me. "The pier. It's breaking apart. C'mon."

Maricel's olive skin turned ashen. "The pier?" she asked, voice shrill.

Stomach hard, I yanked off my apron. I hurried into Hyperion's office and grabbed my trench coat off the antler coat tree.

"Come on," he urged.

I jammed my feet into my red rain boots and followed him into the tearoom. Tad's head turned to watch us leave.

A river flowed down the sloping road and flooded the brick sidewalks. Main Street had become a cascade.

We picked our way down the street. Swathed in a belted black raincoat, Archer trotted ahead of us.

"What was Tad doing at Beanblossom's?" Hyperion asked.

"Amateur sleuthing, I think." I maneuvered around a brick planter box. Water splashed against its side and shot into the air.

My partner sniffed. "When everyone's doing it, it's not cool anymore."

At the base of Main Street, the ocean was pushing up our hill, waves lapping at the shop fronts. Front Street along the beach was flooded. Pacific waves flowed up the road's ankle-deep water.

I stared, briefly paralyzed. "I had no idea it was this bad," I breathed.

"Come on."

We sloshed down the street toward the pier and joined a group of onlookers jammed between a coffee shop and a surf shop at the edge of the beach. Whitecaps pounded against the pier's pilings. The structure trembled with each blow.

"It'll be okay," Archer said, panting. "The pier was built to withstand big storms."

"Not this storm," Hyperion said, grim.

The pier shuddered, and murmurs rose to shrieks. The crowd shifted backward, pushing Hyperion and me along with it.

There was a terrible, rending noise, and I grasped his arm. The middle of the pier ripped free and dropped into the roiling ocean.

Chapter 23

THE CROWD SCREAMED. HYPERION was yelling, and I was shouting helplessly right along with everyone else. A second section of the pier splashed down.

More sections crumpled like dominoes into the foaming waters. The collapse continued toward the pier's end, where the fish restaurant stood. It was unstoppable, a slow-moving disaster.

And then the disintegration did stop, roughly ten feet from the fish restaurant. A relieved sigh rose from the crowd.

Sagging, I braced one hand against the yellow stucco wall of the surf shop. Waves pounded the remains of the pier, sweeping shattered wood toward the beach. The nearest chunks of wood flowed into the street.

I cursed and grabbed Hyperion's arm. But he'd already seen the danger. We were too close, the waves coming in too fast.

"Get back," he shouted, grabbing my hand.

Hyperion and I turned with the others and raced into the street. The waves were faster. We splashed through ankle-deep water.

Waves surged higher, pushing us forward, tripping us up. We stumbled against a metal bicycle rack and held on.

Glass crashed. A few others in our group caught hold of the bike rack as well. Archer shot me a terrified look.

Icy water sloshed against the blue stucco wall of the bank at our backs, flinging spray upward. And then it receded, dragging us and the bike rack toward the Pacific.

The rack jerked to a halt, a chain clanking, anchoring it to a lamp post. I tightened my grip on the cold, slippery metal. There was a chorus of shrieks. Not everyone in our group had grabbed onto something solid.

Half a dozen people's feet were swept from beneath them, and they tumbled into the water. The surge pulled them toward the ocean.

Releasing the bike rack, Hyperion turned. "Aaaah!" He splashed toward the flailing victims of the rogue wave.

My eyes bulged, black spots dancing before them. "Don't—!" Was he crazy? He'd be pulled into the Pacific too.

The pressure on my own legs lessened, the ocean receding. I cursed and waded after him.

A woman in a green rain poncho spun slowly through the water on her backside. It would have been comical if it hadn't been so terrifying.

I made a grab for her and caught her rainboot. Her weight pulled me forward, knocking me off balance. I grabbed wildly and caught a wrought-iron stair railing. Straining, I hooked the top of her foot to one of the balusters. "Hold on!"

Releasing her, I floundered toward another hapless spectator washing toward the beach. I reached for her grasping hand, caught it.

The water swept my feet from beneath me, and I fell. My pulse thrashed in my ears. I floundered, the wave dragging me toward the Pacific.

My foot caught on something beneath the water, yanking me to a stop. Pain flared in my ankle, but I stiffened my foot, hardening the hook I'd made between my foot and calf.

I grit my teeth against the pain. Whatever held us, it was the only thing keeping us from being pulled out to sea. Salt water rushed past. I bent my foot higher, tethered to whatever it had caught on.

And then the water was gone, leaving us gasping in an ankle-deep puddle. I relaxed my foot. An iron hook stuck into the pavement had saved us. I didn't know what it was or why it was there, but it had saved us both.

Shamefacedly, shakily, we rose. Hyperion, Archer, and the three others stood huddled against the wall of a shingled bar.

"Let's get out of here before another wave comes in," I said, panting. I needn't have bothered. Everyone else was already jogging up the street, away from the shore.

"I've got video." Archer gasped, waving his cellphone in the air. "Video!" He trotted up the street.

Shivering from our soaking, Hyperion and I returned to Beanblossom's. He marched straight to his yellow Jeep in the parking lot, got in, and drove off, presumably on a quest for dry clothes.

I stood outside for a long moment, letting the adrenaline rush fade. Then I shook myself and walked into Beanblossom's. I slogged down the tearoom's hall.

Maricel emerged from the kitchen and stopped short. "What happened to you?"

"Rogue wave," I said. "Is Tad still here?"

"No, he left right after you did. Got a to-go box."

"Huh." He'd wanted answers, but he'd been serious about those "skons." I was mildly flattered.

"The pier—?"

"Washed out."

She put a hand to her mouth. "Shut the front door. You mean... it's all gone?"

I shook my head. "The section with the restaurant is still there, and so is the very front of the pier. But the middle's gone. Archer got video."

"Thank God they evacuated it," she whispered.

"Front Street is flooded. The businesses facing the water are too." That glass I'd heard crashing... It had to have been windows breaking, and the thought twisted my gut. All those restaurants had big picture windows facing the water.

"Are there any more reservations this afternoon?" I asked, knowing the answer but wanting to confirm it.

She shook her head. "No."

"Okay, we're closing early." And if we'd *had* reservations, I would have called to cancel. The storm was too dangerous.

"When?" she asked.

"Now." I moved toward the kitchen.

"Ah, Abigail?" Maricel pointed at my rain boots. "You're dripping water all over the floor. Maybe you should just go home. We can clean up."

I hesitated. "I can stay. The mess is my own fault."

"Yeah... But go home anyway."

I went home and changed into jeans, a thick, forest-green henley, and dry tennis shoes and socks.

Grabbing a partially waterproof green jacket, I returned to Beanblossom's in time to clean out the cold storage unit. I locked up, and we trudged through the flooded lot to our cars.

Alas, this defeated the purpose of changing into dry shoes and socks. My feet would be itching by the time I got home.

But instead of returning home, I drove to the police station. Yes, it was only a couple blocks away. But I had an Amphicar.

It was starting to seem like a superpower.

Unsurprisingly, given the weather, I found a spot on the street near the station and parked. I hurried up the concrete steps and onto the arcade, roofed with Spanish tiles, then inside.

I stopped short in the brutalist-style reception area. A lone, burly cop sat behind the counter. The room was otherwise empty. It was also stuffy. Moisture misted the high, narrow windows.

I approached the high counter. "Hi. Is Detective Baranko available?"

"He's about the only one who *is* available." The desk sergeant picked up the phone receiver and pushed a button. "Detective Baranko, you've got a visitor." He cupped his hand over the receiver. "What did you say your name was?"

"Abigail Beanblossom."

"Abigail Beanblossom," he repeated into the phone. After a long moment, the desk sergeant grinned and replaced the receiver. "He'll be right here."

"What's so funny?" I took a step backward, my pulse quickening.

He shook his head. "I don't know what you did to get on his bad side, but lady, you're on it."

Great. I folded my arms over my jacket. My shoes were sopping.

Baranko ambled into the waiting area. His suit, for once, did not look like it had been pulled from a dirty clothes hamper. He wore sleek navy blue over his massive frame and a red power tie. "Any other evidence you're withholding?"

Heat rose in my cheeks. "I didn't mean to withhold that pendant."

"Have you got information for me?"

Did I? I wracked my brains. "Ah, no." I'd come to get information, not give it.

He turned.

"There was someone lurking outside Katey's bookstore Friday night," I said quickly.

He turned back. "What were you doing at her bookstore?"

"There was a book signing. And a Tarot—oracle deck," I said. "Is, er, Verbena... out?"

"No."

"Does she have a lawyer?"

"Nope. Ms. Pillbrow is acting as her own attorney. She'll be arraigned on Monday."

"She's representing herself?" I asked, aghast.

"She says she's innocent and doesn't need a lawyer."

"But... That's crazy."

The detective scratched his fleshy cheek. "Crazy as someone who'd murder her business coach to stop him from manipulating other people."

The air in the reception area grew closer. "Is that what Verbena said?" I asked.

"She hasn't admitted to the murder." He shifted his weight and studied a pair of empty, plastic visitors' chairs.

I stared hard at him. He didn't meet my gaze.

"Do you really think she did it?" I asked.

"She had means, motive, and opportunity."

"How?"

"He was poisoned with oleander," the detective said. "There's a bush in front of Ms. Pillbrow's apartment—"

"This is California. There are oleander bushes everywhere."

"And she was in Falkner's house before the murder."

"Oh." Dammit. *Verbena*. I didn't ask how he knew that, but I trusted that he did. "What about Anna's death?"

"Dumped her at your place to make you look guilty."

"Wait. Dumped? Anna was killed before she got to my house?"

Baranko adjusted his necktie. "Looks that way."

I pressed my palms to my eyes. Selfishly, knowing she hadn't died in my backyard made me feel a little better. I dropped my hands.

"Ms. Ogawa's car was left as dead as she was in the Apothecary parking lot," he continued. "And Ms. Pillbrow is one of the few people in that group who knows where you live. Didn't you wonder why Pillbrow was so hot for you to investigate this? She was framing you up."

I deflated. Though hadn't Jose said Anna had been having off-and-on car trouble? That might explain the car she'd left behind. Not that a dead woman would have much use for one.

"How was she killed?" I asked.

A phone rang behind us. "San Borromeo PD," the desk sergeant answered.

"Not with your shovel," Baranko said. "We found blood on it, but the shape of the impact in her skull didn't match. The blood was a frame-up too. You should be thanking me for clearing your name."

"Thank you," I muttered.

His fleshy chin lifted. "Anna Ogawa was bludgeoned with one of those weird-shaped glass jars she kept at her shop. We found a shard on her floor and the broken jar in her dumpster."

"A shard?"

"The killer cleaned up good, but not good enough."

"So, she'd been killed at her shop and taken to my house... How?"

The big man shrugged. "Not in Ms. Ogawa's car. When we checked it, it wouldn't start. The garage is looking at it now."

Hold on. My eyes narrowed. Baranko was being way too helpful, but I decided to push my luck. "I don't suppose you know Anna's time of death?"

"Between six PM and midnight on Wednesday."

Something was definitely *Up*, capital letter. I squinted at him. "Why are you telling me all this?"

"I dunno. Why do *you* think I'm telling you this?"

"If I knew I wouldn't have asked," I said testily.

A dour smile played about his lips. "Tell your friend to get a lawyer. A good one." He turned.

"Verbena and I aren't friends."

He flapped one hand dismissively and vanished into a hallway.

I stared after him. My lips parted. There was only one reason why he'd told me way more than he should have about the investigation.

He didn't think Verbena was guilty.

Chapter 24

I DROVE TO JOSE'S place of business barefoot, heater blasting my toes. When I arrived, my socks and shoes on the seat beside me were still wet.

I couldn't bring myself to put the socks back on. But this being California, I doubted Jose would notice or care. I climbed the steps of his purple bungalow, shook out my umbrella, and rang the bell.

He answered the door barefoot. "I was just going to do some grounding. Want to join me?" Rain drummed on the roof of the covered porch.

I hung my head. "Will I have to take my shoes off?" I glanced over my shoulder at the soggy lawn.

"That's the only way it works."

I toed my sneakers off in his entryway beside the painted tin sacred heart then followed him outside. The lawn was pleasantly cold and unpleasantly squishy.

"Now what?" I asked, my umbrella wobbling.

"Now we stand here and absorb the negative electrons. They'll balance the positive electrons we're bombarded with all day."

"For how long?"

"Usually I do thirty minutes," Jose said.

My feet sunk deeper into the mud. *Augh*. But if we were stuck on the lawn, I might as well get to the point. Either it would drive him inside (win), or...

Actually, I didn't know what the other side of that equation might be.

"Anna was killed sometime between six PM and midnight last Wednesday," I said.

"That would explain why that detective was asking my whereabouts on Wednesday night."

"What *were* you doing?"

"You and Hyperion really are playing amateur detectives, aren't you? Why do you care? We have a perfectly fine police department. Why not leave it to the professionals?"

"Verbena's sitting in jail. She didn't do it."

"You don't like her very much," he said, "do you?"

My face heated. "She's not a killer."

"That's not an answer."

I thought of all the answers I could give him. That I'd been a murder suspect a couple years ago, and I sympathized. That the police got it wrong sometimes, and so did juries. Or that murder mattered. We *all* should care.

"People are often driven by old wounds to do inexplicable things," he continued.

I glanced down. Clippings of grass were plastered to the tops of my feet. "Everyone has wounds." I shrugged. "We get past them or we don't. I'm past mine."

Verbena had called Falkner a Svengali, but it was hard to keep up walls around Jose. I didn't owe him my childhood history though. I didn't owe him that morning, alone in the airport, staring at my little white shoes and waiting for my parents to come back. That was in the past, and the past didn't exist.

"Are you? That's good." He looked toward the street. The orange traffic cone had fallen on its side and washed against the tire of a Subaru. "More people have that abandonment wound than you'd think."

"I never said I'd been abandoned." My voice was hard and unpleasant, and I realized once again I'd given the game away.

He smiled. "What made you think I was talking about you?"

A car drove past, spraying water across the sidewalk.

"But you're right," Jose said, "our past doesn't have to be our future."

I shifted my weight. Rain pattered on my umbrella. "So?" I finally asked. "What would you tell a client who came to you with an abandonment wound?"

"That those kinds of wounds tend to lead to a distrust of authority figures—"

Well, damn. Maybe I *hadn't* gotten completely over it. But distrusting authority just made good sense. "Check."

His smile broadened. "Engagement in unhealthy relationships, pushing people away before they can be abandoned again, obsession, paranoia—"

"Nope. Not me." Except for the paranoia. But you're not paranoid if someone's thrown a rock through your window and left a body in your garden. I raised my chin. "Tell me about that online class."

"I taught it from six to eight," he said. "You can check out the replay, if you like."

The patter of rain on my umbrella was hollow and flat. "I *would* like. And from eight until midnight?"

Jose flushed. "I was on a date."

"With whom?"

"Tad."

My eyebrows shot upward. "Tad Trzaskalski? The psychic?" It didn't surprise me that either were gay, but Tad didn't seem like Jose's type.

"He really *is* psychic you know. Tad had a serious illness when he was a child. He died and came back. It changed him. Since then, he's been trying to… figure things out." He looked toward the street. "I think Falkner took advantage of that."

"What do you mean?"

"They were seeing each other."

Tell me something I don't know. Was there anyone Falkner *hadn't* been seeing? "When did you find out?"

"I didn't know until, well, last night. Though I'd always suspected. There was a certain energy between the two. It's freezing out here. Want to go inside?"

"Yes." I toyed with the idea of Jose murdering Falkner in a jealous rage and discarded it. He wasn't the type.

We trooped up the steps and inside. Jose handed me a towel, and I scraped wet grass and bits of dirt off my feet. He toweled off as well and led me into the sitting room.

A spider dangled from one of the plants in its macrame hanger. I sat in a worn leather chair, my back to the spider. A deck of Tarot cards lay neatly stacked on the low, round table.

"I'd like some tea," Jose said. "You?"

"Tea would be good."

He left the room. I rose and walked to the windows, blurred by the rain. A car drove slowly past on the street outside. The fallen traffic cone wobbled in its wake.

When Jose returned, he handed me a blue mug. I sipped but didn't taste the tea.

"I haven't met anyone who didn't have a childhood wound," he said. "But I've met a lot of people who have a hard time moving on from theirs."

I nodded. It was rational to feel uneasy when you found a strange woman wearing your boyfriend's bathrobe. *Trust but verify*. But that had been a nothing burger.

I still felt a lingering uneasiness about Jude though. And I needed to let it go. Brik had been dealing with her for years and managing it the best he could.

"Who do you think killed Falkner and Anna?" I asked, the mug warming my hands.

"I don't want to think about it, because it's probably someone I know and like." His dark-eyed gaze met mine. "I'd hoped Falkner's death was random. But with Anna gone now too..." He shrugged.

I turned from the window and sat in the leather chair. A deck of Tarot cards on the low table beside me had been stacked neatly beside a car magazine. "Tell me about Wednesday night. You finished your online class at eight?"

Jose came to sit across from me. "Yes, Tad picked me up from here. We drove up to San Francisco and met a friend of ours in the business for drinks. We got back after midnight. I think it was around one."

It was a perfect alibi. *Maybe.* Jose could have pre-recorded his online class.

Jose sat, legs sprawled, cup in both hands. He looked perfectly at ease, an innocent man. Or a sociopathic killer.

My breath quickened. I rose. "Thanks for the tea."

I returned to my bungalow and checked the web link Jose had gave me. He hadn't been lying. His class on Wednesday night hadn't been pre-recorded. Students had asked questions, and Jose had responded.

So that was that.

I sat back on my blue couch and studied the gold and red charm I'd bought from Jose before I'd left. He'd said it boosted personal power. He'd given it to me with a selenite holder to clean and recharge it each night.

I put it around my neck and touched the golden spiral on my chest. I'd only bought it because I'd taken up so much of his time, and he'd given me free advice. And it was pretty.

The pendant's stones glimmered against my green henley. A killer was still out there. I'd take all the personal power I could get.

I called Brik. He answered on the first ring.

"You home?" I asked.

"No. I'm with Jude. There was an incident."

I stilled. "What sort of incident?"

"Jude went to talk to her trustee," Brik said, "and I guess she got weird. The police are here. She called me before they arrived."

"How weird?"

He sighed. "Nothing violent. Just weird, and I guess she wouldn't leave. Look, I'm sorry, but can we talk later?"

"Sure. Call me when you can."

"Thanks. I love you." Brik disconnected.

I touched the little charm at my chest. The feeling of unease was gone. Was it the work of the charm? Or in my decision to buy the charm as a symbol that I had changed. I wasn't that little girl in the white shoes. I had power.

I could take risks. I could fail, and I'd get up again.

It was a bit like love, which was also a risk. We loved, we lost. But I'd come through the loss of my parents—the worst sort of loss, intentional abandonment. I'd survived.

Loving again was a risk I chose to take. The alternative was unthinkable.

Chapter 25

Loss. Abandonment. Bad relationships, obsession and paranoia. What Jose had said plucked at my mind—not because of my past, because I felt he'd been trying to tell me something.

Was there something I'd forgotten or should have understood about the murders but didn't? I shook my head, as if I could jangle the missing pieces in place. But they'd come when they were ready.

I pulled my pink trench coat from my dryer and slipped into it. Its warmth was delicious. Grabbing my purse, I headed for the front door. A gust of wind buffeted my bungalow's French doors. I looked over my shoulder, stopped, turned.

Slowly, I walked to the rear of the bungalow and peered through the paned windows into the gloom. Where normally I'd see nothing but fence, low lights glimmered near the ground—the solar lights from Brik's backyard.

The six-foot fence between my house and Brik's had fallen completely on its side. The windows in the blue house were dark.

The fence was no big thing for a contractor. We'd repair it together. But it felt like an omen. If I was superstitious, I'd think either a barrier had fallen between us... or the fallen fence was a warning.

I called Hyperion.

"Are you drowning?" he asked.

"The fence is down between Brik's place and mine."

"Hm... Sounds symbolic."

"Yeah, that the weather's a nightmare." I told him what I'd learned from Jose, omitting the metaphysical stuff. *Had* Jose been hinting at something more? "I watched the replay of his class though. It was live, all right."

"It's a decent alibi," Hyperion said, "assuming Tad verifies it, and you know he will."

"But we should ask anyway." I adjusted one of the blue curtains on the French doors. The silhouette of the dogwood tree thrashed in the wind.

"I thought you were worried we were making things worse?" he asked.

"It's just... I feel like things are coming to a head. Verbena's innocent, and Baranko knows it." A breeze shivered beneath the plywood covering my front window. A flyer for solar panels stirred on my dining table.

Hyperion sighed. "I'm torn. Yes, you are correct, things are *obviously* coming to a head. But it is *also* the storm of the century, and only someone with a death wish or a boyfriend who has turned their quaint and quirky domicile into a sterile, hallucinatory anomaly—"

"What?"

"It's Lovecraft. You were right about the old-timey language. It wasn't working."

Lovecraft wasn't exactly modern lingo either, but okay. "But—"

"Everything's a mess." He groaned.

"At your house? I thought Tony was cleaning—"

"I can't find *anything*. Tony's alphabetized my Tarot decks, removed the dripping wax from all my favorite drippy candles, and..." He lowered his voice. "He shaved half of Bastet because the cat hair was, and I quote, out of control."

My mouth puckered. "Ah, only half?"

"You have no idea how dire the sitch was. Bastet was furious. I had to take him to your grandfather's to cool off. Peking laughed at him. Bastet was mortified."

"But those two are such good friends." Peking adored Bastet. The cat even let Peking ride around on his back.

"It's not the duck's fault. I laughed at Bastet too. I'm a terrible person," he wailed. "Why is it that I'm perfectly happy with the scent of vinegar and bleach at Tony's house, but smelling it in *mine* is causing generational trauma?"

"Maybe you just need a break."

"If you're trying to trick me into going with you on more investigative shenanigans, don't bother. I'm outside." His fist thundered against my front door.

I opened it. Hyperion had changed into a green velvet blazer, fresh brown skinny slacks, and a brown button-up top. He looked me up and down, taking in my trench coat, umbrella, and scarlet rain boots. "To the Amphicar," he bellowed.

We raced through the rain to the tarp-covered car. Hyperion and I whipped the covering off, and he jumped inside while I disposed of it in my side yard. I joined him inside the Amphicar and rubbed my hands together for warmth.

"Heater." His teeth chattered. "Where's the heater?"

I started the car and turned on the heat. The Amphicar might be big as a boat, but the heater got going quickly.

Hyperion sagged against the faded passenger seat. "So... Off to Tad's to confirm their alibis?"

"I guess." I checked my watch. It was almost four. If the roads were as bad as I suspected, we were pushing it. But I didn't want to phone-in this interview. I wanted to see Tad's face when we asked about alibis.

I pulled from my driveway. My headlights spotlighted wind-tossed eucalyptus trees, their slender reddish branches strewn upon the road.

"I haven't seen much of Brik lately," Hyperion said casually.

"He's been busy with the storm. Also, his dead friend's homeless and mentally ill sister is in town."

"Uh... What now? There's a dead friend with a cray-cray sister and you haven't mentioned either? Talk about burying the lede. Is she staying with him?"

"No," I said. "He's gotten her a hotel room." I turned the car down the street. A glimpse of black where the ocean should be slivered between the trees and vanished.

"Uh, huh." He nodded. "That sounds totally normal and fine. But, uh, how do you feel about it?"

"If you're asking if I'm jealous, no. Though I admit, it shook me at first. Jude found Brik's spare key and broke into his house. She answered his door in his bathrobe."

"Whoa. Brik wasn't home, I take it?"

"No. He got the key back from her."

"Brik wouldn't get involved with someone who was mentally unstable. He'd consider it taking advantage."

I smiled. "I know. But thanks for saying that."

"I'm saying it because it's OH MY GOD!"

I slammed on the brakes. "What?"

"That street's flooded." He pointed.

We'd been going steadily downhill. In front of us, the road rose. Our headlights glimmered in a water-filled depression before the rise.

I made a face. "Hello? Amphicar?" I switched to boat mode, and we chugged across.

Hyperion rolled down his window, stuck his fist in the air. "Whoo-hoo!" Rain splattered his face, and he quickly rolled the window back up. "I like seeing you getting back into the spirit of things."

"Me too."

We continued on without incident to Tad's tiny blue stucco building. The neon palm was lit, so his business was still open. We splashed across the flooded lawn and up the steps to his sunshine yellow door.

Hyperion opened it, making an after-you gesture. We walked inside.

Tad emerged from his office. "Ooof. You two again?" He rolled his eyes. "May as well come in. And don't drip on anything."

We followed him into his tent-like office. The Turkish lamps glowed evocatively in the gloom, their light reflecting off the crystals in the front windows.

Tad lowered himself into his thronelike chair. The two of us remained standing on the oriental rug.

"Let me guess." Tad pressed a finger to his temple and squinted. "Where was I the night Anna was killed?"

"Jose again?" I guessed.

"Bingo." Tad dropped his hand. "From five to eight I was giving emergency psychic readings at the crummy long-term care facility down the road."

"Really?" I furrowed my brow. I'd driven past that facility. It was hard to imagine anyone inside could afford Tad's prices.

Tad looked away and frowned. "My mother died in one of those places. I couldn't afford..." He swallowed. "The storm was scary, and they were bored. Those places are warehouses. The staff steals from the inmates, and no one does anything about it."

I grimaced. Those places *were* awful. I didn't care what it took. Gramps was staying in his own home as long as he wanted. I'd find a way to pay for a nurse if he ever needed one. And I hoped he'd never need one.

"You can call the staff to check my alibi," Tad continued.

"I will." Hyperion pulled his phone from the pocket of his velvet jacket. "Shady Acres?"

"Shady staffing is more like it," Tad said.

Hyperion's thumb skated across the screen. He wandered from the room. "Hi. Was it true you had a psychic...?" He rounded the corner, and his voice faded.

I studied Tad. "Pro bono?"

His broad face pinked, his lips firming. "If you tell anyone," he said, "*everyone* will want a discount. So, keep your trap shut."

I raised my hands, palms out. "Your secret's safe with us. How's business?"

"The economy's down, so business is great. The psychic industry grows during recessions."

"I've heard that." Had Beanblossom's been doing better than most because of the Tarot readers?

His mouth twisted. "But not even Falkner could save a bookstore in this economy."

"Katey's, you m—?"

"You're in the clear." Hyperion returned, pocketing his phone.

"Thanks so much, mate," the psychic said, caustic.

"And you were with Jose the rest of the night?" Hyperion asked. "On a date?"

"Jealous?" Tad waggled his eyebrows.

"Just as an FYI," Hyperion said, "that long-term care residence is evacuating."

Tad started in his chair. "What?"

The lights went off. Hyperion and I stood frozen for a moment, unmoving.

Tad fumbled his way to the window. "Power's off on the whole street."

"Let's go, Abigail." My partner felt his way from the room, and I followed.

We got into the Amphicar. Rain pounded its canvas top. I started the car and turned on the headlights. And if my muscles loosened when the headlights lit the street, it definitely wasn't because I was scared of what might be in the dark.

Nope. Not me.

"It's getting late," Hyperion said. "Maybe we should just phone Katey for her alibi."

"Fine." I called her and was a little surprised when she answered. I almost put the phone on speaker, but the noise from the rain was too loud.

"This is Katey," she said cautiously.

Ah. She'd answered because she *hadn't* recognized the number. I pressed the phone closer to my ear. "It's Abigail. We learned Anna's time of death. Roughly. I thought you might want to know."

"Oh?"

"She died between six PM and midnight on Wednesday."

"Oh."

"Has Baranko asked you for an alibi for that time?" I asked.

"No," Katey said. "I haven't seen him. I heard he arrested Verbena."

"Right. So, you won't mind if I ask where you were between six and midnight that Wednesday?"

"I was volunteering at the community center," she said. "It's become an emergency shelter."

"The whole night?"

"I got home around one. Satisfied?" Katey disconnected.

"Well?" Hyperion asked.

I told him what she'd said. It was a decent alibi, if it could be believed.

"So, if it's a shelter," he said, "it'll still be open, right?"

I started the car. "Let's go."

Chapter 26

I BOATED DOWN A flooded city street in the dusky gloom. The lights in the shop windows we passed were dark. So were the streetlamps. The whole downtown had been hit by the power outage.

A city works employee in an orange vest gaped at the Amphicar. Hyperion waved through his car window. The man shouted and splashed toward us from the other side of the street.

"Gun it," Hyperion said.

I stepped on the gas. The Amphicar roared forward.

Hyperion twisted in his seat and shook his fist at him. "It's an Amphicar!"

I glanced in the rearview mirror. The man in orange spoke into a radio, and my insides gave a little jump. *Dammit.* Was he calling the cops?

Hyperion faced front. "There wasn't a barricade. I don't know what that guy's problem is. If we could make it down the street, so what?"

"Ignoring the guy was still probably illegal."

"California has too many rules," he grumbled.

"Yeah," I said uneasily. The Amphicar was fun, but I hoped the city works employee hadn't gotten our license plate. "They really evacuated the long-term care facility?"

"Only as a precaution," Hyperion said.

I gnawed my bottom lip. At first the storm had had the feel of a roller coaster ride. It was scary, but interesting. I'd been certain everything would be okay. I wasn't so certain anymore.

Time to think of something I could control. "Let's review the suspects."

Hyperion drew a deck of Tarot cards from his blazer pocket. He pulled out three cards and laid them on the gray seat between us, avoiding the tuft of stuffing sticking up between the frayed seams. "Okay, I'm thinking Queen of Swords reversed for Tad..."

I raised a brow.

"The Queen of Swords can be a real pill," Hyperion said. "Reversed, she's a troublemaker, and so is Tad."

"How so?" I asked, interested. Had Hyperion seen something I hadn't?

"Please, all those catty remarks? Don't you see it? Every time I've been in a group with him, he causes problems between people."

"There's a big jump between being catty and being a killer."

Hyperion sighed. "I know. I just don't like him."

"He's not all bad."

Hyperion snorted. "Just because he volunteers—"

"I meant his relationship with Jose. If Jose likes him—"

"Jose can be fooled. He likes to see the good in people." He turned over the Knight of Cups.

"And they alibi each other," I reminded him.

"Which makes me wonder... Is it possible *two* people killed Falkner?"

"Collusion?" I grimaced and splashed through a puddle too low for the Amphicar and a bit too high for a normal car. "I hope not. That will be hard to prove. But... it can't have been Verbena. She didn't leave that warning for me to stop beneath my windshield wiper. Verbena was with me when I found it."

And Tad had answered the door afterward with his hair soaking wet... He'd just come in from the rain, like us. Had he been following us the whole time? Or had Jose followed us?

"Which brings us to Katey," he said, and flipped the Queen of Swords from reversed to upright.

"That just seems lazy."

"But accurate. Katey's a tough customer."

"I don't know. She—"

A fox darted in front of my headlights, and I braked hard. The Tarot cards slid across the seat. Hyperion slapped them down before any could fall to the damp floor mat.

"What was that about?" Hyperion asked, accusing.

"Fox," I said wildly. "There was a fox. Didn't you see it?" I edged the car forward and scanned the road.

"We've got foxes? No. Those are a sign of good luck."

"It wouldn't have been lucky for the fox if I'd hit it," I said and sped up.

"But you didn't hit him. Lucky." He drummed his fingers on the door's armrest.

"If Tad and Jose's alibis check out, Katey is the only one left." Aside from Jude. But Jude hadn't known Falkner. She was only a wild card.

I hoped.

My toes curled in my shoes. I should have told the cops about Jude.

"I hate to say it," Hyperion said, "but maybe Tad doesn't have such a great alibi. He could have slipped out of the old folks' home with none of the staff the wiser, and none of the inmates *compos mentis* enough to complain."

"That's the type of thing a cop could check out better than us." I piloted the Amphicar around a sharp corner.

"The problem with poisoning Falkner, is anyone could have done it," he said. "All of them had probable access to his house to plant the poison, since they were all having affairs with him."

"Not Jose," I reminded him.

"And then all they had to do was wait for him to take it," he said. "There's so much we don't know. How was the poison delivered?"

"Tea," I guessed.

"Where did you hear that?"

"I didn't. I'm just guessing. But if it was oleander leaf, it would make sense." I shrugged. "Also, I'm a tea person."

"So was Falkner," Hyperion reminded me. "He was always sipping tea on his online videos. The only thing that kept him out of Beanblossom's was the knowledge that I was a part owner."

I nodded. "Okay, so opportunity is out for Falkner, because they all could have gotten in, save, possibly Jose. They all had motive, and they all had means to kill him—oleander grows all over the place in Northern California."

"Which leaves Anna's murder. If the motive was to shut her up, again, that could have been any of them."

"She'd been bludgeoned," I said.

"Front or back?" Hyperion asked.

"Back." My gorge rose, and I swallowed queasily. "Baranko told me Anna was killed in her apothecary shop and her body brought to my house."

"When did you talk to Baranko?"

"I went to the police station to find out what was going on with Verbena. He said she died between six and midnight. The cops impounded her car. I guess Baranko thought something was fishy about it." I thought it was too. "I was surprised he gave me that much."

"Could have been any of 'em then."

"Yeah. They all had means. Though it would have been a lot easier for a man to lug Anna's body into my yard…" I frowned.

"What?"

"Lost my train of thought. Sorry." I pulled up to the sidewalk outside the community center.

Welcoming lights gleamed through the windows. Round windows on its second floor gave the blue and white stucco building a ship-like appearance.

Water covered the lawn. Wind whipped miniature whitecaps across the concrete path to the front door.

Leaving my umbrella in the Amphicar, I raced down the path after Hyperion. My shoes were soaked by the time we reached the front door. Panting, we stumbled inside a wide foyer with a thin green carpet. A generator hummed.

A harried-looking woman glanced up from her high desk. "Volunteers or clients?"

People bustled in and out of a set of swinging doors at the back of the foyer. A rumble of voices rose and fell with every swing of the door.

"Uh... Neither?" Hyperion said.

The older woman put down her pen. Her expression pinched. "What do you want?"

"We're checking on a volunteer who was here last Wednesday," I said.

Her expression shifted to concern. "Is he missing?"

"She," I said, "and n—"

"Yes." Hyperion pressed a long hand to his chest. "This was the last place anyone saw her."

Her eyes widened. "She's been missing for three *days*?"

"The police are so busy," Hyperion murmured. "The storm, you know."

"I know it." She stretched to pull a ledger-like book from the far corner of the desk and slapped it open. "What's her name?"

"Katey Molina," I squeaked out.

Her crooked finger scanned down the page. "Yes, she checked in at 6:15 and checked out at 11:45 Wednesday night."

"What was she doing here so late?" I asked.

"We're a temporary shelter," she said. "She was doing what everyone else was doing, I suppose. Providing food and comfort to the people sheltering from the storm."

"How do people sign in and out?" I asked.

"They just sign out when they leave," she said, angling her head down and looking up with an *obviously* expression.

"I mean," I said, "do they go through you to sign out, or just do it on their own?"

Her graying eyebrows slashed downward. "I don't have time to hand-hold every volunteer. They know where the book is."

"Oh, totally," Hyperion said.

"Mind if we take a look around?" Hyperion asked.

Her nostrils pinched. "Our guests aren't zoo animals."

"Because we'd like to volunteer," he said.

I glared at my partner in crime solving. Pretending we were going to volunteer when we had no intention of doing so was just mean.

"Our volunteer coordinator is Parker Gonzalez." The woman pointed with her pencil to the double doors. "If you can find him."

We entered a cavernous hall lined with cots. People huddled, clutching their belongings, reading to children, sipping coffee. We eventually found Parker ladling soup to a buffet line.

"Yeah, Katey was here." He poured soup into an elderly woman's bowl. "She was pitching in wherever she was needed, like most of us."

"Was she here the entire time?" I asked. "From six until midnight?"

"I didn't have eyes on her the whole time." He motioned around the hall. "Look at this place. It's a zoo. I don't have time to micromanage."

A frizzy-haired woman with an empty bowl elbowed me in the stomach, and I grunted. She glared at me and stepped up to Parker. Shooting me an apologetic smile, he ladled her soup.

Hyperion and I thanked him and left the shelter. "So that's that," Hyperion said, caustic. "No one did it. Everyone's innocent."

"Or no one is." I started the Amphicar.

He clicked his lap belt together. "You don't think they're *all* responsible? That's so Agatha Christie." He jiggled the buckle, testing it.

"I don't know what I think," I said, weary. But I was starting to suspect I'd need to tell the police about Jude. She had no reason to kill Falkner. I tasted bile. But could she have killed Anna and left her in my garden?

Chapter 27

"This isn't the way to Beanblossom's." Hyperion frowned on the seat beside me.

"No," I said, "it's the way to my garage."

I navigated the Amphicar through the twilight gloom and into a warehouse district outside town. Fishing shacks hung with nets jammed side-by-side with industrial buildings and the occasional bar, oil lamps lighting the windows.

"You're not giving up the Amphicar in this weather?"

"No. I have an idea."

"And you're leaving it as a surprise?" Hyperion crossed his arms and sunk lower in his seat.

"Not anymore." I explained my idea.

He nodded. "He's not going to tell you, but we might as well give it a try."

I turned a corner. Lights gleamed from the dirty windows of the corrugated metal building, and I relaxed. Mike's place was still open.

I parked in the driveway, and Hyperion and I hurried to the office door. He yanked it open. We scuttled inside the office.

A desk piled with yellow receipts. A bulletin board hung with car keys. An empty swivel chair. No one was home.

"Hello?" I called.

Mike emerged through an open door. "Hey. There's not something wrong with the Amphicar, is there?" The mechanic wiped his hands on a dirty rag.

"No," I said, "it's been great. By accident, we even took it for a test swim. It floats. The motor works."

"Yes." He punched his fist in the air. "That's great news. Hey, if you're here about your Mazda, it should be ready by Wednesday."

"I'm actually here about Anna Ogawa's car," I said. "Did the police bring it in?"

"Uh, yeah." He shifted his weight and tossed the rag onto the desk.

"Do you know why her car wasn't working?" I asked.

His eyes narrowed. "Yeah, but I can't tell you."

"Even if it was a matter of life and death?" Hyperion asked.

"Is it?" the mechanic asked.

"It could be," Hyperion said, glancing away and gesturing vaguely.

"I don't need the details," I said. "All I need to know is, was it sabotaged?"

The mechanic's mouth pinched. "Look, I can't—"

"Because I think it was," I said. "But Hyperion thinks it wasn't. We have a bet, and I'd prefer not to lose it."

Hyperion grinned and folded his arms. "Forget it, Abs. You lose. You'll be paying my Tarot readers for a week."

"It *had* to be sabotage," I whined and turned to the mechanic. "Didn't it? It's just too big a coincidence otherwise."

"I told you." Hyperion wagged a finger at me. "Coincidences do happen occasionally."

"Sorry. You're both wrong." The mechanic shot me a regretful look. "Loose wire on the battery. According to records, she'd gotten a new one recently. It probably wasn't installed correctly. Or it was sabotage. Right now, it's indeterminate."

Mike pulled his neck back, his chin lowering. "She had some problems before—sugar in the gas tank, that sort of thing. I can tell you that, because it had nothing to do with the police bringing it in. When they brought it in, it worked."

"Then why'd the cops bring it to you?" I asked.

"But there *was* sabotage," I said. "What about the sugar in her gas tank you mentioned? How did you know about that?"

Mike scratched his head. "Because by chance, she brought the car to me after the sugar incident. Look, I shouldn't have said anything at all. Don't tell anyone. Okay?"

"We were never here," I said, "and this never happened. And thanks again for the loaner. I think the Amphicar may literally have been a lifesaver."

The mechanic's brow creased. "You need to be careful with that car."

"Oh, we will." Grasping my arm, Hyperion steered me toward the door.

"Hey," the mechanic said, and we turned. "There was blood in Anna's car. I didn't find it. The other forensics team did."

I hesitated. "Thanks."

Hyperion maneuvered me into the rain. "Anna's body was transported in her own car," he said.

"Which was dead." But a loose wire might have been easily fixed. And then loosened again? Why? "Now we know she was transported there in her own car, and someone returned it to her parking lot."

"Now where?"

"Beanblossom's. I'm going to have to cancel Sunday's reservations." I should have done it earlier, but I'd been hoping that the storm would ease.

It hadn't. The windshield wipers had a hard time keeping up with the rain. I didn't start to relax until I entered the parking lot behind Beanblossom's.

The wheels of the Amphicar lifted off the pavement. My muscles tightened, and I straightened in my seat. Hyperion shot me a panicked look, the angular shadows across his face darkened by the parking lot lamps.

The wheels touched down again, and I exhaled. I piloted the car toward his Jeep.

He swallowed. "You don't think the sandbags have failed, do you?"

"Let's look." I turned the car and drove as close to the sandbags as I dared without swamping them.

Hyperion rolled down the window and leaned out. "The water hasn't topped them yet. Hang on." He unbuckled his seatbelt, twisted and stuck his feet through the open window, and slithered out.

He teetered atop a sandbag then hopped to the ground. "Come on." My partner stuck his hand through the open window.

I turned off the ignition. Opening the door, I followed him into the damp island of calm behind the sandbags.

Hyperion unlocked the tearoom's metal door. "We've got more, right?"

"Yeah. Inside your office."

"My office is not a storage space." He sniffed and walked inside.

"I didn't know where else to put them. I didn't want anyone to stumble over them in the hallway." I followed him into Beanblossom's.

He jiggled a light switch. The hallway remained dark. "No power."

"The lights are on in the parking lot," I said. "Maybe we've blown a fuse." I checked the fuse box beside the door to Hyperion's office. All the fuses were okay. "Weird."

Using my phone's light, I walked down the hallway and into the tearoom. No lights glowed through the front windows. My shoes splashed in a puddle at the front door. "Water's coming through," I said, my voice unattractively high. *Don't panic.*

I aimed my light at the laminate, faux-wood floor. Water seeped from beneath the blue front door, and I cursed.

"Coming." Hyperion grunted. His lean shadow emerged from the hallway.

THUMP. SCREE.

My heart jumped. "What's that?"

"Ow," Hyperion said.

I gripped my umbrella more tightly. "What happened?"

"Bumped into a table." He came closer, a sandbag hugged beneath both arms.

I grimaced. "You ready?" How much water was behind the front door?

He nodded. "Open it."

I opened the door. More water flowed inside the tearoom, but not the tidal wave I'd dreaded. Hyperion sloshed outside and stacked two sandbags to the left of the door.

I stuck my head out. If I'd thought Main Street had been a river before, it was a torrent now.

The lights were off up and down the street, but I could hear the roaring of the water. Most of it flowed around the sandbags Hyperion had added. Most.

Hyperion unclipped a mini flashlight from his belt. He aimed its beam up the street.

"Where did you get that?" I asked.

"Brik gave it to me. He said real men didn't use their phones as a flashlight."

"And you listened to him?" I laughed. "He uses his phone light all the time."

"Yeah, but my flashlight's better. Look. I can see the t-shirt shop." He aimed it at the darkened windows across the street.

A shadow bobbed and skidded down Main Street. Its movements were choppy. Something in its lurching shimmy made my heartbeat slow.

"What's that?" I pointed up the street.

Hyperion reoriented his flashlight. A baby carriage jounced against a brick planter then skimmed into the middle of the street. It bobbed in a quick spiral.

I sucked in a breath, a damp ache swelling in my chest. A *baby...*

"Oh, God." Hyperion hopped over the sandbags and staggered in the rush of water. The carriage swept toward him. Lurching forward, he grabbed its handle.

I swayed dizzily. *No, no, no. Not a baby...* I dropped the hand I'd pressed to my mouth.

Hyperion dragged the carriage to Beanblossom's. I helped him maneuver it inside.

We peered inside the carriage. It was empty. The fabric was an old-fashioned pattern, faded and dingy and torn in places.

My insides plummeted. "You don't think..."

He touched the dingy fabric lining. "Dry. If it had tipped over, the lining would be soaked."

My shoulders sagged. No one had been inside it. At least, that was what I wanted to believe. I exhaled shakily.

"This thing's ancient," Hyperion said. "It was probably junk in someone's yard, and it got swept away."

Please, let him be right. But what if he was wrong? "I'm calling the cops. Just in case."

"Yeah." He studied the insides of the carriage, the skin bunched around his dark eyes. A muscle jumped in his jaw. "Yeah. Call them. I'm getting more sandbags." Shoulders slouched, he trudged to the back of the restaurant and vanished into the hallway.

I stared after him for a moment. The carriage had unnerved him too.

Shaking myself, I phoned the police station and explained what we'd found to the dispatcher. He told me there'd been no reports of missing babies, but he'd make a report. I hung up, both relieved and dissatisfied.

I got a mop and towels from the kitchen. It didn't take long to clean up. Hyperion dropped sandbags on the dam around the front door. I finished about the time Hyperion declared the sandbags done.

"Take a look." Hyperion braced his fists on his hips.

Cautiously, I stepped outside. Water flowed harmlessly around the sandbags. "Nice job," I said.

A dark, rectangular shape barreled toward us down the sidewalk. I gasped. "Look out!"

I yanked Hyperion toward the door. This didn't budge him at all, as he was significantly bigger than me.

"What?" he looked up the street. "Aaah!" He pushed me inside Beanblossom's and scuttled after me into the tearoom.

THUNK. The shape hit the sandbags. Water splashed across the front windows and sloshed through the open door. The shape reared up on one end.

CRASH. It collapsed atop the sandbags.

"What the hell was that?" Hyperion asked.

I opened the door. It banged against something solid and stuck. We wedged our heads through the narrow opening and gawked.

Archer had been right. He'd warned us. I'd thought he'd been exaggerating. I should have known better. "That's a—a—"

"Coffin," Hyperion whispered. "And it's *beached*."

A muddy coffin lay upside down across our sandbag dam. I pressed a hand to my stomach. "You don't think there's someone ins—?"

"Call the cops. Call the cops!" He yanked me into the tearoom and slammed the door.

I called the cops and got the same dispatcher. He was more interested in the coffin than the baby carriage, given the potential for human remains. The dispatcher promised to send someone.

"You think we should stick around?" I asked. Because I really didn't want to. And it wasn't as if the coffin was *inside* the tearoom.

"No. Let the cops do their thing."

"Yeah." Because sometimes, you just need to trust. Also, I didn't want to know what was left in that coffin.

A breeze tossed my hair and ruffled the hem of my trench coat. I clutched my arms to my chest, my shoulders curling forward. The back door slammed shut.

Hyperion and I froze. Whoever it was, it couldn't possibly be the police. Not so soon.

A bulky shape emerged from the rear hallway, and I tensed. A flashlight clicked on, blinding.

Chapter 28

"Abigail?" The flashlight beam lowered.

My shoulders relaxed. "Brik." I wound through the tearoom's bare tables. "What are you doing here? What's wrong?"

"Nothing's wrong. I was worried about your sandbag situation. I've got more in my truck." He kissed me, keeping me at arms length so his black rain jacket wouldn't get me wet. "You okay?"

"Yeah. We may need more sandbags, but we're okay for now."

"And I wanted to give you this." Brik dug into the front pocket of his jeans and pulled out a key. "It's to my place. I thought you should have it."

My heart stumbled. *His key.* It shouldn't have been that big a deal. We lived next door to each other. But it seemed like a big step. I swallowed. "Thanks, but if this is because of the bathrobe thing—"

"It is, and it isn't. I'm not trying to prove anything. But it's time."

"No, you don't have to prove anything."

Hyperion pressed his nose to the windows and pretended not to listen. "Uh, guys?"

"Not now." Brik placed his hands on my shoulders. "Jude opened my door wearing my bathrobe. Anyone would wonder."

And I had, briefly, because love *isn't* blind. It's a choice, and it's a practice. And I chose to love Brik. "Honestly, that worried me for all of two minutes, before I came to my senses. Where is she now?" I asked him.

"I'm not sure. She didn't ask me to pay for her hotel last night. I think she's moved on."

"Guys?" Hyperion said. "I really think you should—"

"Am I an awful person for being glad about that?" I asked.

"If you are, then we're both awful."

"I do trust you," I said.

"Guys," Hyperion said loudly, "why doesn't anyone *listen*? The coffin is *moving*."

"Coffin?" Releasing me, Brik strode to the window and peered out. "Damn. I'd heard parts of the cemetery were washing out. I didn't realize they'd lost some residents."

"The police are on their..." I trailed off, my breath slowing. Someone was *inside* that coffin. Someone whose loved ones had mourned them. If the storm washed the coffin off our sandbags, it might be lost in the Pacific. "We need to stop it."

Hyperion turned from the window. "Whoa. What?"

"Someone's *in* there," I said.

Hyperion dragged both hands through his wet hair. "Why do you think I want to let the police deal with it?"

I grimaced. "If the coffin goes into the ocean—"

"Okay, okay." Hyperion groaned. "I get it. We're on coffin duty." He strode to the front door and cautiously swung it wide. "Ruh-roh."

"Don't tell me it's gone?" I hurried to join him.

The coffin teetered on the edge of the sandbags. Slowly, it swiveled, tipped.

Hyperion lunged and grabbed one of the brass handles. "I got it." The handle pulled free with a damp groan. The coffin drifted onto Main Street. "Whoops. I don't got it."

Brik pushed past us. Wading into the water, he grabbed both sides of the coffin's base. "I can't get a good grip." He grunted.

Hyperion splashed after him to the other end of the coffin. He braced it with his hands. "Now what?" he gritted out.

A police car turned down Main Street. Its blue lights flashed. The sedan chirped a warning.

The car pulled up beside the coffin. A window rolled down, and a police officer stuck his head out of the passenger window. "What are you two doing?"

"I called it in," I shouted.

"Thanks, ma'am," the officer said. "We'll take it from here."

"Thank God," I muttered.

"Put your hands up," he told Brik and Hyperion, "and step away from that coffin." The blue lights from the squad car flickered weirdly over the two hunched men.

"No," I shouted over the roar of water. "You don't understand."

"We can't," Brik said. "There's someone in here."

"Uh, oh." Rain streamed down Hyperion's face. His dark hair was plastered to the sides of his head.

"You're tampering with human remains," the cop bellowed. "Step away from the coffin."

"We can't," Brik said. "If—"

"We don't have time for this." The cop stepped from the car. He wore waders beneath his navy raincoat. Pushing the raincoat aside, he rested his hand on the butt of his gun.

"We found it this way," Hyperion bleated. "We're trying to help."

"Sickos," the police officer snarled. "We got reports of grave robbing with the cemetery washing out. You two jokers fit the descriptions of the perps. A big blond guy and a skinny dark haired one."

"Skinny?" Hyperion said, outraged. "I'm *lean*. I've got muscle tone."

"You don't understand." Brik spat water. "We're trying to stop it from going into the Pacific."

The second cop stepped from the car. He was even bigger than the first, his face dark beneath his plastic-covered cap. "Secure the coffin, then you're both coming to the station."

"What?" Hyperion squawked.

"But they're telling the truth," I said, motioning toward the open door of the tearoom behind me. "The coffin washed onto my sandbags."

"All right," the first said.

My muscles relaxed, shoulders dropping. *Thank God.* They believed us.

"You two pick it up and move it inside," the cop told Hyperion and Brik.

My shoulders jumped to my ears. "What? Inside where?"

"You said that was your place, didn't you?" He jerked his chin toward Beanblossom's.

"Yes, but... You can't," I sputtered. "There are health regulations. It's a restaurant. You can't put a used coffin in a restaurant."

"Where else are we going to keep it?" he asked.

Oh. My stomach sank. The coffin wouldn't exactly fit in the squad car. "But it's a *tea*room," I wailed.

"Tea and Tarot room," Hyperion snapped.

"Move it," the second cop roared.

"It's the best solution." Brik got to his feet and swiveled his end of the coffin toward me. Grumbling, the two men hefted the coffin into the tearoom.

The lights came on in the tearoom, and I blinked, my eyes adjusting. A chunk of earth loosened from the coffin. It thudded wetly to the laminate floor.

"All right," the second cop said. "Back to the car. You two can explain at the station."

"No," I said. "Wait. They're who they say they are. Brik and Hyperion were just helping me put sandbags out—"

"Sorry," the first cop said. "The station's two blocks away, and we're too busy to sort it out here. The town's sliding into the ocean, if you haven't noticed. There are people who need to evacuate who haven't, and you're wasting our time."

"Forget it, Abigail," Brik said. "They're right. We'll clear it up at the station."

"But—"

Hyperion shot me a wry smile. "Bail us out, will ya?"

At least the police officers didn't handcuff them when they put them into the back of their squad car. The car made a slow turn and pulled up the road, water sluicing off its front grill.

I wanted to race after them to the station. But they were safe, and I had responsibilities here, too. I stacked more sandbags around the front and rear doors. At this point, I wasn't leaving anything to chance.

I dropped the final bag in the small dam around the back, metal door and huffed a breath. The lights flickered in the parking lot, and I looked up. Brik and Hyperion waded toward me.

I smiled, straightening. They were free. Of *course* the cops had let them go. It had all been a silly misunderstanding.

Hyperion jiggled the handle on the Amphicar. Brik laughed.

I frowned. That wasn't Brik's laugh.

The men moved closer, and I scrunched my forehead. They matched my friends' builds and hair colors, but they weren't Brik and Hyperion.

My pulse jumped. *You two jokers fit the description of the perps.*

The grave robbers.

The men turned and sloshed toward the wine bar on the other side of the lot.

I grabbed my pink umbrella, locked Beanblossom's rear door, and hurried after the two. It would be a lot easier for Brik and Hyperion to prove their innocence if I could identify the *real* grave robbers.

Plus, they were *grave robbers*. They deserved to be caught. I mean... *Ew.*

But instead of going inside the wine bar, the men made their way through the alley between it and another building. The very *dark* alley.

I detoured as quickly as I could around the stucco building. The two men's silhouettes ambled toward the pier. I hesitated, then followed.

To my relief, the men avoided Front Street, which surged with ocean waves. They took a roundabout way to the row of pastel apartments that arced along the beach. The grave robbers turned onto a flagstone sidewalk with a low rock wall facing the beach.

A wave crashed over the wall and surged against the apartments' ocean-facing walls. Water roared down the sidewalk toward me.

I grasped a nearby lamp post. The wave tugged at my rain boots then overflowed them, pulling me backward. I gripped the lamp post more tightly. Wind howled through the narrow passage.

The grave robbers turned up a set of concrete steps, their shoulders bumping. The wave receded. I took a breath and squished after them. One of them opened the door of a yellow motel room.

I nodded. *Yellow room number five.* I'd be able to find it again. I turned to retreat back to my car.

Katey stood in front of me in a black rain poncho. The light from an iron streetlamp glittered off the knife in her hand.

Chapter 29

THE CORRIDOR BETWEEN THE motel rooms was too tight. A chill zapped from my heart to my hands, and my fingers trembled in response.

I couldn't move fast enough or far enough to escape that knife, cold and colorless in the dim light. If my fear would even *let* me move.

The knife was long, its tip serrated, like something used for hunting. My legs tightened. How long had Katey been hunting me?

"I really hope that's for the grave robbers," I squeaked out.

Rain streamed down my pink umbrella, and I realized I might actually have the advantage. True, there was nothing pointy on my umbrella, but at least I could use it to keep some distance.

She rolled her eyes. "Seriously? Everyone knows that grave robber story is fake news." A wave crashed on the concrete steps beneath her.

"The cops don't," I said loudly. Could the guys in the yellow motel room hear us? But if they were grave robbers, it was doubtful they'd come to my rescue.

"Stop talking." Her black poncho crinkled.

"Then what's with the knife?" I asked, trying to keep my voice casual.

"And stop pretending. You know why I'm here. You *must* know. You've been asking all the wrong questions. And if you didn't know before, you know now. Where's your partner?"

"In jail," I said. "So, I wouldn't bother trying to pin my murder on him."

"I won't need to." She flattened herself against a pink stucco wall and motioned with her knife toward the stairs. "Move."

I took a hesitant step, then moved, feet dragging, toward Katey. *My umbrella.* I could hit her with it. It would work.

"Your alibi was weak," I said. "There were so many people coming in and out of that community center, it was easy for you to slip out without being noticed."

I didn't want to get anywhere near that knife. But I moved closer anyway, coming into line with her. I whipped my umbrella down.

Her knife thrust through the pink fabric, her hand striking the umbrella's metal frame and pressing me backward. I grunted, twisting the umbrella, and yanked sideways.

The knife flew from her hands, clattering to the cement walkway.

"Help!" I shrieked.

She drove forward, shoving me against the building. I didn't have a chance to dive for the knife. Wind screamed around us, pink fabric and rain blinding me.

No one would come. The wind and waves were too loud. Anyone with any sense had evacuated these motel rooms. I was on my own, and I hated it.

Twisting, I wrenched free, my grip releasing on the umbrella. The wind tossed it along the concrete walk and up the steps. I raced after it.

Maybe adrenaline had heightened my hearing. I'd swear I could hear Katey's footsteps over the noise of the storm. Her hand grasped my shoulder. She yanked me backwards, and I tumbled down the steps.

I splashed into icy water. A wave receded, dragging me with it. I clawed frantically for purchase, spinning. My foot struck something hard, and I straightened my leg.

Water flowed past me, leaving me beached and panting against the door of a purple stucco motel room. I struggled to standing.

A cold blade pressed against my throat. "Don't scream." Katey panted.

My guts somersaulted, and I was almost sick right then and there. Honestly, I wasn't much of a screamer anyway. Now, that seemed like a defect on my part.

"You found out Falkner was having an affair with Anna," I gasped out. "You killed the both of them out of jealousy." It was the oldest motive in the book.

And what had Hyperion told me about knife defenses? To turn my head so it wouldn't strike the carotid? But that made no sense.

"I didn't care about that," she snarled. "Falkner couldn't save my bookstore. He had no idea. I can't lose it. It's all I've got, and he took advantage of me. He took my money when he knew he couldn't help."

Obsession. Paranoia. Bad relationship choices. My head swam. Jose had been describing Katey. Her father's suicide must have felt like the ultimate abandonment.

"I'm sorry," I whispered.

"What do your *sorrys* help?" she spat. "You run a *tearoom*."

My fists tightened. If she was going to be that way about it... "You poisoned him with leaves from the oleander bush in your parking lot, didn't you?"

"It was easy. I added the dried leaves to the box of tea in his kitchen." The pressure against my throat released. "He had no idea what I was doing, because he had no idea what *he* was doing. Falkner was a fraud. He never cared about small business owners. He only cared about himself."

"Did Anna find out you poisoned him? Is that why you killed her?"

"Start walking toward the beach."

That was the *last* place I wanted to be in this storm. "You were the one who kept messing with Anna's car. Your father owned a garage—I saw the photo of it in your store. That's where you worked when you were a kid. But why disable her car? Were you trying to keep her at her shop that night?"

"Yes," Katey said from behind me. "I told her I'd give her a ride home, and then I made her wait for me until no one was around."

"And then you rewired her car so you could bring her body to my house." My gaze darted around the narrow passage between the hotel rooms.

"One snoop deserves another. Besides, I didn't want any of her DNA in *my* car."

Water blurred my vision. "How did you move her into my yard? My wheelbarrow?" And the rain had washed out the wheelbarrow tracks.

"Obviously."

"And then you smeared her blood on my shovel."

"Also obvious."

"Now what?" I asked.

"You're the amateur detective. You figure it out."

I figured she'd leverage the storm to make my death look like an accident. Hyperion would never believe it, but others might. After all, I *had* walked into the storm of my own accord.

"Were you the one who put those threatening notes on my windshield?" I asked.

Katey snorted. "I should have thought that would have been obvious by now."

In other words, *yes*. "Then who was lurking outside your bookstore the other night?"

"I have no idea. Just someone walking by. I wanted you to think I was in danger too."

At least the person who'd left the threatening notes hadn't been Jude. She might be crazy, but she hadn't been trying to scare me. But Brik...

Brik. My heart lurched. He'd lost one girlfriend to a madman years ago. I didn't know how he'd handle losing another.

My spine straightened. He wasn't going to lose me. I wasn't going down without a fight. Katey had a knife, but she was roughly my size—

"Turn right here," Katey said, forcing me around the corner of the building. A low cement wall was all that held back the black ocean.

The storm roared, turning the Pacific waves to mini mountains. The buildings facing the ocean were dark. I could just make out their rectangular shapes and what remained of the pier.

Pursing my mouth, I forced my breathing to slow. *Now. Make your move now.*

"I'm sorry I have to do this," she said, her tone firming. "You're a struggling business owner, like me. But—"

Swiftly, I turned. A wave swept over the low wall and took my feet from beneath me. Katey shrieked.

I landed hard on paving stones, and then those vanished beneath my fingers as well. I bumped against the low wall and struggled to grasp it.

The water lifted me, helpless. I clawed at the top of the wall, and the ocean took me.

Chapter 30

CALIFORNIANS JOKE ABOUT THE Pacific. When Magellan discovered it in 1520, all he experienced were calm waters. But the Pacific off the coast of California is cold and rough at the best of times. And this was the storm of the century.

I flailed, but the ocean was stronger. Of all the awful feelings in this life, helplessness is one of the worst. And as I was swept through the darkness, the cold realization struck that my life would soon be ending.

My pulse grew sluggish. No one had seen me go into the water except for Katey. And judging by the occasional feminine cry, she was in desperate straits too. It gave me small satisfaction.

A surge swamped me. I choked on salt water. *Fight*. But it was no use. My clothing weighed me down. The current was too strong. The night grew blacker.

A hand grasped the collar of my trench coat. Someone dragged me, sputtering, across rough pavement.

I bicycled my legs beneath me until my shoes found purchase. Lurching to my feet, I turned, fists clenched.

And faced a creature from a nightmare. Lank, black hair dripping over sloped shoulders. Impossibly tall. A gaze that burned a trail to—

"You okay?" Jude asked. She wore a cheap, black raincoat, belted at the waist over what appeared to be waders.

Jude? Where had she come from? I looked around. We stood on a small, paved rise, the loading dock to my favorite Mexican restaurant. Two metal railings climbed the wide slope to the rolling metal door.

CRASH. A wave struck the rear of the restaurant, and I winced. Black water surged up the squat street where we sheltered and swirled against our little concrete island.

Relieved, I blinked and swiped the hair from my face. I was alive. I'd worry about how Jude had found me later. "You— Where's Katey?"

"The other woman? I got her." Jude motioned behind her. "She's all right."

My hands went limp. "Oh, no," I said thickly.

"Oh," Katey said, "yes." Beside the opposite railing, she racked the gun she held in her hand.

My lips flattened, my muscles quivering with impotent rage. *Seriously? Just when I thought I might survive the night...*

The bookstore owner stood on higher ground, roughly five feet away from Jude. Katey stood flattened against the white stucco wall and out of arm's reach.

Not that being any closer would help. A bullet could move a lot faster than either of us.

Jude turned and patted the pockets of her raincoat. "That gun's mine."

"Finders keepers." Katey smiled crookedly.

"You're the other one." Jude glared. "You threw the rock through Abigail's window. If I'd recognized you earlier, I wouldn't have saved you."

Another mystery solved, I thought wildly. "Jude," I said, my voice cracking, "this is Katey Molina. She killed her lover and business coach, Falkner Fiore, and then she killed one of his other clients, Anna, who basically knew too much."

Water dripped from Katey's rain poncho. "She didn't know a damn thing," she snarled. "Anna was ruining my business. I had enough problems without arguing over that parking lot. And then she was going to sell Jose's amulets, when he told me I couldn't. She didn't even *believe* in them."

"But those are... Those wouldn't have ruined your business," I said, and not because I hated being wrong. Those sorts of problems were small potatoes. Annoyances. Bumps in the road.

"My father *died* for his business," Katey shrieked.

But every bump in the road might seem like a mountain to someone like Katey. "And that's why you sabotaged her car," I said.

"She deserved it," Katey said.

"Were you the one who pushed the dumpster into my car?" I asked.

"I followed everyone from Falkner's to your tearoom that night. I knew they never liked me. Sneaking around behind my back. I knew you were all plotting, trying to blame me for his death."

My nostrils flared. "You killed him!"

"I don't like murderers," Jude said.

"Yeah," I babbled, "most people don't. But Katey's no common killer. She owns a bookstore." The absurdity of the statement almost made me laugh. Was I becoming hysterical?

"That metaphysical bookstore you were at last night?" Jude asked. "That's *hers*?"

"Wait," I said. "You were the person in the parking lot?"

Jude shrugged. "Like I said, I was following you."

The storm surged around us. Everything was in motion, the rain, the waves, the bits of broken pier surging against the buildings. All we could do was hold on. I grasped the metal barrier behind me.

"If she knows metaphysics," Jude growled, "she'll know all about the rule of three."

Katey's mouth compressed.

"What's the rule of three?" I asked, stalling.

"Whatever you do—be it good or evil—comes back to you threefold," Jude said.

My chest warmed with pathetic gratitude. Jude was stalling too. But this was a terrible place to dawdle. Storm surge had already washed across Front Street, just above us. The next big wave would wash us out.

"I'll worry about my karma later," Katey snapped.

"It's not karma," Jude said. "We're all connected. Everything's connected. The backlash is happening in real time. It's blackened your soul. You just don't feel it yet."

"I knew I should have opened a mystery bookstore instead," Katey muttered.

My hand tightened on the cold metal. "Katey, this has gone too far. I get wanting to kill me—even though it's a terrible idea. But now you're going to kill an innocent good Samaritan?"

"Not so innocent," Katey said. "She was carrying a gun."

"You'll never get away with it," I said. "It's too much."

"It's too perfect," the bookstore owner responded. "This isn't my gun. It's hers. If they find your bodies, they'll trace the bullet back to her." She waggled the gun at Jude.

"Jude, were you following me?" I asked. The answer was obvious, but Katie didn't know that. *Delay.* There had to be a way out of this.

"Sometimes," Jude said, her voice a low growl.

"Why?"

Jude met my gaze. "Brik has a problem with pretty women," she said seriously. "He gets these chivalric complexes. I wanted to make sure you weren't taking advantage of him."

I gaped. *She... What?*

"What are you two talking about?" Katey asked. "Who's Brik?"

"No one," Jude and I said simultaneously.

I glanced at the taller woman. She was trying to protect Brik, and warmth sparked inside my chest. If the two of us survived tonight, we might actually become friends.

"Do you work for my brother?" Jude snarled.

Katey's eyes widened. She took a step backward, bumping against the metal railing. "I don't know what you're talking about."

Jude's delicate nostrils flared. "You do. Him or my cousin, or both. They paid you off, didn't they?"

"You're crazy," Katey said.

"You're the one with the poison." Jude's lips peeled back in an animalistic snarl.

Jude had known about the oleander...? No. She couldn't have. She was talking about the poison she thought people administered to her in her sleep.

"You know about the poison?" Katey said above the ocean's roar. "How many people know? That wasn't in the papers."

"Ah..." I glanced between the two women. "I don't think—"

"You admit it," Jude shrieked. "Do you have any idea what you've done?" She lunged at Katey.

BANG. The shot rattled the teeth in my skull. Something struck me in the cheek. Automatically, I dropped, shielding my face with my arm.

Slowly, I lowered it. I wasn't hurt. I was alive.

And Katey still had a gun. I looked up.

The two women grappled. Jude, who was taller, had the advantage. She bent Katey backward over the railing.

CRASH. A wave roared up our street. There was another shot. I gripped the metal railing and cried out.

And then the ocean was on us, flowing over us. I clung with both hands, crouching, pressed against the railing by the force of the water, my eyes and mouth shut tight.

Something struck my head, and stars danced before my vision. My grip loosened. Then I remembered myself and hung on tighter.

And then the water was receding, sucking me away from the metal barrier. My hands were ripped free. I shot backward, banged against the opposite railing and tumbled over it. The water scraped me across pavement, and I was drowning, drowning, my lungs compressing.

Hands grasped me, pulling me from the ocean's grip. I was too wrecked to struggle. It was over. Done. And Brik...

Sputtering, I looked up. A guy in a long raincoat and floppy hat grinned at me. "You okay?"

I nodded, floundering for purchase, and my hand touched a metal hubcap. I stood, staggered once, and stared up at the black monster truck.

"You—" I sputtered. I stood on the sidewalk that curved along the beach. The monster truck sat easily on the road. Bits of broken boards littered the street.

The man tipped his hat. "We're just here to help, ma'am. Name's Maddoxxx. Three X's."

"Are you *kidding* me? *You're* Razzzor's—? How—?"

Another man leaned out the driver's window and exposed rows of white teeth. "We thought you folks on the coast might need an assist."

Never mind. I whipped my head back and forth, searching. "Where is she? Where are the other women?"

They glanced at each other and shook their heads. "Other women? We only saw you."

We searched for Katey and Jude, me shivering in the backseat of the monster truck, the men shining spotlights from the windows on the water. But Katey and Jude were gone.

Chapter 31

THE SOUNDS OF PUSH brooms and distant chainsaws reverberated down Front Street. Beanblossom's was safely above the disaster on Main, but I pushed a broom too, cleaning up mud and debris.

The tearoom was closed for the day—not because it was a Monday—because San Borromeo needed a breather.

Hyperion, in gloves, worn jeans, and a hoodie, tossed bits of broken wood and seaweed into a metal garbage can. He wiped his forehead with the back of his wrist and studied the destruction.

Maddoxxx and Harry from the monster truck shoveled debris into another bin. They'd come to San Borromeo to try to talk me into working for Maddoxxx. But they'd altered their plans when they saw the damage the storm was causing.

I still didn't trust Maddoxxx—not because he was an inconsiderate driver. He'd been poaching Razzzor's employees. But at least he wasn't afraid to roll up his sleeves and get dirty. The tech billionaire couldn't be all bad.

None of the town's buildings had been swept away, but their first floors along the beachfront were wrecked. I had no idea how long it would take for Front Street to get back on its feet. But I knew it would.

There'd only been one official fatality—Katey. I scrubbed my hand over my face, dullness settling in my body. Jude's body hadn't been found. I hadn't given up hope she'd escaped alive.

I glanced at Verbena, sweeping up glass across the street. She hadn't exactly been humbled by her stint in jail. She also hadn't bothered to thank me for getting her out. But she was here.

"My garbage can's full." Jose sloshed through the muck toward me carrying a garbage bag. "Mind if I dump this in yours?"

"You're awfully far from Santa Cruz." I arched into a stretch and rubbed my lower back. "And go ahead."

He dumped his bag into my can. "Yeah, but this could have been Santa Cruz."

I nodded. San Borromeo hadn't been the only town damaged by the storm, but it had been the worst hit. A lot of people were thinking *it could have been me* right now. If I was being honest, it was part of the reason I was out here.

"All those things you said about the abandonment wound... Were you talking about Katey?"

"I was talking about all of us."

"Yeah, but Katey—"

"I'm needed elsewhere." He ambled down the street dragging his empty bin behind him.

"But you were talking about Katey," I shouted. "Right?"

He raised his free hand and waved over his shoulder without looking back.

At the other end of the block, a handful of men stood leaning on shovels and brooms. Tomas handed a cup of coffee from an oversized thermos to a worker. My grandfather pantomimed a falling tree and leaping sideways.

Verbena approached me, her broom bumping and scraping on the ground behind her. "There's something I need to tell you."

My neck stiffened. *What next?* "Oh?" I steeled myself.

She drew a deep breath. "I can't come to the tearoom for a while."

"Oh... That's..." *Amazing. Delightful. Wonderful news.* "Ah..."

"It's not me, it's you. After what happened at Beanblossom's, I need a break."

"You mean after getting arrested? I get how that would be trau—"

"I mean how you lured me into detecting," she said hotly. "Because of you, I nearly went to jail."

My hand clenched on my broom. "Hold on. I didn't—"

"I know you can't help it. It's a weakness of character. But I need to draw boundaries. It's not only for my own spiritual health, but for yours. I have to honor the energies around me. Goodbye, Abigail." Verbena strode away.

I stomped my foot. She thought it was *my* fault she'd broken into Anna's Apothecary? I breathed noisily, heat flushing through my veins. After all I'd done to clear her name, that was... She was just...

Gone.

I stared after her. Verbena grabbed a green garbage bin and pulled it around the corner of a t-shirt shop.

She was really gone.

Heh.

Brik's blue pickup bumped down the street and stopped beside me. He hopped out. "How're you doing?"

I leaned my broom against his truck. With a sigh of pleasure, I pressed against him, the fabric of his navy hoodie soft against my cheek.

His arms, warm and strong, came around me. We stood in silence for a long moment. And then he exhaled heavily, and we broke apart.

"Any word?" I asked him for the *nth* time.

He shook his head. "No. But I have a feeling Jude will be back."

"So do I. She's a survivor." She'd survived a fall, a coma, insanity. Jude would be back.

We gazed into each other's eyes, and what I saw was love. Not the burning love of desire, though we hadn't lost that—last night was proof of that. In his eyes, I saw a warm, solid, gentle love—the kind I wanted. The kind I needed.

Brik took my free hand. "At least I'm not a suspect in a grave robbing anymore." He laughed shortly, and I smiled in response.

The grave robbers had still been in yellow motel room number five when the police caught them. They'd found a good bit of old jewelry in the room too.

Apparently, the coffin we'd rescued had gotten away from the robbers. The coffin, and its resident, had been safely returned to the cemetery. Hyperion, Brik, and I planned to attend the reinternment next week.

"I still can't believe Katey killed that guy because he didn't give her enough value for her money," Brik said.

"It wasn't only that. Katey's business meant everything to her, and it was failing. She thought Falkner was a lifeline. Instead, he put her deeper in debt. It was too much."

"Still—"

"Her father killed himself when his mechanic's shop went under. For Katey, her business was more than a business. It had meaning. It was a part of her."

Just like Beanblossom's was a part of me. If we had been closer to the ocean, I might have lost the tearoom. I'm not sure I could have recovered. I hoped the businesses that had been washed-out by the ocean could get back on their feet.

But that was the risk of living on the ocean I loved. There was always a risk.

Brik squeezed my hand. He looked down at me, the corners of his blue eyes crinkling, and my heart expanded.

The risk was worth it.

<<<<>>>>

Note from Kirsten:

San Borromeo is based upon the town of Capitola, CA. In January, 2023, a violent storm wrecked its double-wide pier and wreaked havoc on the street and shops along the beach. This was the inspiration for the storm in *Matcha Murder*.

And yes, Amphicars were a thing, and Lyndon B. Johnson really *did* own one. When he was driving visitors around his ranch, he liked to pretend he'd lost control and plunge the Amphicar into his pond.

But Abigail and Hyperion's adventures aren't over. Next up, a Jane Austen fan-fic group hosts a séance in the tearoom, and murder is the result, in *Séance and Sensibility!*

In the beach town of San Borromeo, (patron saint of heartburn suffers), Abigail and Hyperion have brewed more than just the perfect cup of Darjeeling. Their latest endeavor? Hosting a séance for the local Jane Austen fan-fic group in Beanblossom's Tea and Tarot.

But when the candles flicker and plunge the tearoom into darkness, the gathering takes a turn to sense and suspicion. Because when the lights come on, a guest is dead. Abigail's grandfather is at the top of the suspect list, and the situation is brewing into a real a problem.

Our amateur detectives must sift through the clues faster than Abigail can pour a cup of Earl Grey. Will they manage to read the signs before the killer serves them their last cup of tea?

Join Abigail and Hyperion in *Séance and Sensibility*, a new novella in the Tea and Tarot mystery series. In this culinary cozy mystery, only one thing is certain: the truth will be as hard to catch as the perfect Mr. Darcy.

Cherry Lemonade Scones

SCONE INGREDIENTS:

3 ¾ C bread flour*

¼ C sugar

3 T baking powder

¼ tsp salt

8 T cold unsalted butter

Zest of one large lemons

1/8 C lemon juice (juice from approximately one large lemon)

1 1/8 C milk

1 tsp. vanilla extract

1 C dried cherries

Lemon Glaze Ingredients:

2 C powdered sugar

1 T + lemon juice

Directions:

Heat oven to 375 degrees F.

Mix flour, sugar, baking powder, and salt in a medium-sized bowl. Cut butter into cubes and mix into the flour mixture with your fingers or with a food processor, crushing the butter, until the mix is coarse and sandy. Mix in the dried cherries.

Combine the vanilla extract and lemon juice with the milk and add to the dry mix. Stir until almost combined. You may need to add extra milk, a tablespoon at a time, until the mix is incorporated.

Knead dough in the bowl. Roll out to 1" thick. Cut circles 2 ½ inches in diameter, or cut into triangular wedges 2 ½ inches at the base.

Bake on ungreased cookie sheet until light golden brown. Circles take approximately 15-20 minutes. Triangles will usually take 20-25 minutes.

While the scones are baking, mix the lemon glaze ingredients, adding additional lemon juice 1 tsp at a time to reach desired consistency.

Remove scones from oven and let cool five minutes, then spread lemon glaze on them.

Serve with lemon curd.

* You can use all-purpose flour instead of bread flour, and it will give the scones a denser, more cookie-like texture. Bread flour will "lighten" up the scones, so they're a bit more like biscuits (but not—they're still scones).

Birthday Cake Scones

3 ¾ C BREAD flour*
　¼ C sugar
　3 T baking powder
　¼ tsp salt
　8 T **cold** unsalted butter
　1 ¼ C milk
　1 T almond extract OR cake batter extract
　1/3 cup rainbow sprinkles, plus more for topping
　¾ cup white chocolate chips
For the Glaze:
　2 cups powdered sugar
　2-3 tablespoons milk or cream
　½ teaspoon vanilla extract
　Extra sprinkles for decoration
Directions:
Heat oven to 375 degrees F.

Mix flour, sugar, baking powder, and salt in a medium-sized bowl. Cut butter into cubes and mix into the dry mixture with your fingers, crushing the butter, until the mix is coarse and sandy. Add rainbow sprinkles and white chocolate chips and mix thoroughly.

Add the almond extract to the milk and add both to the dry mix. Stir until almost combined. You may need to add extra milk, a tablespoon at a time, until the mix is incorporated.

Knead dough in the bowl. Roll out to 1" thick. Cut circles 2 ½ inches in diameter.

Bake on ungreased cookie sheet until light golden brown. Circles take approximately 15 minutes. Triangles will usually take 20-25 minutes.

While they are baking, mix the ingredients for the glaze. Spread the glaze over the warm scones. Decorate with extra rainbow sprinkles before the glaze dries.

* You can use all-purpose flour instead of bread flour, and it will give the scones a denser, more cookie-like texture. Bread flour will "lighten" up the scones, so they're a bit more like biscuits (but not—they're still scones).

Matcha and Almond Scones

SCONE INGREDIENTS:
3 ¾ C bread flour*
¼ C sugar
3 T baking powder
3 T matcha powder
¼ tsp salt
8 T cold unsalted butter
1 ¼ C milk
1 tsp. vanilla extract
1 tsp. almond extract
¾ C slivered almonds

Glaze:
2 cups confectioners' sugar
1 T+ lemon juice

Directions:
Heat oven to 375 degrees F.

Mix flour, sugar, baking powder, matcha powder, and salt in a medium-sized bowl. Cut butter into cubes and mix into the flour mixture with your fingers, crushing the butter, until the mix is coarse and sandy.

Combine the vanilla and almond extracts with the milk and add to the dry mix. Stir until almost combined. You may need to add extra milk, a tablespoon at a time, until the mix is incorporated. Mix in slivered almonds.

Knead dough in the bowl. Roll out to 1" thick. Cut circles 2 ½ inches in diameter, or cut into triangular wedges 2 ½ inches at the base.

Bake on ungreased cookie sheet until light golden brown. Circles take approximately 15-20 minutes. Triangles will usually take 20-25 minutes.

Mix confectioners sugar with 1 T lemon juice. Keep adding lemon juice, 1 T at a time, until sugar reaches somewhere between frosting and drizzling consistency.

Frost or drizzle with glaze.

Serve with raspberry jam.

* You can use all-purpose flour instead of bread flour, and it will give the scones a denser, more cookie-like texture. Bread flour will "lighten" up the scones, so they're a bit more like biscuits (but not—they're still scones).

More Kirsten Weiss

THE DOYLE WITCH MYSTERIES

In a mountain town where magic lies hidden in its foundations and forests, three witchy sisters must master their powers and shatter a curse before it destroys them and the home they love.

This thrilling witch mystery series is perfect for fans of Annabel Chase, Adele Abbot, and Amanda Lee. If you love stories rich with packed with magic, mystery, and murder, you'll love the Witches of Doyle. Follow the magic with the Doyle Witch trilogy, starting with book 1, *Bound*.

The Mystery School Series

The Doyle Witches have created a mystery school, and a woman starting over becomes a student of magic and murder...

This metaphysical mystery series is perfect for readers who love a good page-turner as well as the deeper questions that accompany life's transitions. These empowering books come with their own oracle app, the UnTarot, plus downloadable mystery school worksheets. The Doyle Witch magic continues, starting with book 1, *Legacy of the Witch*.

The Perfectly Proper Paranormal Museum Mysteries

When highflying Maddie Kosloski is railroaded into managing her small-town's paranormal museum, she tells herself it's only temporary... until a corpse in the museum embroils her in murders past and present.

If you love quirky characters and cats with attitude, you'll love this laugh-out-loud cozy mystery series with a light paranormal twist. It's perfect for fans of Jana DeLeon, Laura Childs, and Juliet Blackwell. Start with book 1, *The Perfectly Proper Paranormal Museum*, and experience these charming wine-country whodunits today.

The Tea & Tarot Cozy Mysteries

Welcome to Beanblossom's Tea and Tarot, where each and every cozy mystery brews up hilarious trouble.

Abigail Beanblossom's dream of owning a tearoom is about to come true. She's got the lease, the start-up funds, and the recipes. But Abigail's out of a tearoom and into hot water when her realtor turns out to be a conman... and then turns up dead.

Take a whimsical journey with Abigail and her partner Hyperion through the seaside town of San Borromeo (patron saint of heartburn sufferers). And be sure to check out the easy tearoom recipes in the back of each book! Start the adventure with book 1, *Steeped in Murder*.

The Wits' End Cozy Mysteries

Cozy mysteries that are out of this world...

Running the best little UFO-themed B&B in the Sierras takes organization, breakfasting chops, and a talent for turning up trouble.

The truth is out there... Way out there in these hilarious whodunits. Start the series and beam up book 1, *At Wits' End*, today!

Pie Town Cozy Mysteries

When Val followed her fiancé to coastal San Nicholas, she had ambitions of starting a new life and a pie shop. One broken engagement later, at least her dream of opening a pie shop has come true.... Until one of her regulars keels over at the counter.

Welcome to Pie Town, where Val and pie-crust specialist Charlene are baking up hilarious trouble. Start this laugh-out-loud cozy mystery series with book 1, *The Quiche and the Dead*.

A Big Murder Mystery Series

Small Town. Big Murder.

The number one secret to my success as a bodyguard? Staying under the radar. But when a wildly public disaster blew up my career and reputation, it turned my perfect, solitary life upside down.

I thought my tiny hometown of Nowhere would be the ideal out-of-the-way refuge to wait out the media storm.

It wasn't.

My little brother had moved into a treehouse. The obscure mountain town had decided to attract tourists with the world's largest collection of big things... Yes, Nowhere now has the world's largest pizza cutter. And lawn flamingo. And ball of yarn...

And then I stumbled over a dead body.

All the evidence points to my brother being the bad guy. I may have been out of his life for a while—okay, five years—but I know he's no killer. Can I clear my brother before he becomes Nowhere's next Big Fatality?

A fast-paced and funny cozy mystery series, start with Big Shot.

The Riga Hayworth Paranormal Mysteries

Her gargoyle's got an attitude.

Her magic's on the blink.

Alchemy might be the cure... if Riga can survive long enough to puzzle out its mysteries.

All Riga wants is to solve her own personal mystery—how to rebuild her magical life. But her new talent for unearthing murder keeps getting in the way...

If you're looking for a magical page-turner with a complicated, 40-something heroine, read the paranormal mystery series that fans of Patricia Briggs and Ilona Andrews call AMAZING! Start your next adventure with book 1, *The Alchemical Detective*.

Sensibility Grey Steampunk Suspense

California Territory, 1848.

Steam-powered technology is still in its infancy.

Gold has been discovered, emptying the village of San Francisco of its male population.

And newly arrived immigrant, Englishwoman Sensibility Grey, is alone.

The territory may hold more dangers than Sensibility can manage. Pursued by government agents and a secret society, Sensibility must decipher her father's clockwork secrets, before time runs out.

If you love over-the-top characters, twisty mysteries, and complicated heroines, you'll love the Sensibility Grey series of steampunk suspense. Start this steampunk adventure with book 1, *Steam and Sensibility*.

Beanblossom's Swag Shop!

Be a Beanblossoms Patron!
Would you like to sip tea from a Beanblossom's mug? Check out Kirsten's swag shop HERE.
By purchasing our hoodies, t-shirts, and mugs, you're backing the *Tea and Tarot* series. Your love for these books fuels future hilarious adventures!

Other misterio press books

Please check out these other great *misterio press* series:
Karma's A Bitch: Pet Psychic Mysteries
by Shannon Esposito
Multiple Motives: Kate Huntington Mysteries
by Kassandra Lamb
The Metaphysical Detective: Riga Hayworth Paranormal Mysteries
by Kirsten Weiss
Dangerous and Unseemly: Concordia Wells Historical Mysteries
by K.B. Owen
Murder, Honey: Carol Sabala Mysteries
by Vinnie Hansen
Payback: Unintended Consequences Romantic Suspense
by Jessica Dale
Buried in the Dark: Frankie O'Farrell Mysteries
by Shannon Esposito
To Kill A Labrador: Marcia Banks and Buddy Cozy Mysteries
by Kassandra Lamb
Lethal Assumptions: C.o.P. on the Scene Mysteries
by Kassandra Lamb
Never Sleep: Chronicles of a Lady Detective Historical Mysteries
by K.B. Owen
Bound: Witches of Doyle Cozy Mysteries

by Kirsten Weiss
At Wits' End Doyle Cozy Mysteries
by Kirsten Weiss
Steeped In Murder: Tea and Tarot Mysteries
by Kirsten Weiss
The Perfectly Proper Paranormal Museum Mysteries
by Kirsten Weiss
Big Shot: The Big Murder Mysteries
by Kirsten Weiss
Steam and Sensibility: Sensibility Grey Steampunk Mysteries
by Kirsten Weiss
Full Mortality: Nikki Latrelle Mysteries
by Sasscer Hill
ChainLinked: Moccasin Cove Mysteries
by Liz Boeger
Maui Widow Waltz: Islands of Aloha Mysteries
by JoAnn Bassett
Plus even more great mysteries/thrillers in the *misterio press* bookstore

About the Author

I BELIEVE IN FREE-WILL, and that we all can make a difference. I believe that beauty blossoms in the conscious life, particularly with friends, family, and strangers. I believe that genre fiction has become generic, and it doesn't have to be.

My current focus is my new Mystery School series, starting with *Legacy of the Witch*. Traditionally, women's fiction refers to fiction where a woman—usually in her midlife—is going through some sort of dramatic change. A lot of us do go through big transitions in midlife. We get divorced or remarried. The kids leave the nest. Our bodies change. The midlife crisis is real—though it manifests in different ways—as we look back on where we've been, where we're going, and the time we have left.

Now in my mid-fifties, I've spent more time thinking about the big "meaning of life" issues. It seemed like approaching those issues through witch fiction, and through a fictional mystery school, would be a fun and a useful way for me to work out some of these ideas in my own head—about change and letting go, faith and fear, and love and longing.

After growing up on a diet of Nancy Drew, Sherlock Holmes, and Agatha Christie, I've published over 60 mysteries—from cozies to supernatural suspense, as well as an experimental fiction book on Tarot. Spending over 20 years working overseas in international development, I learned that perception is not reality, and things are often not what they seem—for better or worse.

There isn't a winter holiday or a type of chocolate I don't love, and some of my best friends are fictional.

Sign up for my **newsletter** for exclusive stories and book updates. I also have a read-and-review tea via **Booksprout** and I'm looking for honest and thoughtful reviews! If you're interested, download the **Booksprout app**, follow me on Booksprout, and opt-in for email notifications.

bookbub.com/profile/kirsten-weiss

goodreads.com/author/show/5346143.Kirsten_Weiss

facebook.com/kirsten.weiss

instagram.com/kirstenweissauthor/

youtube.com/@KirstenWeiss-Writer?sub_confirmation=1

Made in the USA
Middletown, DE
11 July 2025